To Candy...my sweet inspiration.

September, 2013/1st printing/4,000 copies
Copyright 2013
all rights reserved

Thanks again, Tony, for your art.
Cover Design by Anthony Conrad

Spring of Knowledge

It was a cool, sun-bright day in May 1962. A shabbily dressed encyclopedia salesman had been going door to door—striking out again and again—in Pittsville, a small town twenty-four miles north of Kansas City, Missouri. The obscure middle-aged salesman with wrinkled slacks, bunions and smoker's breath had no way of knowing he was about to do the one critical thing that would eventually put this dinky town on the map. And it would all start by changing the life of an insecure nine-year-old boy. One ordinary act by an anonymous, underachieving salesman became the instigation for an ordinary boy with the odds stacked against him to become nothing less than extraordinary.

It all started when this salesman with a gouty shuffle stopped and set his worn brown oversized sales case on the sidewalk and lit a Camel non-filter, satisfied that the cigarette didn't seem quite as harsh to his lungs on the bright spring day. The old, unkempt Victorian house behind him on the big corner lot was a place he'd never tried to call on. He'd seen it earlier and passed on it while in the throes of hoofing the quiet streets of Pittsville for some four hours, all without a sale or even so much as one presentation. Plenty of housewives had been home when he knocked, but they just weren't interested. Standing on Pitt Street and able to see the name of "Pitt" on the mailbox, his interest in the ramshackle house piqued anew. He had been unconsciously saving the unlikely prospect for his last call of the day—that glorious moment in time when salesmen know they are about to make or break the day they have endured. Failure loomed for the apathetic salesman with zero sales and no commission for the week. It was all in the timing. Any professional knows that.

To everyone in town, including nine-year-old Adam Pitt, the three-story Victorian "Pitt House" was a dilapidated box of flaking wood. Its white paint was ashen gray, and the once charcoal-black trim had dulled a deeper gray that screamed "Poverty!"—not only to the whole town and visiting salesmen, but most especially to the boy who lived there. Yet there was a certain dignity about the old house that also said, "With a little money and work this could once again be a magnificent, well-respected house." But that was the problem with Bill and Penny Pitt—they had little money and even less ambition.

The desperate and now nicotine-anxious encyclopedia salesman inhaled his smoke deeply then reached into his trouser pocket for a coin. *Heads I try that house ... tails I go home.*

He flipped his nickel, letting it land in the tall grass beside the sidewalk. Stooping down, he gingerly parted the overgrown green blades in need of mowing and peered down at the head of Thomas Jefferson, knowing now that he had one more call to make. He followed the sidewalk to the driveway and could see a man asleep on a lawn chair in front of the garage. It seemed odd that the sleeping dog beside the lawn chair did not even bark at a stranger walking up to the front door. The tired salesman was indeed aware that timing is everything in sales. At the front door he saw a bad omen, a welcome mat that read "The Pitts."

Forty-two-year-old Penny Pitt answered her door and seemed strangely happy to see the visitor once he identified himself as an encyclopedia salesman, and she quickly invited the man in for a presentation. After exchanging pleasantries about the weather, Penny invited the salesman to sit with her at her dining room table that was cluttered with open magazines, newspapers, and piles of winter clothing waiting to be hauled upstairs and stored in the attic. The condition of the table was no different than the rest of the house. Penny Pitt was slattern in her housekeeping and appeared to be the very likeness of her lazy husband sleeping outside. While waiting for his prospect to bring him a glass of water, the skeptical salesman could see in the dark living room two matching plaid-patterned black-and-gold recliners with standing aluminum TV trays that held empty cocktail glasses and full ashtrays. The floors and furniture were strewn with newspapers, shoes, coats and clothing. It appeared as though a dust rag and mop had never seen the inside of the Pitt House. He took the glass of cold tap water Penny handed him and watched her push away a stack of clutter to make room for his sales case. The sunlight streaming into the kitchen illuminated the lingering blue haze that revealed the pack-a-day habit both she and her husband had of smoking Pall Mall non-filters.

"My son'll be home from school any minute. I want him to hear this," the anxious mother told her guest.

"Very good," he smiled while opening his sales case to make ready his presentation to the mother and son, which meant to him from experience he had a good chance of getting a sale. "What's your son's name?"

"Adam."

"How old is he?"

"He's nine."

"And so Adam's about finished with the fourth grade?" the salesman surmised.

The woman's little laugh before she talked about her son was strange, as if she were talking about a funny little guy who lived in the attic instead of her little boy. "Well, that's the problem. Yesterday I found out from Adam's teacher that he's being held back a year and has to repeat the fourth grade. I can't believe he flunked fourth grade!" Penny declared with a palpable disgust and resignation that made her get up and get her pack of cigarettes on the TV tray by her recliner. She invited her guest to light up a Camel if he wanted.

4

Meanwhile, outside on the sidewalk a red-headed boy with exceptionally long arms and marked bowed legs opened the "Pitt" mailbox at the front of their long driveway, just like he did every day when returning home from school. Excitedly, he riffled through the mail and smiled at the bulging manila envelope he'd been expecting from Charles Atlas, the fitness guru. It had been three weeks since Adam had responded to the ad at the back of a *Boy's Life* magazine and sent in his seven bucks for the Charles Atlas Fitness Course. Adam was self-conscious about his primate-like arms and legs and the awful, humiliating nickname his peers had given him: "Ape." And it didn't help his self-esteem that his initials were A. P. Sensitive Adam knew that it was just a matter of time before the whole school figured that out.

Burdened with the all-consuming news that he had to repeat the fourth grade, Adam needed the Charles Atlas course more than ever. He stuffed the big envelope under his jeans and underwear and halfway down his butt. Then he pulled out his tucked-in shirt to cover the visible part of the envelope that stuck up above his beltline. He didn't want his mother to see what he had ordered, since he feared she would tease him about it. And she would have. Penny Pitt was more like an obnoxious big sister than a nurturing mother to her son, a bright boy who was starved for the love and positive influence his parents refused to give him.

"There's my little flunky!" Penny called out to her son in her disparaging, teasing voice. The salesman didn't know whether to laugh or feel sorry for the poor kid, whom the salesman's keen eyes could tell was doing his best to be invisible and get away from his mother.

"Front and center, buddy boy!" his mother barked while rapid-butting her cigarette.

He stepped into the dining area, approaching the table cautiously with a pronounced reddened face that was blushed from embarrassment along with the bad news he knew was coming his way. The salesman couldn't help noticing the boy's bowed legs and long arms that reached almost to his knees.

"I want you to sit down and listen to this man," his mother ordered while pulling out and positioning a dining room chair so that her son faced the salesman during his presentation.

It was the most uncomfortable, boring, and physically painful forty minutes Adam had ever endured, thanks to the manila envelope's sharp paper edges cutting into his butt each time he squirmed on the hard chair. And he squirmed a lot at the presentation that was, unbelievably, even more boring than school. And even though Penny Pitt was sold on the encyclopedias before the presentation ever began, she made her aloof son sit through every boring word anyway because of the humiliating lecture she had to endure in the school principal's office. Mrs. Goetz, Adam's teacher, had stated over and over, "Adam's problem is he doesn't pay attention in the classroom."

By the end of the salesman's insufferable speech, Adam was the proud owner of twenty-four of the biggest books he had ever seen. "Your new set will be delivered by express mail in three to five days from the home office in Chicago," the salesman smiled while Penny Pitt wrote out a check for $149.00 to Global Encyclopedia. It was obvious to the salesman that Mrs. Pitt was slaking her desire to not have a dumb kid; and that by buying this expensive set of encyclopedias, she was eliminating a problem she and her husband earnestly wanted handled.

Later that same day, after his mother had bought the set of encyclopedias, it became clear to the couple's only child why his parents wanted him to have all these big books that would take forever to read. Adam's father, Bill Pitt, had been living off a small inheritance from his dead father's defunct sand and gravel business, which at one time was the town's biggest employer. "Your dad's laziness was caused by your selfish grandfather," was the excuse Penny always gave her son when he questioned his father's excessive drinking and stay-at-home lifestyle. Adam was becoming conscious that both of his parents were alcoholics. Neither had any desire to do anything with their lives besides drink, smoke, and watch television. Many times Adam felt he was more of an inconvenience to the self-absorbed, indolent couple

6

than their legacy. He felt he was tolerated by his parents because of some innate sense of duty they had, but he certainly wasn't loved. There was no room in their selfish hearts to love their son—at least not until he could be something other than another mouth for them to feed. His parents no doubt saw these encyclopedias as a means to that end.

That night when Penny told Bill what the set of books cost, his response to his son was curt and final. "If I'm gonna spend a hundred and fifty bucks for these books, I expect you to read every one of 'em. Maybe this way you won't flunk again. See, Grandpa Pitt's money is runnin' out one of these days, and there won't be any money if you want to go to college. You'll have to get smart and get a scholarship. Those are the facts, son."

❖ ❖ ❖

School had been out for summer break for two days when the set of books arrived. Adam had been feeling even lower since it had sunk in that he would be repeating the fourth grade with Mrs. Goetz. He opened the heavy shipment, and it took him three trips to haul all twenty-four books up to his attic bedroom. Right away he arranged the brown, new-smelling, hardcover books in alphabetical order into three stacks of seven books each against the foot of his twin-sized bed. The top books of each stack were even with the top of his mattress. The "flunky" had been unspooling in his mind his plan for the last three books in the set. He placed them on the floor as close to the sloped ceiling as he could get while still remaining standing, then he stood on them while performing his exercises to strengthen his calf muscles as instructed by Charles Atlas. Sarcastically, he mused how he had promised his dad that he'd use every one of those books.

There was only one exercise in the entire Atlas course of twenty-two exercises that interested Adam: "Increasing Your Spring." He saw the drawing of a boy standing with only his toes on the edge of stacked books as if a diver on the edge of a diving board. As instructed, by holding onto a nearby wall for balance while standing on the books, he was to raise his body up and down on his toes, letting the heels extend down below the level of his toes. He would stretch and build his calf muscles while raising and lowering his body with his toes. This exercise was designed to build toe strength for maximum takeoff and calf muscle enhancement that would guarantee increased jumping ability.

Adam Pitt had a plan. He started out slowly, as Mr. Atlas suggested, doing ten repetitions of toe and calf muscle builders. Then he hopped off his new books and went over to the stacks of books at the foot of his bed. He removed the first book, sat down on his bed with it, and began reading from page one. He would read for an hour, mark his spot with a bookmarker, and do ten more repetitions of the toe and calf muscle-builders. Then he'd go back to reading, constantly reminding himself to like it, because he had two goals by the time school began in the fall. The first was to finish reading the entire set of encyclopedias. The second was to have enough spring in his legs to block Steven Kaladi's jump shot.

Why do I hate Steven Kaladi so much? Oh, yeah, now I remember, Adam answered his own query while resting on his bed. He remembered the exact day his hatred for Kaladi began. Adam had walked to school carrying a box of twenty-four Hershey candy bars to share with his class, which was a birthday custom back then in Pittsville. Adam's mother had given him the box of candy bars on the morning of his sixth birthday with the admonishment, "Don't you eat any of those on your way to school."

On his way to school, somewhere on Sycamore Street, little Adam's selfish mind convinced him that it was okay to find a hiding place for his birthday treat and get it later after school. To a six-year-old boy, the curbside mailbox marked "Bach" seemed like a safe and dark place. It even had a door he could close. *If I shove it all the way into the back of the mailbox and close the door tight, no one will ever know they're in there,* Adam reasoned. But later that day at lunchtime, he saw that rich kindergarten brat Steven Kaladi eating a Hershey chocolate candy bar before having his lunch and handing out bars to his friends at the table. He teased Adam with his laughing taunt, "Want a candy bar, Pitt?"

Adam was sick to his stomach the entire afternoon of his birthday. Sure enough, on his way home from school the mailbox was empty when he checked it for his stashed treat that he did not want to share with anybody. Especially Steven Kaladi. Worst of all, that box of candy bars was the only present his parents gave him that year for his birthday.

Kaladi (Sounds Like Potty)

E arly on in the next school year, Adam was constantly in his head about repeating the fourth grade. All his peers had advanced to the fifth grade, and he could tell that most of them looked down on him now as a dumb kid who wasn't smart enough to keep up with them. Even Clark Bach and Bobby Taggit, Adam's only friends whom he frequently watched cartoons with on Saturdays, had somewhat turned cold shoulders to Adam since he flunked a grade that everybody else passed. At least that's what Adam thought.

In school, lunch period was now a big kick in the face to Adam's self-worth because he still had to eat with the kindergarten through fourth grade kids, which was a staggered ten minutes earlier than the fifth through eighth grade lunch period. He always ate his lunch fast, wanting to avoid seeing his ex-classmates and taunting boys. Unfortunately, he was stuck with Steven Kaladi, who was now a fourth-grader with Adam and always seemed to be making some joke about Adam flunking.

One day right after lunch when Adam went into the boys' restroom, all three stalls were occupied. The obnoxious voice coming from behind the third stall must've recognized Adam's old red Keds that he wore year round.

"Hey, Pitt! I got somethin' for ya!"

Adam couldn't ignore Kaladi's big mouth because he had to go "number two" really bad. He paced in front of the sink basins hoping one of the other two stalls opened up for him. Unlucky again. The third stall door jerked open fast, and sharp-dressed Steven Kaladi's smiling Italian face stood in the stall doorway. His face reminded every poor kid like Adam Pitt that Kaladi was one of the very few rich kids in Pittsville, a town named after Adam's grandfather.

Purposely, Kaladi stayed in the doorway of the stall as Adam kept his distance. Adam was always expecting some prank or a slap across the back of his head from the class clown who had stolen his candy bars.

"Hey, Pitt … ya know what dumb kids who flunk do when they graduate?"

Adam looked down and away from the big brown eyes that taunted him as he slipped past the doorway, closing and locking it behind him. Right when Adam turned to face the toilet bowl, he saw the carefully positioned layer of toilet paper covering the down toilet seat. A step closer and he saw the full bowl of giant snake-like coiled turds left unflushed by the animal named Steven Kaladi. That's when Kaladi answered his own question. "They clean up other people's shit!" the cocky classmate laughed all the way out of the bathroom and above the sound of Adam rushing to a sink basin to dry-heave.

Adam rushed out the bathroom door, suddenly not having to go to the bathroom anymore. He had to reach the outside air to breathe again and lose the image of what he'd seen. Right when Adam pushed open the door and could breathe again, the school bell rang signaling the end of lunch period and the beginning of hating Kaladi even more.

11

Neck Flaps, Highballs, and Gop

Adam's goal to read his entire set of encyclopedias by the time his second fourth grade school year started was way off the mark. But he did finish the first book—all of letter A and a little of B—by early October. He read every night for three to four hours on weekdays and more on the weekends, which meant his calf muscle growth and toe strength were definitely showing signs of increased jumping ability. By the end of summer, he was able to jump up from a standing position and lay his palm against the ceiling at its highest point in his attic bedroom. Before Mr. Atlas came along, he was at least four inches short of touching his ceiling with his fingertips. He was incredibly happy with his progress in that department of his life. At school he was getting rebounds in basketball games, which was a nice change for Adam Pitt. As a bonus, he was also a much better reader.

The increased reading had another effect on Adam. He was noticing things in his family life that were odd or different from most of the people in town. For example, his dad's most remarkable feature was a three-inch-long neck flap that looked just like the one on the family dog, Gop. It hung as a tapering clump of skin under and back a ways from his weak chin that Bill Pitt tried to keep concealed with a neck beard. The buttery-yellow beard hair with streaks of gray looked to Adam like a hairy slab of chicken skin. More and more, little Adam would notice the repulsive soup spills and fallen scraps of food that would sometimes stick to his dad's neck flap until he showered.

That's why Adam started inspecting his inherited double chin every morning in the mirror and doing his own "neck flap" exercises faithfully. What bothered the only child of Penny and Bill Pitt was that his parents didn't seem to care about anything except smoking cigarettes, watching television, and drinking scotch-and-water highballs in their matching recliners. Their atrophied bodies melded into the comfortable chairs that held them in an invisible grip; and each recliner had a side pocket that held newspapers and magazines, old *TV Guides*, and wooden back scratchers they bought from a mail-order catalog. Every night if Adam was on the floor with Gop (a great floor pillow for Adam's head) watching television with his folks relaxing behind him, he'd never fail to hear that familiar sound of the wooden, curled fingers scratching an itch on a thigh, a back, the backside of an arm, or a foot. It was all so hideously hilarious, yet it was normal behavior in the Pitt House. It always started after a few of their late-night highballs that they sometimes switched up with whiskey sours. The scratching was always louder than any commercial or commotion on their twenty-four-inch black-and-white Zenith.

This period in Adam Pitt's life was when he first started seeing himself as being "stuck."

❖   ❖   ❖

Gop was one of those fat, sausage-shaped, brindle-colored mutts that looked like a walking gym bag stuffed with ham. Gop was born on Election Day one November. Since the Pitts were registered Republicans, the name "Gop" seemed like a perfect moniker. Ironically, the Pitts were one of those couples who had no business voting the Republican ticket. They were poor, and everybody in town knew it. They took advantage of every freebie, handout, and giveaway that they could find. Whenever health

13

issues arose, they would drive the twenty-four miles into Kansas City to visit the free clinic.

And Gop was one of those lazy dogs that in time started to resemble his owners in the face more and more—the flabby jowls and neck flaps, the sad gray-green eyes that were the same color that Adam and his father inherited from Grandpa Pitt, and the Pitt scowl that longtime residents recognized immediately.

The main reason Gop was so fat and lazy is because nobody ever walked the poor dog. They would let him outside to do his business on the front or back yard, or even on the driveway, then leave it there until the dog's business turned white and eventually crumbled into the earth with rainfall. Plus, Gop's diet consisted of table scraps from every meal, which meant Crisco in everything. Neither Bill nor Penny Pitt would ever consider spending their dwindling inheritance on such a thing as dog food bought at the store. "That stuff's just a waste of money," they would say.

Gop's diet was so similar to Adam's diet that one time when Adam was checking Gop for ticks on his face, Adam was certain the dog's face had the very same pimples that Adam had on his. That was a discovery that led Adam to changing his diet. *Poor Gop ... Crisco-soaked food mixed with Pittsville tap water. How can he live this long?* Adam often wondered.

Crazy Little Women

When Adam was twelve, usually every other Saturday morning he would ride along with his parents to Kansas City. While his parents spent the day warming the barstools at Marv's Tap—Bill and Penny's favorite watering hole—Adam would prowl downtown Kansas City, always ending up at his favorite spot in the city, Union Station. It was one massive train terminal. On weekends the station played the song "Kansas City" on its loudspeaker system. Lyrics about "crazy little women" filled the air inside a building that kid from Pittsville knew as well as any kid in Kansas City.

It was a two-mile walk from Marv's to the historic train station. On the way he would pass some of the tallest buildings in the Midwest. Adam knew this from reading his "M" encyclopedia and poring over the black-and-white photos of the Kansas City skyscrapers as well as the population statistics listing Missouri's most populous cities from the 1960 census.

On each Saturday visit to downtown Kansas City, Adam would pick a different building to explore. He would always take the stairs so he'd have a chance at reaching the top floor, or at least as high as he was permitted to go in the stairway. Faithfully, he'd been doing his Atlas exercise for his spring, thus keeping his promise to his parents of "using every single book." It was on one of these skyscraper explorations that Adam knew with certainty that his legs were getting stronger, even though his lungs would nearly burst by the time he reached the end of his climb in the stairway. He'd stop several times to rest in the taller buildings, his deep breathing echoing in the empty skyscraper stairwells. The windowless marble cylinders of space surrounding him never failed to leave him exhausted and recovering on his back by the time he'd reached as far as he could go.

Once recovered, he'd find a window to survey the view for as far as he could see. Far beyond the snaky bends of the Missouri River, he could see deep into Kansas. Oftentimes he could see foreboding weather fronts above the city or moving in from the west. During storms, the changing light from the tempest of gray-black massive clouds riding blustery winds shuddered the glass in front of his face and made the building scream and howl through a thousand different cracks and crevices. In some inexplicable way, he knew his brain was wired to feel inferior on the ground; however, up there—standing high with those incredible skyscrapers he'd marveled at a thousand times on the pages of his books—he felt like he was above all the insanity and far removed from the judgmental labels he hated.

On most of his Saturday treks to Union Station, Adam would walk around to the back of the station to the service depot where all the trains waited to be serviced for their next run. And he would breathe in all those familiar smells of fuel and oil and steel mixed perfectly with city air to a degree that made this a welcome place to explore. Oftentimes, as on this particular Saturday in September, the world of the depot was soundless except for the noises made by employees cleaning, vacuuming, resupplying and making ready the magnificent, heavy, rust-red passenger coaches that Adam would sneak onto and explore without being noticed. Except this time.

A tall Negro man, old to Adam, wearing sparkly clean company overalls with snazzy blue-and-white-striped suspenders, saw the red-headed trespasser. To Adam the man looked like a tall Louie Armstrong, except he wore brown tortoise-shell glasses that had lenses with different magnifications that made one of his brown-and-white eyeballs appear much bigger than the other. He walked over to and smiled down at Adam, appearing to be not at all perturbed or upset or wanting to be the imposing adult with rules to follow. "I'm Grover," the man extended his massive right hand. Grover was always good at sizing up strangers fast, and boys were easiest to figure out. This boy was no trouble; he was a loner with low self-esteem, as revealed by his limp handshake and reticence. "What's your name, son?"

"Adam."

"Adam. You live in K.C.?"

"No. Pittsville." He didn't want to tell the nice railroad man his last name because sometimes it caused people to make a joke about "Adam Pitt from Pittsville."

"Well, Adam from Pittsville ... you like trains?"

The boy's positive nod caused the weekend crew chief to smile big. "You wanna see where the engineer drives the train?"

Another more enthusiastic nod. Adam followed Grover through the elegant dining car. Teenaged boys were busy polishing its brass fixtures, washing the windows inside and out, cleaning the lush maroon leather dining booths, and vacuuming every square inch of the plush dining car with a seventy-foot suction hose that was attached to the platform.

Between the dining car and kitchen car, Grover waved to a man on the platform who was riding by in a golf cart filled with trash bags. Just inside the kitchen car, Grover ducked into a door that revealed his cubbyhole office, and he picked up a clipboard from atop his desk. They then continued on through the spotless stainless steel kitchen car where every single thing appeared to be in its orderly and secure place. This was a new world of clean order for the boy who lived with two slovenly alcoholics. Immediately, he liked this kind of world.

Since there were two giant black-and-orange locomotives and Grover's knees bothered him, they walked to the second engine car. Grover invited Adam to sit down on the engineer's control seat that faced more gauges than Adam could count. Grover said, "Don't ask me anything about them there things ... 'cause I don't

17

know one from the other!" Then the big man's laugh made Adam laugh—a rare thing for the quiet boy from Pittsville.

"You come here with family?" Grover asked from the co-pilot's seat.

"My parents drove me. I like to come here while they do their thing."

"Uh-huh," Grover said with a nod. "Ya know, it's about dinnertime, and I was just gettin' ready to go to Rudy's in the station to grab a bite. And ... ya know ... I hate to eat alone. How 'bout lunch, Adam from Pittsville?"

That marble-tiled walk with Grover to Rudy's Diner located at the end of Union Station was packed with more positive energy than Adam had seen in an entire year in Pittsville. It began when Grover's big feet stepped into the station and started dancing to the song "Kansas City" being piped throughout the vast station. There weren't many people in the station's Grand Hall because there weren't any trains coming or going during that time. But the ones who were there didn't miss Grover gliding and dancing to "Kansas City." Strangers and fellow employees would smile at the longtime railroad employee. It was as if they were lit up and happy to see someone who could celebrate life with absolute abandon, giving himself over to the lyrics "they've got some crazy little women there ... and I'm gonna get me one."

Grover's joyous movement under the ninety-five-foot-high Grand Hall convinced Adam that he was far away from celebrating life on this man's level. He followed behind invisibly as Grover's gliding long legs moved across the vast room and over to the shoeshine stand. The elderly shoeshine man seated on one of his three elevated seats reading a newspaper began tapping his shiny black shoes to the music. Then he started shifting and gyrating and rolling his shoulders up and down with his head bobbing to Grover's smooth, gliding dance-away toward the entrance to Rudy's. Adam could hear the shoeshine man's laughter echoing back to them as they entered the casual diner that brightened when Grover walked in waving to waitresses, busboys and cooks. He called each one by name and smiled at each and every face in the

18

diner with genuine love and affection. Grover and Adam took a seat on the red stools at the fountain counter.

"Root beer float, Grover?" the waitress smiled.

"You got me down!" Grover laughed. "What you want to drink, Adam from Pittsville?"

"A Coke, please."

Grover opened the laminated menu after handing one to Adam, who was swiveled around and scrutinizing historical black-and-white photos on the wall behind them. He hopped off his stool and walked over to one of the framed pictures of travelers in the historic station. Then Adam stepped over to a photo of a tall and gangly Negro baseball pitcher throwing a pitch in a game for the Kansas City Monarchs in the Negro Baseball League.

"You know who that is, Adam from Pittsville?" Grover asked.

Adam turned back to Grover and shook his head that he didn't know.

"That's Satchel Paige ... one of the greatest pitchers of all time."

"You ever meet him?" Adam asked.

"Oh, yes, many times. I served him a whole bunch of times in the dining car."

"Was he rich?"

"Oh ... in his day he was doin' well. I wouldn't say he was rich. But Satchel could throw a fastball so fast it would disappear when it left his hand ... until ya heard it pop in the catcher's mitt. I talked to this umpire one day who told me he couldn't see Satchel's fastball. So he says, 'I watched the catcher's mitt; and if that mitt didn't move ... I'd call a strike,'" Grover recalled with knee-slapping laughter.

It was the animated way Grover told a story with his bulging eyes and big hands that kept pace with his whiskey voice that made time spent with him so memorable to Adam. When their waitress brought their drinks and Adam returned to his stool beside Grover, Grover pointed to Adam's menu and said, "May I suggest the chicken salad special, Adam from Pittsville?"

The boy's positive nod made Grover laugh while holding up two fingers, indicating two chicken salad specials to their waitress.

19

First Entry

When Adam was fourteen in 1967, he started keeping a journal to record what was going on in his life. On May 22nd when he was walking home from school, one particular incident triggered an insatiable desire inside him to write down how he was feeling. Three blocks from school on his walk home, he saw an ambulance parked in the Collins driveway. There was no siren or flashing lights. Celia and Joey Collins were a few years younger than Adam, yet he knew them to be troubled and quiet and unkempt with few friends. Burt Collins was their father and worked day labor jobs in the area for contractors needing a good all-purpose man who could do just about anything.

Standing on the sidewalk across the street from the Collins house, he overheard the awful news about what had happened. It was spooky, thrilling and very surreal to know that such tragedy had happened to someone he had seen before. Neighbors were discussing the tragedy in hushed tones at the exact moment Adam saw a covered body under a white sheet wheeled out from the side door.

"Burt hung himself in the basement. I guess he had big problems … a bunch of old debt he wasn't payin' down. It's just awful."

"Where are his kids?" another neighbor asked.

"The Sheriff drove their mother to the school and she got 'em out."

"Thank God," another neighbor commented just when the back doors to the ambulance were closed and it drove away without making a sound.

That was the event that triggered Adam to do what thousands of other American students were doing after reading *Diary of a Young Girl* by Anne Frank. He made his first entry in his notebook upon returning home from school that day:

> *5/22/67 — Walked home from school and heard that Mr. Collins had hung himself. Ambulance was there and loaded his body. I remember he fixed our roof one time. It will be strange when it rains because I will think of him and how he fixed the leak that almost got my encyclopedias wet.*

Pittsville

By the time Adam Pitt was seventeen and at the end of his sophomore year, he was a celebrity in Pittsville. However, by the end of his junior year he wanted every bit of it to go away. Incredibly, in his sophomore track season he broke two Missouri high school track and field records. Even more incredibly, at the end of his junior year track season he held two national high school track and field records that brought every major college track recruiter to Pittsville, Missouri, in the first two weeks of June 1971.

Why did Adam want it to all go away? Because he believed he was too ugly to be seen in public. It all started when his winter-blanched face broke out with acne early in the eighth grade. Month after month it kept getting worse. Adam believed the older he got, the uglier he got; and about the time he thought he couldn't possibly get any uglier, he did. To make matters worse, even Gop, the family dog, stopped licking Adam's face.

As far as Adam was concerned, he was "The Freak from Pittsville." Alfred E. Newman was handsome compared to Adam, who still carried the moniker of "Ape" courtesy of his peers at school. Oh, how Adam dreaded his senior year! *How can I ever face classmates and teammates and all those coaches when I tell them I'm done with basketball and track?* His low self-esteem couldn't take it anymore; all those ineffable memories of being ignored because of how he looked had taken their toll, so he vowed to never put his ugly face out there for public viewing and scrutiny. *Never, ever again,* he'd sworn to himself a thousand times in his moonlit attic bedroom, the very place and private sanctuary where he had developed his incredible spring from doing thousands of Charles Atlas exercise repetitions designed to increase his jumping ability.

Yes, his memories of being gawked at were too painful to repeat in his senior year, a time when he'd turn nineteen in November and be eligible for the draft.

Varsity basketball games were especially painful in the dreariness of the Missouri winter. Every possible bleacher seat was filled at both home and away games under the bright gymnasium lights. Adam knew each person there just wanted to see The Freak from Pittsville, a five-foot-eleven junior who could jump out of the gym and make much taller opponents look silly.

Adam was not a basketball star. And yet he was. He was a freak of nature who was used by the coach to center-jump at the beginning of each quarter. To Adam's self-conscious ears, that's what the crowd was buzzing about—The Freak from Pittsville with state and national records in the long-jump and triple jump. It would all start during pre-game warm-ups when younger fans would stand under the Pittsville Pirates' basket when the team was doing lay-ups and yell, "Stuff it, Adam!" "Dunk it, Ape!"

But he never did. In 1971 it was against the rules to slam dunk. Aside from that, Adam's hands were too small to palm the basketball. In practice he would easily dunk it forward and backwards with both hands when horsing around before a scrimmage. He'd stand under the rim and sergeant-jump straight up with both hands to stuff the ball easily.

Then would come that awful time at the beginning of every game when his pimpled face was under a glaring spotlight. He would walk with the other four starters to the center of the court in his short, cherry-red shorts and white jersey. He knew the colors

23

exposed and magnified his pale skin and pimples. Every morning Adam would get up and count the pimples on his face. He would have anywhere from forty-five to fifty-seven pimples at any given time. Sensitive Adam had convinced himself that everyone was looking at him while mouthing familiar words about him that made him even more paranoid about his body.

In those few seconds just before the start of every game, Adam had taught himself to read their lips and know exactly what they were saying. They would point and laugh at his bowed and hairless simian legs and his ape-like long arms that dangled halfway down his legs and belonged on a player who was six-foot-eight, not five-foot-eleven. He would see their wizened brows in laughter when pointing out his thin patch of fine red hair that he believed looked like it had been grafted from his armpits. And always he would see someone explaining that Pittsville was named after his grandfather Lawrence Garfield Pitt. That was too much attention for his blushing face because of the inherited shame his parents had heaped on him. L. G. Pitt owned and operated the state's largest gravel pit that had produced enough material to all but cover nearly every road in Missouri by the end of World War II. At one time Pitt Gravel employed half the men in the county. But no more. By 1950 Pitt Gravel was closed for good without explanation, and all of the men who had worked there were left jobless. And by 1970, Bill, Penny and Adam Pitt were knocking on the front door of the poorhouse. Yet the town's third-generation Pitt was the one player they all came to see jump out of the gym. Yes, they wanted to see Adam Pitt more than any prolific scorer or powerful rebounder.

In those crucial seconds between shaking hands with the opposing center jumper and the referee stepping up to toss the ball to begin the game, Adam's self-conscious fear intensified. The silence of the crowd would be shattered by the deafening roar of "SKY APE!"; or a chorus of students chanting "JUMP! JUMP! JUMP! JUMP!" while stomping the bleachers with their feet. Adam's most dreaded fear was the inevitable chant of "APE! APE! APE! APE! APE!"

Adam quieted his mind by looking into the eyes of his much taller opponent and seeing the fear of humiliation coming from the

24

opposing center who was anywhere from four to ten inches taller than Adam. It didn't matter how tall the opposing center was. Every taller player knew he was facing The Kid from Pittsville who could jump so high he could actually touch the top of the backboard—which was rare even among NBA players.

Some of the centers didn't even bother to jump against Adam. That really got the crowd booing, because they all came to see David out-jump Goliath. Whenever the center didn't jump or only half-tried, to spectators it was as if a baseball pitcher had intentionally walked a home run king. Cries of "BOO! BOO! CHICKEN!" would fill the gymnasium.

High school basketball referees around the area knew to toss the ball extra high for "the Pitt kid from Pittsville." And it wasn't the chanting growing louder and louder that shot adrenaline to Adam's muscular calves and to the balls of his feet. Rather, it was what inspires most boys to excel in sports. Girls. Specifically, a certain girl he knew was watching him now. She was one of the varsity cheerleaders, and her brother Clark was starting with him.

Adam liked senior forward Clark Bach ever since grade school because Clark was always a friend even after Adam was held back a year. Clark was a redhead like Adam; and so was Clark's sister, Helen, who was a junior with Adam. Adam could never tell Helen Bach that she was his inspiration, the one he jumped so high for.

At the start of every basketball game, his timing had to be perfect. Otherwise, he could mess up the center jump and lose the opening tip that his somewhat average team counted on. He was aware that he could be out-tipped but never out-jumped. When the referee tossed up the ball extra high, Adam would launch himself at the perfect time—into the rafters, it would seem to the gape-jawed crowd who knew collectively they had witnessed something extraordinary.

Upon successfully tipping the ball to a teammate—usually Clark Bach—Adam would be cheered by his fans. But the boos would never fail to come when the coach pulled "Ape" out of the game, usually within a minute after the center jump. That's how Adam helped his team, by getting them the ball at the start of every quarter. He wasn't a shooter or a defensive player; and, surprisingly, he wasn't a good rebounder because he wasn't aggressive and would get out-muscled and out-positioned by the bigger, stronger Missouri farm boys in their division. And Adam always felt he was the target of the other team's center who had just been embarrassed again by The Freak from Pittsville.

From the bench or during a timeout, Adam would cast his shameful furtive glances to the cheerleading area where Helen would be watching the game on her knees or performing a routine in her red-and-white cheerleading outfit. She'd be jumping and dancing or doing the splits with her red-and-white pompons in each hand. From across the floor he could watch her, but never up close.

Game after game he could always tell that Helen was like all the other girls—watching the "cute guys" on both teams. Deep down he could tell girls were not that impressed by his jumping ability. They were impressed by the boys who could score. In more ways than one. Bobby Taggit was Pittsville's leading scorer and considered "a hunk" by the girls. Bobby was a senior forward, six-foot-two and muscular with wavy black hair and zero acne. Helen would watch Bobby and jump for joy whenever he scored. Bobby was Helen's boyfriend. They could be seen together walking the school halls hand in hand. Adam had liked Bobby since grade school, yet he was jealous of Bobby because Helen was his girl. Bobby was another of the few who had stayed friends with Adam after he flunked the fourth grade.

Worse than the attention Adam got every game was the attention Adam did *not* get. Adam's parents never went to one of his basketball games. Since his games were in the evenings, Bill said they interfered with Dragnet and Hogan's Heroes and Marcus Welby M.D. But Adam knew it wasn't so much the television that kept them home, it was the scotch. Although Adam tried to convince himself that it didn't matter, it bruised him to the core that his parents found the allure of alcohol and television more appealing than their own son's basketball games.

As a high school junior, Adam Pitt believed he was a freak to look at in talent and in appearance. He could no longer put himself through that kind of attention—or the lack of it. So by the end of his junior year when he'd jumped even further and had set the national long jump and triple jump records at 25'-8" and 52'-8", respectively, he quit sports. He wanted nothing more to do with basketball and track.

❖ ❖ ❖

The summer of 1971 was hard on Adam's complexion. For the first few weeks in June, college track coaches from all over the country were dropping by to recruit the record-breaking long-jumper and triple jumper.

Adam met with several coaches during the first weeks of summer vacation. He never allowed any of the coaches to enter the filthy, cluttered Pitt House. Instead, they all took turns standing at the front door of the eighty-year-old Victorian house on the corner of Pitt and Elm. Adam's parents had allowed the town's oldest historical residence to get rundown to the point that the exterior white paint and black trim had flaked off in so many places that the original wood was exposed and rotting.

That's exactly how Adam felt. Exposed and rotting. Each rejected recruiter left his business card with the taciturn high school phenom, and each coach had the feeling that the Kid from Pittsville was really in the throes of a deep depression. They all left town puzzled about Adam's lack of direction or concern for his future. One by one each college coach had talked to Adam's coach at Pittsville High, and they had all been told the same thing. "That amazing, pimple-faced leaper never worked out or practiced at all in the long-jump or triple jump pit built especially for him for his junior year."

Yes, they all left Pittsville dumbfounded by their pathetic-looking prospect who had told each of them, "I quit jumpin'. I'm not goin' to college. Bye!"

Coach Tubbs, the head track coach from Kansas State University, was the only one who pressed Adam for an answer. "Why are you so dead-set against college, Adam? I mean ... it's your life ... but my school sent me all the way out here to offer you a full scholarship with all expenses paid. I don't understand why that doesn't get you excited or at least willing to consider such an offer."

Adam, wearing cheap sunglasses with his face dotted with dried acne cream in forty-seven places, decided to level with the sincere coach. "Coach, I'm ugly. I don't want that kind of attention because it doesn't feel good at all. I hate it. I'm done with track."

Coach Tubbs was flabbergasted at Adam's response and didn't have a quick comeback. All he could say was, "Adam, if you think you're ugly … then that's what you'll be. So you've got acne. You'll grow out of that soon enough like others have."

"I don't want to go through that as a freshman … starting all over." Adam turned headed for the side door to his house.

"Adam!" the coach from Lawrence called out. But as soon as he heard the back door slam shut behind his prospect, he turned and headed for his car. The sad-eyed coach, feeling groggy from hay fever medication, looked over at Gop's lazy body and felt even more sluggish and enervated after his strange visit at the Pitt House.

History Revisited

Bill and Penny Pitt were known as the town drunks who lived off the ten-day period before the July fourth holiday. During that time they were able to take in about ten thousand dollars from fireworks they sold from a trailer parked in their driveway. From the first day of summer until the night of Independence Day, the Pitt Fireworks Stand was open for business twenty-four-seven. The Pitt seasonal home business was just a few days away from opening for its twentieth season, and Pittsville's only celebrity couldn't have cared less. As usual, he would have to work the firework stand's graveyard shift from midnight until eight in the morning when all the drunks, crazies, and early birds would buy their fireworks. Adam thought it ironic that America's history is celebrated with bombs and explosions, but that was exactly what the future held for him depending on how he fared in the upcoming Draft Lottery.

Adam was dreading his parents' return the day before they arrived back in Pittsville from their annual trek to a Tennessee fireworks wholesaler with their trailer restocked with fireworks. They'd been gone since the middle of June, staying with friends they visited every year on their fireworks run. Adam enjoyed having the house to himself, and he stayed downstairs most of the day and night. He didn't have to watch his parents drink themselves into a stupor every night, or listen to their cutting remarks about how expensive it is to have a do-nothing teenager in the house. He still slept in his attic room, though, atop the Victorian that was once upon a time a very majestic home. Lately, he had the feeling that his room was shaped like a breadbox, with its low slanted unfinished ceiling. With his parents gone and the blue haze of cigarette smoke clearing from the house, he realized his room smelled like mothballs and decided to remove them from the pockets of the winter clothing stored at the back of the attic. His parents rarely climbed the black-painted steps that led to the black attic door. The light bulb in the fixture at the top of the attic steps had burned out when Adam was in the sixth grade, but his parents had never bothered to replace it.

In Adam's restless foreboding of his parents' return and the Pitt House resuming life as usual, Adam decided to go into the garage to snoop around in some of the old boxes and crates that had been stored out there since before he was born. One time Adam had asked his dad what was in all those old boxes. "Just ugly old memories of an ugly old man that are best left closed up in them boxes. Leave 'em alone and don't ask me about 'em again," he had been told in his dad's whisky-slurred words.

Adam had always been intrigued by an old wooden box stored high on a shelf in the garage. It was covered with ornate carvings and had been stained a deep, rich mahogany. Despite the decades of dust collected on it, Adam could tell it was lacquered and shiny and probably worth a small fortune if someone would just take the time to clean it up. After carefully placing the rickety old wooden stepladder next to the shelf, Adam gingerly climbed the ladder and retrieved the box—knowing that if he slipped and fell it would be over twenty-four hours before someone would find him. And then his parents would probably be too furious to take him to the doctor, anyway.

Safely back down on the ground with the box, Adam quickly returned the ladder to its place and hurried to his attic bedroom with the box. After wiping off dust and dirt that was older than he was, Adam marveled at the beauty of the ornate box. He opened the lid and realized immediately he was looking at his family's history. The very first item he pulled out of the box was the death certificate of Lawrence Garfield Pitt, who died of tuberculosis on August 2, 1950. Adam figured his father threw the death certificate in the box, then put the box on the shelf in the garage.

Beneath the death certificate were pictures of his Grandpa and Grandma Pitt, as well as pictures of his father as a young boy. Adam watched with fascination the progression of his grandparents as young courters to a newly married couple to proud parents. Adam also saw how happy and vibrant and energetic his father was as a youngster. *How can someone who is such a happy child become such a miserable adult?* Adam wondered as he flipped through the pictures.

Tied together in a bundle were letters his grandparents wrote to each other while his grandfather was overseas during World War I. In reading through the letters, it was apparent how deeply his grandparents loved one another and how fearful they were that they could never have a life together because of the war. His grandmother's words mirrored the sentiments of many of Adam's peers when she wrote,

> *Oh, how I hate this awful war! When will it end, my love? How I long to feel your arms around me! How I dream of the day when I will take your name and be yours forever! The waiting is endless. My nights are filled with fear and terror that I may never see you again. Please, my darling, be safe. Please, my beloved, come back to me unharmed by that awful war that has killed and crippled so many of our young men.*

Adam carefully retied the letters into a bundle. *Wow! ... My grandparents understood the devastating effects of war just like my generation does. I guess it wasn't all patriotism and waving Old Glory for them, either.*

At the very bottom of the box was the Pitt Family Bible that Grandpa had bought the year he and Grandma were married to mark the births, marriages and deaths of the Pitt family for generations to come. The first birth noted was that of Lawrence Garfield Pitt, born May 16, 1897. The next was Mary Alice Hunnaker, born June 19, 1899. The last entry was William Randolph Pitt, born October 9, 1923. The page next to it was for marriages. Lawrence Garfield Pitt to Mary Alice Hunnaker, married June 19, 1920. *Funny,* Adam thought, *Grandma's birthday and anniversary were the same day. I'll bet she never forgot their anniversary.* The next entry was William Randolph Pitt to Penelope Eunice Burton, married August 23, 1947.

Turning the page Adam saw the death register, along with a piece of paper folded up and stuck in between the pages. The only entry on that page was Mary Alice Pitt, died January 29, 1929. Adam unfolded the piece of paper to see it was the Certificate of Death for Mary Alice Pitt, confirming her date of death as January 29, 1929, from cirrhosis of the liver. *Interesting,* Adam thought.

Adam placed the family treasures back into the beautiful wooden box and carefully placed it back on the shelf in the garage. He threw an old blanket over the box so his father wouldn't notice it had been moved and cleaned up. The contents of the box had answered some questions but had also created many more.

Adam Pitt had a good case of teenage angst in the summer of 1971. He was stuck in Pittsville, Missouri, some twenty-four miles north of Kansas City. America was still at war in Vietnam. Adam knew that on August 5th the Draft Lottery was going to be held that would determine his future and the future of many of his classmates. It was a big deal to Adam because his nineteenth birthday was on November 30th. If his number was low in the lottery, he could be drafted and end up in Vietnam.

Should I stay in track and go to college? he asked himself after watching the six o'clock news and seeing more U.S. casualties being loaded onto helicopters. *No ... I'll take my chances with the lottery,* he answered himself from his father's recliner.

It's Impossible

The high in Pittsville was ninety-eight degrees on July third in 1971.

"A wet-ass day," forty-eight-year-old Henry Bach called it as he sat on his front porch with his wife and daughter around 11:40 p.m. The temperature was still well into the eighties.

"Oh, Dad … you say that every Fourth of July," Helen jokingly complained.

Her mother agreed with a laugh that compelled her husband out of his chair and on his way to bed.

"Goodnight, Dad!"

As soon as the door from the front porch to the front room closed, Carol Bach reached behind her chair for an aqua-blue plastic ashtray that held a half-spent butted cigarette and a lighter.

"Mom, why don't you just smoke in front of Dad? He doesn't care."

"I don't like to smoke around him."

The sound of distant firecrackers reminded Helen that her boyfriend Bobby was over an hour late coming over. She had sunbathed in her backyard that afternoon; she was working on her tan because Bobby wanted her to. He was taking her to Kansas

City the next afternoon for a Fourth of July concert in a downtown city park, and she knew that her boyfriend of about two years wanted to show her off to his buddies who would also be there with their girlfriends.

Bobby Taggit had just graduated from Pittsville High and was planning on going to Mizzou in Columbia. It was at least a three-hour drive from Pittsville for the jock whose "girl" would be a senior in the fall.

"Bobby's late," Carol reminded Helen.

Helen rolled her cornflower-blue eyes and smiled at her thought: B*etter he's late than me.*

"You got some color today," Carol remarked, referring to her daughter's reddish-brown legs contrasted with her white denim shorts and dark purple T-shirt.

"I used Clark's tanning oil," she smiled with a wince, "all of it. And, by the way, where is Clark?"

"I don't know," her mother smiled, enjoying her smoke.

"Mom, do you think Clark will ever get married?"

"I hope not soon. He doesn't even have a girlfriend. … How about you?"

"Me? And Bobby? I don't know, Mom. I don't know," she repeated and shrugged her shoulders.

Soon the familiar sound of Bobby's black '65 Mustang could be heard in the distant darkness. She could tell by the way the engine roared that he'd been drinking with his friends. Barefoot, she hurried over the front yard's cool grass and waited by the driveway so she could hop into his car when he pulled in. That way her mother might not realize he'd been drinking. But her mother had already butted her cigarette and hurried inside to join her husband, not wanting to stay up any later.

His headlights were on high. She shielded her eyes, unable to see him when his front bumper dipped and bounced onto the Bach driveway. Buffalo Springfield playing "For What It's Worth" blared from his tape player. She peered into the front passenger window as soon as the car stopped and could tell right away that he shouldn't be driving. She hopped into the front passenger seat and could smell the stink of beer mixed with stale cigarette smoke. She

34

turned down the music and knew by the smell that he'd been partying in his car with friends she didn't really care for.

Bobby's tan and dimpled smile looked different to her when she saw that his small brown eyes looked dull and tired from drinking all day in the heat. "You shouldn't be driving now, Bobby." She was getting more and more agitated as she watched him fumble with his keys to turn off his engine.

"Aw c'mon, Helen … it's the Fourth," he whined with that drunken stupid face she hated.

"Did you get those bottle rockets for Clark?"

"Huh?" he frowned.

"The bottle rockets. You said you would get some for me. It's Clark's birthday tomorrow, and I always get him bottle rockets."

Bobby scratched his head and licked his upper lip. "I'm sorry. I forgot. Let's go get some ." He reached for his keys but Helen pulled them from the ignition.

"You're not driving now."

Helen got out of his Mustang with his keys, and he followed her up to her front porch steps. When she turned back to him, she caught a whiff of his repulsive breath that smelled of meat and beer. The awful smell repulsed her so much that she told him, "Just wait outside. I'll be right back after I put on my shoes and get some money."

On her bedroom dresser she looked at Bobby's framed graduation picture. She couldn't keep from thinking about that dreaded day only a month away, the day of the Draft Lottery. It would be an awful, prophetic day portending possible death for thousands of young men like Bobby who couldn't get a scholarship or ever get his parents to pay for his college.

Outside, Bobby plopped his tired body onto one of the front porch chairs, blinking his glossy eyes lazily at the dull glow of street lights. The familiar blaring horn of the midnight freight train on its way north from Kansas City was coming from three blocks away behind Main Street. He could hear the thudding pulse of the steel wheels rolling on the tracks. In his slumberous trance, he pictured the train carrying his sleeping body safely to Canada before the approaching Draft Lottery.

Helen came bursting onto the porch in her red Keds with the fluorescent yellow shoestrings she'd bought at a flea market in Leavenworth. "Let's go," she said with enough authority to get her tired boyfriend to snap out of his stupor and stagger to his feet.

"I can drive," he announced.

"Oh, no ... the walk might sober you up. And if it doesn't, I will drive you home."

"No, no, no ... I can drive, Helen," he waved his arm in protest.

From the front sidewalk she motioned for him to catch up with her. Bobby thrust his hands into the front pockets of his jeans, and they walked down the Sycamore sidewalk with her arm around his waist.

"Where we goin'?" he asked in a slurred tone that annoyed her.

"To get some bottle rockets for Clark."

"Bottle rockets for Clark?" he scoffed. "There's nothin' open now."

"The Pitt House. They're open all night tonight."

"Adam Pitt," Bobby droned. "Man, that guy can jump! Wow! He's got the national record ... No! Two records! For the long jump *and* triple jump. Did you know that, Helen?"

"Everybody knows about Adam. He's the only thing Pittsville's known for."

"No kiddin'," Bobby agreed with drunken laughter before cynically adding, "I'll never forget the time Coach King tried to get Ape to high jump. So ...," Bobby had to laugh at his memory getting ahead of his words, "Coach takes Ape over to the high jump pit and puts the bar at five feet or somethin'. I mean ... Ape could jump that high from his knees!" Bobby cackled just like he did when the scene played itself out for the very first time. "So Ape tries to jump over the bar by straddling it from the front," he demonstrated for Helen, "Like this ... with one leg over ... and he gets ... I mean ... Ape launches himself straight up in the air so high I bet he would've cleared seven feet! Helen, I'm not kiddin' when I say he had to be two feet above the bar when he came straight down on it! I mean ... he hits his nuts real hard, and he missed the whole pit! Ape ended up landing face-first on the cement!" Bobby laughed as they walked.

"I don't think that's very funny."

"If you'd of been there … Even Coach had to laugh."

"Adam's lucky he didn't get hurt."

"Oh, he got hurt all right," Bobby laughed. "Let's just say that's the last time Ape ever high jumped. See, what's so strange about Ape is that most guys that can jump are pretty good all-around athletes. Not Ape. He can center jump, long jump and triple jump like nobody's business. But if there's ANY technique involved … like clearin' the high jump bar, dribblin' a basketball or even shootin' a layup … he can't do any of those things!" Bobby roared with laughter. "But, man … that guy can jump!"

From a half-block away they could see the neon-lit, multi-colored interior of the fireworks trailer parked near the end of the Pitt driveway. This season Adam had hung fishnet on the trailer ceiling and had a black light that lit the nets. And again this year, the Pitt graveyard shift customers would hear Led Zeppelin's "Stairway to Heaven" playing from a portable cassette player standing on the lip of the trailer's back door. The silhouette of a barefoot Adam wearing a baseball cap pulled down over his eyes could be seen seated on a kitchen chair that was leaning back on two legs against the trailer. Next to Adam was the pull-out aluminum ramp that led up and into the cargo area where the colorful fireworks were displayed. The ramp wasn't for customers; it was for Adam and his parents to use when entering and leaving the trailer.

Bobby and Helen saw that a carload of teen boys were walking up to Adam to buy fireworks. They were local boys who were coming back to show off Adam to other boys from the area who'd heard of his incredible track records—somewhat like a small-town celebrity. Adam knew these underclassmen and liked them, all soon-to-be sophomores. They were but a few of his legion of fans who would come to his games and meets just to see "The Ape Man." Nevertheless, this fireworks gig had taught him that people get crazy on Independence Day. Yes, "Independence Day" could only be for the rich or guys like Adam Pitt who had a real talent that could be measured. That's what these kids thought of Adam. They idolized him. Bill Pitt's words rang true for Adam when he told his son, "People are looking for any excuse to blow off steam and do crazy stuff."

The boys closed in on Adam, who could hear these boys were saying things about him that he'd already heard a thousand times. Adam could tell they'd been drinking as he reached up with his ape-like long arm to turn down the volume on Led Zeppelin. Over his frayed cut-offs he wore a carnival vendor's apron that was stuffed with cash and change. He could see them all looking at his famous legs as if he were a racehorse. Or a celebrity who held records that put their hick town on the map. These were the boys of Pittsville who admired Adam Pitt.

Adam rocked forward on his chair to stand on his powerful feet when he saw to his left on the sidewalk Bobby Taggit walking with the girl who secretly inspired him to jump into the record books. Always, always, he would feel his shame and embarrassment whenever she was near him. It was there again as the boys stood looking at the fireworks display behind him. One of them discreetly lit a cigarette and cupped it to hide it from Adam, but Adam saw everything.

"Put that out, Casey!" Adam ordered from inside the trailer.

Right away the boy butted out his smoke so as not to get the town's living legend upset with him. "Sorry, Ape," the offender sheepishly replied.

Ape! Adam hated that nickname that was started by tough and good guys like Bobby Taggit—guys he had admired since grade school. That awful name reminded him of his freakish long arms and bowed legs.

"APE MAN!" Bobby called out when he and Helen reached the end of the Pitt driveway. Adam waved back to his teammate and felt anxious because Helen was there to get Clark's bottle rockets for his birthday. Adam was used to being around obnoxious drunks; two of them were inside his house at that very moment snoring off their gin and tonic nightcaps that began around noon every day of his eighteen years and didn't take a break even during the Fourth of July holiday.

"Ape, how far'd ya jump to get the national long jump record?" one of the sophomores asked.

Bobby answered for Ape, "'Bout ten feet further than you could EVER jump, Porter!"

The other boys laughed with Bobby and acted submissive around the graduated jock Bobby Taggit. "Tag" was Pittsville's all-conference defensive end for three years straight.

Adam tried not to smile at Tag's comment, fearing he would crack open a zit or two at each corner of his mouth.

"Hi, Adam," Helen smiled, looking up at him as he stood inside the trailer pretending to be busy.

"Hi," he returned with zero animation and eye contact for the beauty who gave him abounding energy to reach incredible numbers.

Helen began sorting through a stack of cassette tapes piled near the cassette player, most of which belonged to Penny Pitt. Adam clicked off Zeppelin.

"I'll take two packs of Black Kats and a box of sparklers," Casey ordered from the celebrity vendor. As soon as he asked for the sparklers, his friends started laughing and taunting him.

"They're for my sister!" he shot back, obviously embarrassed.

"How do ya keep track of all those fireworks?" Bobby slurred in amazement.

"How much, Ape?" Casey asked.

"Eight bucks," Adam answered, swiping the ten dollar bill with his long arm and handing back two dollars from the big wad of bills inside his apron pocket.

"Perry Como! I love Perry Como!" Helen exclaimed while holding Perry's cassette. "'It's Impossible' is on here. Adam, can you play 'It's Impossible' for me?" she pleaded to her shy classmate while he looked into her slumberous blue eyes.

Adam took the tape from her hand, looked at the song selection order, and queued up the song Helen wanted.

"How much are them Roman candles?" Casey's friend Hal pointed inside the lit trailer.

"Three bucks each. Five for twelve bucks," Adam said.

"I'll take five for twelve bucks," Hal said, handing Ape a twenty.

While handing him back his change, the lyrics to "It's Impossible" began on low volume. Helen turned up the volume, which caused the boys to leave the area faster. Besides, Bobby was known to have a temper on the football field or when he had been drinking.

Adam watched Helen close her eyes and get lost in Perry's smooth, dreamy love song. He also saw that Bobby, the tough guy, was struggling with feeling the softness of love coming from the music. It was a strange thing to see since his father was a tough ex-Marine and martinet who expected excellence in everything his son did.

"Ape, give me a couple bundles of bottle rockets. How much are they?" he asked above Perry.

"Twelve bucks total," Adam said when handing Bobby the bottle rockets just as more customers were arriving and parking near the Pitt House.

Bobby paid Adam then rolled his tired eyes when the song ended and Helen came back to reality. She clicked off the cassette player and told the fireworks vendor staring down at her, "That was beautiful."

"Let's go," Bobby said, grabbing her hand and pulling her away.

"Clark's bottle rockets?"

"I got 'em," Bobby showed her.

"Bye, Adam!" Helen called back and waved.

Adam stood on the end of his trailer waving back at her, his half-smile cracking open one pimple, then another. He winced from the pain around his mouth as more night owls and bar people were arriving to buy their annual supply of fireworks on the first hour of Independence Day.

When will I ever be free from this shameful blush? Adam asked his busy mind as he was yet in the throes of his blush from waving back at Helen Bach.

Just then those "stupid sophomores" tossed an exploding package of Black Kats from their car window that every resident on Pitt Street had to hear. And that was bad because every year more and more neighbors were complaining about the dangers of having a fireworks stand on a residential street. And every year the Pitts were more and more surprised that their permit was approved for another season.

Scary Numbers

B efore the first of August, Adam's dreams—at least the ones he could remember—were usually about jumping and not fouling in a big track meet. Or he would be making an important center jump in a basketball game. Sometimes he'd be blocking the last-second shot of a much taller opponent to win the game. Once August arrived, he was still jumping in his dreams— but instead he would be in Vietnam. He would wake up sweating after jumping from one perilous cliff to another, trying to get away from armed Viet Cong chasing him. Or he would be running as fast as he could to jump into a waiting helicopter he could never quite reach before it flew off without him.

August 5th was the real cause of Adam's nightmares. That was the day all boys born in 1952 had to watch and see when their day of birth was drawn in the Draft Lottery. The numbers 1 through 366 were placed into plastic capsules which were placed in a cage and spun around to ensure they were mixed. One ball was released for each day of the year, beginning with January 1. The lowest numbers drawn would be drafted into the army first after the draftee graduated from high school. That is, *if* the draftee did not have a college or medical deferment. The lottery was televised starting at ten in the morning in Pittsville.

There had been 162,746 troops drafted to Vietnam in 1970. That bothered Adam. He knew he faced a very uncertain future. He had decided not to compete in track his senior year, which more than likely meant that he would not be sought after for a college track scholarship. Since there was no money for his education, his parents would not send him to college. Besides, he had decided not to go to college, anyway. Almost certainly, Adam would be drafted.

Adam's face was a mess and on fire with fifty-six pimples the morning of August 5. Half of them had been picked and repicked a dozen times in the last few days leading up to the Draft Lottery. At the breakfast table, Adam sat staring at the little black-and-white television set on the kitchen counter waiting for "The Lottery" to begin. Bill was looking at the morning paper, and Penny was stirring pancake batter at the counter. The stove fan was sucking up the rising smoke from her cigarette in the ashtray next to the bowl where she stirred the batter. Adam despised the reality of his situation—a future that included either an unpopular war on the other side of the world, or life with oppressive parents who clearly were not interested in giving Adam any kind of a promising future.

Bill dropped his paper long enough to ask Adam, "What're ya gonna to do if ya get a low number?"

Adam just shrugged. *This would be a great time for you to act like a real parent and offer me a few helpful suggestions,* Adam thought.

"You can go to Canada," Penny said, almost as if she'd heard Adam's thoughts.

Bill answered his wife's suggestion like he knew what he was talking about. "Too cold up there to spend the rest of your life. If ya volunteer, you'll spend four years in the Navy or Air Force. If they draft ya, it's two years. I'd take the two years if it was me."

"The ones that get drafted're the ones that get killed!" his mother yelled above the stove fan at what she thought was insane logic coming from her husband.

43

"Either way it sucks," Adam complained as his hands perspired from anxiety and the three cups of coffee sloshing around inside his stomach.

"A bunch of boys from K.C. have been killed in Nam. It's in the paper all the time. And most of them are young Negro kids from K.C.," Mr. Pitt stated while hunting for a section of the newspaper piled on the table to prove his point.

❖ ❖ ❖

Bobby Taggit stared at the portable radio in his dad's gas station. He was in shock because his birthday, January twenty-fifth, was number two in the Draft Lottery. That meant he would be one of the first draftees to be inducted into the service if he didn't get a school deferment. He really had been counting on getting a football scholarship at Mizzou. He'd been telling everybody—and had even convinced himself—that he'd be contacted for sure this summer to play defensive end for the Missouri Tigers in Columbia. But there were no letters or phone calls from any school. He knew his parents couldn't afford to pay his tuition, and now he had to make a decision whether to volunteer and spend four years in the service, wait to be drafted, or run to Canada. Since his dad was an ex-Marine, Canada was not an option. He knew he'd never be able to face his father again if he dodged his duty to his country.

Bobby also knew that if he volunteered to be a Marine or was drafted into the army, he would be putting Helen through the nightmare of having a boyfriend in Nam. He had had the conversation with Helen several times. "I've seen what happens to couples separated by war. It's no good," he'd often told her.

Jimmy Taggit came into the service bay of his two-stall gas station and saw Bobby staring at the radio. "What was your number?" he asked his son.

"Two," Bobby answered numbly.

His father sighed, having survived Iwo Jima. He didn't say a word to his son, not wanting to influence what he knew was a life-

or-death decision for Bobby. He just patted his son on his broad
shoulder and walked away.

❖ ❖ ❖

Adam was finishing up with the breakfast dishes as the lottery
ball number was about to be revealed for his birthday, November
30th. His father turned up the volume on the television set, and
Adam turned to the TV screen and moved in closer to look with his
parents. "Fourteen."

"Fourteen," his mother repeated Adam's low lottery number.
"You're going to Canada."

"Honey, be still," her husband snapped at her.

Realization turned into dread which turned into fear for Adam.
He headed to his room in a stupor, knowing now that if he didn't
go to college on a track scholarship, he could be drafted right after
he graduated from high school next spring.

What do I do? Adam's mind kept asking the universe as he
stared at the ceiling while lying on his bed tucked away in his attic
bedroom. His long forearms covered his brow as if trying to keep
his thoughts pinned down. He ruminated on his chances of getting
a track scholarship if he didn't go out for track next spring. It
would still be possible since he had two national records under his
belt.

But I'm still ugly ... and I'd be a freshman all over again, he
moaned to himself.

He thought of his recent dreams of Vietnam and how he was
always running and jumping to get away from death. To Adam's
self-conscious mind, the fear of being killed in Nam was just as
bad as being gawked at by strangers, ignored by his parents, or
talking to Helen Bach and being rejected.

Adam got up from his bed and went to his front attic window.
Over the years he had seen hundreds of images on television of the
war's carnage, the dead and wounded being carried from the field.
He kept thinking about all the young men who would die because
of today, because of some number that came up on a random
lottery ball. *Could I be one of them? And for what? Am I going*

from one meaningless day here to another, and all the while a
bullet is waiting for me in a world I know nothing about or even
care to know about? All of the men who died in war have made
our reality ... but does it make this a better world now? Or do we
have to keep killing and dying in wars to validate all those dead
young men from past wars? If we stop going to war, does it make
all those "sacrifices" meaningless? Why can't we stop this
madness and all of us just refuse to go? We can all go to Canada.

The thought of going to Canada froze his thought pattern and charged his brain with the image of fleeing to save his life.

Would that make me a coward in my own eyes and everyone
else's because I'm not like the ones who went and served in the
name of patriotism? I can't live my life this way. Or does everyone
feel like I do and somehow make these choices, deciding what
happens to them ... decisions that may mean life or death. And by
what God-given authority do those old politicians in Washington
have to send us away to die or be wounded or scarred mentally for
the rest of our lives when they will stay home and be safe from it
all?

Adam's thoughts turned to Helen, the fantasy girl who had inspired him to jump into the record books and experience the fame he knew he could never handle. *What would she think of me if I went to Canada? Then again, would it matter? I'd be in Canada ... and alive."*

❖ ❖ ❖

Helen resisted the urge to call Bobby or to walk over to the gas station to console him for drawing such a low number on the lottery. She was in no condition to offer consolation, anyway. For over an hour she had been crying in her bedroom after hearing his birth date called out along with that scary number two. Like her boyfriend, she had been in denial about this possibility. Now all she could think about was how he could be hurt or even killed in Vietnam.

She also knew that Bobby could never aim a weapon to kill somebody. He had told her that several times. Even though Tag was known to be violent but "clean" on the football field, he wanted no part in ever going hunting with his dad. As a boy he refused to aim a weapon at any animal, let alone pull the trigger. But that scary number still meant he would be drafted soon if he didn't get a football scholarship and get a college deferment. Jimmy and Evelyn Taggit were not believers in paying for their son's college when he could go for free on the G. I. Bill after serving in the Corps, just as Bobby's old man had done.

Train of Thought

Two weeks after the Draft Lottery, Bobby Taggit enlisted in the Marine Corps. Helen assured him she'd wait for him, but her confused boyfriend had other ideas.

"It might be better if you didn't. Besides, we've had this talk before. Long separations are hard on couples. My mom said it was by far the hardest part of her life when my dad was in the service," Bobby said.

"Don't you want me to wait for you?" Helen asked in disbelief.

"Yeah, but I think it's better if none of us waits for … I mean … I don't know what I mean, Helen. I know I'd like you to write me even if we aren't together. But I don't want to hear about who you're dating. All I know is I couldn't take it if you broke up with me while I was in Nam. I know how I am, Helen. I'd rather know it was over before I left. Does that make sense?"

"But I wouldn't break up with you," she was trying to understand.

"Helen, two years is like a hundred years when you're young like we are. Remember what you said when you thought I was goin' to college? You said if I loved you, I couldn't be with anyone else … that I wouldn't want to be. All I'm sayin' is *if* we left it open, that we were free to do what we wanted or date other people ... that doesn't mean that we will. It only means that we're not lettin' this world separate us and destroy us by makin' promises to each other we're not sure we can keep."

"But I'm sure," she declared with tears forming in the corners of her eyes.

"Helen, I can't even promise you I'll even come back."

That scared her. Then she said, "If we're not waiting for each other, then why bother to even write each other?"

"I guess you're right," he agreed, much to her dismay.

"So you're saying we should break up because you don't trust me?" she asked.

"I don't trust life. Things happen, Helen. Hell, I thought I'd be in Columbia playin' football now. Instead, I'm a Marine headed for Nam. What I'm sayin', Helen, is if we can keep it open with no promises to each other ... and if we want to be together when I get back ... great."

"But if either one of us goes out with someone else or has sex with someone else, it means we aren't in love with each other and it's not meant to be?" Helen demanded with tears running down her face.

"Exactly! But meanwhile, we aren't forcin' each other to count the days or forcin' each of us to trust each other from so far away," Bobby tried to put a positive spin on it.

"So, it's really about you not trusting me."

"Not you, Helen. People. I don't trust life."

"Because you didn't get a scholarship?"

"That's part of it. And just because life threw me a curve doesn't mean that I have to drag you along with me. In time you'd resent it."

"How do you know that?" Helen really wanted to know.

"I just do. Some things ya just know."

"You've been talking to your dad," she stated with certainty, which made him smile. "I knew it! Bobby, every time your dad gives you advice, you come up with these things from his life that don't have anything to do with us."

49

"That's not true. And I don't know what really is true. I'm confused about everything in my life. One day my thoughts are clear and I feel good about everything … and the next day I'm a Marine headed for Nam."

❖   ❖   ❖

Just before midnight, Adam was feeling depressed while lying on his bed and staring absently out his window at the night's blackness. "It's Impossible" played low from his cassette player. Earlier at Taggit's gas station when filling up his parents' car, Bobby had given Adam the news that he was going to Kansas City in the morning to take his physical because he had enlisted in the Corps.

"Really? What was your number?" Adam asked.

Bobby held up two fingers—and he wasn't indicating a peace sign.

"Two?" Adam asked incredulously.

"Yeah … two," Bobby still couldn't believe his bad luck.

"Man, I thought I had a low number," Adam said.

"What was your number, Ape?"

"Fourteen."

"Wow, that is a low number! But you don't have to worry. You'll get a track scholarship."

"I don't know for sure."

"What are you talkin' about, Ape? You've got two national track records. You got it made."

"I may not go out for track."

"That's crazy, man. Why?"

"I just don't feel like it."

"With number fourteen, you'll end up in Nam if you don't go to college."

Adam was testing the waters when he said, "I might go to Canada."

"I couldn't do that," Bobby shook his head as if trying to shake the thought loose. Then he stated with positive clarity, "I'll do my four years. The government will pay for my college, and I can try out for football as a walk-on. I'll still be in my early twenties. No big deal."

Adam nodded in agreement as if that sounded like a good plan. He couldn't bring himself to ask Bobby what Helen thought about him going into the Marine Corps.

Adam had spent the day thinking about Bobby and Helen and how all their lives had changed since that lottery. Since the lottery, Bill Pitt had been checking the paper for local casualties in Nam. If a soldier had been killed who was from the area, Bill Pitt would let his wife know later when their son wasn't around. But Adam felt everything. He had felt Bobby's fear when he told him he had enlisted, and he felt his parents' fear during breakfast whenever his father was reading the war's casualties in the newspaper. And Adam was feeling what he was certain Helen must've been feeling that night at the fireworks stand when she listened to Perry singing "It's Impossible."

He clicked off the smooth singer's hit and got off his bed. He looked down at his clock radio which read 11:52, and he quickly put on his cut-off shorts, red track shoes, and a black t-shirt. Then he headed outside for the place he always went when he felt like screaming at the world.

For some inexplicable reason, Perry Como had the same power in his voice to move Adam's emotions just as Helen's image had done for him when he wanted to jump. Outside his oppressive house, the equally oppressive humid August night blinked with lightning bugs and roared with chirping insects that seemed to be following him all the way to Main Street, all but wiping out the audible memory of Perry's song—a sound that had sent him out into the night.

Main Street was usually quiet, day or night. The only business open was Red's Tavern on the south end of Pittsville's two-block business district. Adam crossed Main and continued for a block until he passed Solomon's Lumber, then waded into a narrow patch of weeds in front of the railroad tracks. The 11:59 was a nightly freight train of some sixty cars that hauled livestock north to the giant packinghouses in Omaha, Sioux City and Sioux Falls.

Standing between the iron rails, Adam faced south and stared into the lone light of the approaching train he had heard all his life. He stretched out his long arms as if welcoming the train to plow over him. Then, not wanting the train to blare its deafening horn at him, he stepped out from between the rails and remained standing close to the rail on the other side of Main Street and its weathered look of rural Midwest commerce.

The dual engines thundered past him at sixty miles per hour, then the massive freight cars rushed past him, not more than two feet from his body. At the top of his lungs he yelled "IT'S IMPOSSIBLE!" with his head bent back and his arms outstretched. Over and over he yelled the title of "Helen's song" until the last car passed, then fell exhausted onto the gravel and rocks that were from his grandfather's gravel pit.

School was starting in a week, and his acne had only gotten worse over the summer. This had been Adam's final cry-out before he faced another year of shameful introversion. Nothing he'd tried from the drugstore had helped his acne. The day before at the pharmacy counter, he had overheard one woman telling another about how some man she knew had changed his life. "I couldn't believe the difference in Sam," she related to her friend. "He was a totally different man. He told me he did it by drinking boiled water with lemon juice and fasting on only that for one week. His skin is clear, his eyes are bright, and he has tons more energy."

It was the first proactive decision Adam remembered making. He couldn't wait for morning so he could start his fast to clean out the toxins he had accumulated by living with his parents. And he didn't care what he knew they would say about his fasting. He had to see progress. He had to change his life. It was Adam's new train of thought.

The Weak and The Stupid

After two days of fasting on boiled water with lemon juice, Adam felt anxious and weak and more glum than usual. *So much for more energy,* he thought to himself. Bill and Penny's grouchy son came into the kitchen for no breakfast. He sat down at the kitchen table and began ridiculing every little thing his parents said and did.

"Royals are playin' the Cards today in K.C.," Bill remarked to his son from behind his newspaper.

"So?'

"So ... just makin' conversation."

Then Penny asked Adam, "Why, exactly, are you doing this fast, Adam?"

"I'm tryin' to clear up my ugly face. Is that okay with you?" he snapped back at her.

Adam got up from the table, took a big gulp from his glass of lemon water, and walked over to the refrigerator. He yanked open the door and stared at its contents while shaking his head in disgust. "No wonder my face looks like the moon. I've been eatin' garbage and drinkin' polluted water."

"Well, you don't have to eat it," his mother fired back.

"Don't worry! I won't! It's like zitsville around here!" he slammed the refrigerator door and stomped out of the kitchen with his lemon water. *I can't believe how stupid and weak they are,* he complained to himself.

On the evening of day three of his fast, he went outside for the first time since starting his fast. He figured he should go for a walk since his body felt like it was getting weaker every day. He wanted to experience Pittsville in his delirious state of confusion before he was too weak to get out of bed. Like many boys Adam's age, he was stuck in a shameful past and feared the future. Yet after his shower that morning there was a bright spot. Even though he was close to giving in to his hunger cravings, he noticed that his face was clearing up more than it ever had before. There were some places on his face that were now clear that hadn't been for a very long time. *Twenty-two,* he had counted and forced a smile into the bathroom mirror. *But you're still ugly.*

Outside, he walked to keep pace with his anxiety and resolved to not say another word to his parents as long as he was fasting. Everything about them he despised during this cleaning-out period—a process that seemed to magnify their negative habits a thousand times. He now blamed them for his ugliness and his inability to interact with people. They both gloated over his track records only because they knew they wouldn't have to spend a dime for his higher education. That angered Adam because he didn't want his talent to cover for the fact that his parents refused to take responsibility to provide for him. In their minds they didn't have a dime to spend on anything but their own destructive habits. *If they wanted to do the right thing, they might have to actually stop drinking and work,* he griped inwardly when he reached Sycamore Street.

Since his face was clearing up, he decided to turn onto Sycamore. He wanted to walk past the Bach house and see if Helen was on her front porch. And he was curious about Bobby, when he was going to boot camp after having just passed his physical.

It was unusual for Adam to walk on the sidewalk on the same side of the street as the Bach house, but he was numb to his own paranoia and self-consciousness because of the fasting. And except for the intense hunger, he preferred feeling this way. It was as if his body were too busy dealing with starvation to bother with the trivial details of social interactions.

Yet he stopped on the sidewalk before the Bach house came into view because he could hear people talking on the Bach front porch. He looked down at his red track shoes, a reminder of his freakish jumping ability that only magnified his own feelings of worthlessness. He could see the power line lit by the street light and knelt to untie his famous footwear, the same shoes he had worn when he broke the national records last spring. After removing his red track shoes, he tied all four ends of the laces together and tossed them up three times before getting them to hang over the power line in that obscure location. Only he would know they were there.

He continued walking barefoot on the sidewalk until the Bach house was in view. Affable Clark was there on the front porch with Helen and their parents. He saw his teammate walking by and called out, "Ape!" Clark could see by Adam's body language that he would not come any closer, so he left his porch and walked over to Adam, Pittsville's shy celebrity.

"You ready to be a senior?" Clark smiled.

"I guess," Adam shrugged, self-conscious that the rest of Clark's family was watching them.

"I'm goin' to KU," Clark said proudly.

"You get a scholarship?" Adam was curious.

"Are you kidding, Ape? I'm an average student. My parents have been savin' for my college my whole life. They don't want me goin' to Nam. I got a school deferment. Did ya hear that Tag's goin' in the Marines?"

"Yeah."

"Ain't that somethin', Ape? Bobby goin' to Nam?"

"Yeah, that's somethin' crazy."

"I heard you turned down a bunch of track coaches. Did ya commit yet?"

"No more track for me."

"You gotta be kiddin' me! You could get a full ride to any school you want."

"No, Clark ... I'm done with sports."

"Why?"

"I just don't want to do it ..."

"You're stupid, Ape. You want to end up in Nam like Bobby? Your number was fourteen, Ape. You're a dead man if you don't go to college."

Just then Helen came over to them, curious to know what her brother was so excited about. "Hi, Adam. What's up?"

"This dummy's not goin' out for track, and he got number fourteen in the lottery."

"Really?" Helen looked at Adam, who was struggling to relax in his weakened state from fasting and fighting the urge to explode on the next person who wanted him to explain himself. "Fourteen ... Man, that is a low number," she said calmly.

"I know," he nodded.

"Bobby's going to boot camp soon," she told Adam.

"I thought for sure he'd get a football scholarship," Adam said while in the tremulous throes of hunger pangs that intensified with the smell of a neighbor's barbeque.

"So did he. Now all I do is think about what's going to happen to him. That stupid war!"

Clark told Adam, "Ya know, there's a campus protest rally in Lawrence next weekend. Helen's drivin' me there. It's the weekend before classes start. You should go with us, Ape."

"Yeah, you should," Helen agreed.

"Is Bobby goin'?" Adam asked Helen.

"No way. He's into the Marines. His dad was a Marine. Those college protest rallies go against everything his family stands for."

The phone rang inside the Bach house, and Helen hurried inside calling back to Adam, "I'll see you Saturday, Adam!"

Adam asked Clark, "So what time are you leaving Saturday?"

"Early. We want to get out of here by seven. We can have breakfast on campus."

On his walk back home from the Bachs', Adam stopped under the spot where his track shoes were hanging from the power line. Now he wished he hadn't tossed them up there because he didn't have any casual shoes to wear to Lawrence on Saturday. His only other shoes were a pair of brown penny loafers that he last wore at the assembly when he and other school athletes were awarded their letters for the year.

Continuing on home he decided he would cut off his fasting a day early so he could have breakfast with Helen and Clark on Saturday. Thrilling images of spending the whole day with Helen Bach made him vacillate whether or not to spend some of the $120.00 he had made at the fireworks stand on new clothes and shoes.

And will we be driving back alone? he wondered.

All the incredible musings gave him more energy. More energy than even before he started his fast. Then he thought about Bobby and how he was headed for Nam, risking his life for all the weak and stupid reasons that anyone uses when a soldier dies in a war. *If he makes it ... at least he has Helen to come back to. And here I am thinking of spending time with Helen while Bobby's getting ready to risk his life. I will run away to the north, past an imaginary line that says "you are safe here." But will I really be safe? How will I escape being seen as a coward by all the eyes in this town and by those like Bobby who are scared but go to serve their country anyway. I'm stuck. It's a trap that could kill me either way. I'll end up dead on the battlefield or isolated like my weak and stupid parents. All's fair in love and war. Isn't that what they say? So it is fair to want to be with Helen ... and to run away from war.*

Inside his house his intense hunger returned. *Just three more days of this*, he told his frazzled mind as he walked past his parents in their matching plaid recliners. As usual, they were reposing with gin and tonics while watching television and smoking their non-filter Pall Malls. Gop looked dead lying between them.

"I need to take the car tomorrow ... to get some clothes!" he called out into the dark living room area. Only sausage-shaped Gop responded by raising his eyelids to look up at Adam. He knew they would ask him to repeat what he had just said, so he said it again before they could come out of their stupor and ask him. "I'm takin' the car tomorrow to get some clothes!"

"Just make sure you put the gas back the way you found it!" his dad barked from his recliner, which made Gop flinch.

Adam headed for the upstairs to get away from them. Ever since starting his fast, he'd been more sensitive to their second-hand cigarette smoke and was convinced that their smoking in the house contributed to his acne.

More boiled water and lemon juice was waiting for him in a gallon pitcher on his dresser. There was an encyclopedia at the foot of his bed that held the black-and-white pictures of the places he liked to go in downtown Kansas City, places that he would see tomorrow.

Sucker in the Mirror

The morning of day four of his fast, Adam counted twenty zits—the lowest number he could remember ever since his pimple-tracking began in his sophomore year.

The forty-five-minute drive to downtown Kansas City always thrilled Adam. Mort's Clothing on Tenth Street and Vine was a familiar landmark for low-income families who wanted cheap clothes and shoes. Bell-bottom jeans were in style with wide-collared puffy-sleeved shirts that Mort Rabinowitz and his Jewish clan would peddle from inside their massive warehouse-looking discount clothing store. Paper signs advertising "Wholesale Prices" and "Going Out of Business" had always covered the ground-floor windows, obstructing any view of the store's interior.

Sixty-something, beak-nosed Mortimer Rabinowitz was smart. He'd been at this same location for over forty years and still had the same sign posted at the entrance of his fifty-stall parking lot behind his building: *FREE ALL-DAY PARKING FOR CUSTOMERS ONLY.* Since Mort was open seven days a week, his lot was usually full. Even on Sundays. People would park in his lot, come into the store and buy something—anything—and Mort would let them park all day and night in his lot. Mort was a rare businessman who insisted that his employees know every customer's name and, at least, where they lived. Adam was first known as "The Boy from Pittsville" back when his dad, "The Man from Pittsville," would bring in Adam to buy school clothes or shoes or a winter coat.

As Adam entered the big store with the huge ceiling fan near the front door, he noticed his sense of smell had been increased markedly from fasting. He immediately smelled the rubber-soled shoes and boots mixed with mothballs and the sawdust sprinkled on the faded and creaking old oak floorboards. And then came old Mort's greeting, another clue his senses were heightened upon hearing that nasal-rich voice. "There he is! The Jumping Jack from Pittsville!"

That greeting always brought a smile to Adam's usually glum mouth that was miraculously free from the cracking stings of acne sores. Behind him he could smell the hot city pavement and its saturated exhaust fumes. Then he noticed the explosion of the "Back to School" clothing racks that the shrewd proprietor positioned at the front of the store, working his intent on the celebrity senior-to-be.

This time Adam wanted to take his time and find the right colors for his red hair and fine skin, since most dark colors washed him out and enhanced his pimpled face. Until now he avoided bright, cheery colors because he didn't want to draw any attention his way. And Mort would usually rush him by finding his size quickly and ushering him over to the full-length mirrors or a dressing room. For this incredibly strange and rare chance to be around Helen, he had to have just the right shirt in the right color. It had to be a shirt she would like and remember because he looked good in it, not because it magnified his acne and enhanced his ugliness. This time Adam was determined to not let Mort rush him into buying a shirt he hated the next day.

"And what is The Jumping Jack from Pittsville looking for today?"

"A shirt, maybe some jeans, and a pair of shoes."

"I remember you have the exceptionally long arms, so a short-sleeve shirt is what you want," the old Jew smiled, dipping his head down to look at his customer above his black-framed glasses.

Mort riffled through his inventory adroitly and asked Adam if he was looking for a particular color.

"I don't know. I want to try colors on and see what they look like on me."

"I see," the man sighed through his nose and scratched the back of his head.

Adam spotted a magenta tie-dyed t-shirt he liked and took it over to the tri-folded full-length mirrors by the dressing room. He held the shirt up to his neck to see how the color went with his skin tone and hair.

"You want to try it on?" Mort asked.

Adam nodded yes.

Mort unlocked his small dressing room with a key dangling from a brown shoestring looped around his thin, long neck that resembled a chicken leg. It was draped with sagging fat that had yellow creases deeper than wrinkles and visible black hairs he had missed when shaving.

Soon Adam came out of the dressing room wearing the dark-purple tie-dyed t-shirt, wanting to see how it looked in the mirror. Right away he liked the way the color looked on him, and this time he didn't trust Mort's opinion one way or the other. There was something about the mirrors that Adam believed was rigged in favor of the seller, like some carnival trick that made the sucker in the mirror appear thinner or more attractive than in reality. But then Adam noticed that the mirror wasn't hiding anything or trying to trick him at all. His acne was just harder to see and was really clearing up. When Mort came into view behind him holding a charcoal-gray tie-dyed t-shirt, Adam could see himself wearing the gray shirt when he was with Helen on Saturday, and he could imagine her liking the gray shirt. Seeing things in his mind is how he accomplished anything good in his life. Like his jumping records. He would imagine that Helen was in the stands cheering him on to jump as far and as high as he possibly could. That was the only image he needed to launch his body into the record books.

The euphoric feeling of a record leap was upon him as he hurried to put on the gray t-shirt and a pair of flared jeans that he hoped would be baggy around his thighs. He imagined that would help to somewhat diminish his ape-like bowed legs.

He liked the way his new clothes looked on him and wore them when he went over to the shoe section to try on a pair of black high-top Converse. Mort sat on his shoe stool and measured Adam's feet.

"I'll take 'em if you give me red shoestrings instead of white." Adam didn't even glance at old Mort when he said that. Instead, he smiled at himself while walking around the shoe area in the new Chucks that were size 12D.

"Your feet are eleven-and-a-half Ds. You wear a cotton sock, and you'll grow into 'em anyway. Geez Almighty, kid ... the way you can jump ... if I was you, I'd have my track coach buy me the best shoes I could find. And that shoe is not in this store," he started his funny chortle-snort laugh that exited his big nostrils.

While Mort was lacing up Adam's black Converse with red shoestrings, a hippie-looking young man with long white hair walked past the store's open double doors. Adam could hear the song "Ohio" playing from the man's handheld transistor radio. "Tin soldiers and Nixon coming / We're finally on our own / This summer I hear the drumming / Four dead in Ohio."

 Adam stood up and walked a few steps in his new outfit; he liked the way his new gray shirt felt on his skin. He went to the register to pay Mort, who already had his new purple shirt and old clothes bagged.

"You going to break your records next year?" Mort asked as he handed Adam his change.

"I quit track."

"That's good. Savin' your best for college. Smart. Very smart," the old man winked and dipped his chin to smile at Adam.

Adam didn't want to explain himself, so he waved goodbye and left the store.

He put his bag of clothes in the trunk of his parents' car and headed on foot in his new shoes toward Pershing Road. He was on his way to the one place he liked most to go whenever he was in downtown Kansas City: Union Station. Grover would be on his run to Wichita and back, so he wouldn't get to see the friendly weekend crew chief. Union Station was the one place he could go to see the world coming and going to a thousand destinations he had only read about in his books.

It was eight blocks to Union Station from Mort's Clothing Store. Adam's legs felt weak and shaky from fasting, yet his stomach ceased to be hungry. He felt as if his starved body was now consuming his insides. He noticed that he wasn't sweating as much from the heat and humidity, which was always higher downtown because of all the tall buildings and vast concrete pockets of dead air that weighed heavy on every living thing. And it was obvious that his sense of smell was heightened. In a strange sense he felt healthier and more alive than he'd ever been. Never before while approaching the station had he smelled so intensely the city's fumes from buses and cars and trains. It was an acrid smell in the stagnant late-summer air that burned his gray-green eyes to a bright red.

Ahead of him, just a couple blocks away, was the ten-story, 850,000 square foot Union Station. Built in 1914, it was the third largest train station in the country. He had memorized many facts about this place from his books at home. He loved coming to this incredible place where over the years millions of people made their way to and from wars, families and friends at home—all incredible journeys that decided for millions their future and who they would become.

His record-breaking legs were tired and plodding as never before; his fasting had taken his energy and switched on his brain to a survival mode he had never experienced before. He thirsted for the cold water at the drinking fountains located in dozens of places in the North Waiting Room and lobby. Each massive area could hold ten thousand people. He looked forward to letting the fountain's cold water spray on his face, eyes and neck until the cold water literally took his breath away.

Most importantly, he had only eleven pimples that he could see in the bathroom mirror that morning. By far his lowest zit count in years. That's why he so looked forward to Union Station—to see how strangers saw him. It was his ultimate gauge that told him how the world saw him. The closer he got to the station, the more his belly ached and his mouth salivated for his usual order at Rudy's Diner—the $3.95 Special. It was a heaping chicken salad sandwich on rye bread, two large scoops of potato salad and good coffee that made the Folgers used in the Pitt household taste like swill. To Adam, this meal at Rudy's beat anything made in the Pitt kitchen; and to not indulge himself with this treat made his legs bow even more. His mind berated him for not wearing his favorite cut-off jeans instead of these new bellbottom jeans that were heating his body as if wearing leather pants in a sauna.

Right away he hit the first fountain by the door he entered and let the ice-cold water splash onto his face and then his neck before taking a long drink. At first the interior of the station was a vacuum of cooler air. His new shoes squeaked on the station's terra cotta floors until he planted his tired body on a bench where he could see the Grand Hall's ninety-five-foot ceiling. One of the three massive 3,500-pound chandeliers reminded him that he was in his favorite place in the city. With starve-spooked eyes, he scanned the station's central arch and rose-brown marble walls that led up to a vividly painted plaster ceiling. It was hard for Adam to believe the critics of this incredible building who claim that Union Station has deteriorated to a shameful degree. Just a couple weeks earlier his father had read to him an article in the paper about how the nation's largest railway freight and mail terminal was in need of extensive repairs. They said the roof dome alone would cost over a million dollars to repair and restore.

Adam was feeling better, but he was still tired and felt like sitting on the wooden bench for a long time. Better yet, he felt like lying down. But the fear of being booted out by a security guard made him reconsider. He'd often seen vagrants escorted out of the station by armed men. He was glad Grover was on his usual run to Wichita. He was content to just be alone in the station with his thoughts about Helen and their trip to Lawrence on Saturday.

It was a slow time for the station compared to the real busy times he'd seen when several trains were arriving and departing around the same time. To his right on the next row of benches was a young sailor in dress blues sitting rigidly with his stuffed forest-green sea bag standing close to him. Instantly, Adam thought of his low number—fourteen—he had drawn in the lottery and wondered if he should enlist in the Navy in order to avoid the combat on land where most of the casualties occurred. But then he realized he had a sickening aversion to drowning and being confined and claustrophobic on a ship for months at a time with strange men from all over the country. *God, that would be worse than being a freshman again*, he thought.

He decided to get up from the bench and go to Rudy's to have just a cup of coffee. It was a favorite place of his to people-watch. But first he ducked into the men's room to see how he looked in different clothes and a different mirror. Several sink basins were lined up on the counter with one massive mirror that reflected his new clothes and a haggard face that he saw as gaunt and made his fine red hair about as attractive as back hair. Seeing nobody else in the restroom, he leaned in his face closer to his reflection to scrutinize the lone hairs at the front of his hairline that stood out like grasshopper antennae, and he plucked out the ones he could see. Then he stopped himself from counting his zits and opened his mouth as wide as he could just to experience no pain from cracked open sores.

Upon exiting the restroom he read the giant six-foot-wide clock hanging from the ceiling in the station's central arch as arriving passengers from St. Louis were flooding into the Grand Hall. Purposely he walked toward the flow of people moving through the station and stopped in front of the barber shop beside a shoeshine stand where an elderly man sat in one of the elevated shoeshine chairs reading a newspaper. Adam could smell the distinct aroma of shoe polish stronger than ever before as he walked past Kansas City's Largest Barber Shop with "$7 dollars a haircut" posted on the shop's front window. Again the trip to Lawrence with Helen came to his mind, but this time in images of long-haired college boys in their worn, casual clothes. He reached up and felt the top of his fine red hair with the palm of his open hand to gauge how short it already was. It felt so limp and ugly to him that he wanted it all off his head. All gone. *One less ugly feature to look at*, he reasoned as he ducked inside the shop and approached one of the sixteen barber chairs. A white-smocked barber greeted him by gesturing for him to take a seat in the red leather chair he swiveled around for his customer.

Before Adam sat down, he could see in the mirror that his gray-green eyes were ablaze from fasting. He told the barber while still looking in the mirror, "I don't want a haircut. I want it all buzzed off. How much would you charge for that?"

"Three bucks," the man answered after gauging the young man's head of hair.

"Okay," Adam sat down. From then on Adam kept his eyes closed, not wanting to see another mirror that lied to him.

The buzzing was over in less than twenty strokes. Then the barber put hot lather around his ears and on the back of his neck, and quickly shaved the areas clean with a razor. When Adam opened his eyes, he saw all his red hair on the apron before looking at his pale head in the mirror. He paid the man and left the shop.

Once again he was in the Grand Hall, and his head felt cooler as he walked with the increasing manswarm that filtered through the vast train station. It was a swollen rush of lost people with grim faces and no sense of open friendliness. But now he looked at the strange faces to see if he was reflecting some kind of change after his recent buzz job. Nothing seemed to be different in the moving current of humanity living during this period of social unrest toward an increasingly unpopular war, assassinations, civil rights uprisings, and rock music. To Adam, the country was like himself. Stuck.

Rudy's was up ahead. That would be the place where he would truly see if the sucker in the mirror was all in his head and if there was any possible chance of losing his self-image as a cipher—an invisible young man like millions of others who lived and breathed and jumped for nobody now.

The diner was not as busy as it usually was when he was there, but the usual nameless waitress was there walking toward him at the counter in her gray-and-white uniform. Her voice called to him from behind, and he saw her reflection smiling at him when she passed by and said, "Someone got buzzed." From his counter stool he felt too tired to blush. This special spot for his taste buds made his belly ache more intensely than it ever had since he started fasting. Then the waitress surprised him when she passed behind him and asked, "So ... you want your usual?"

"Just coffee, please," Adam replied with a shy smile.

She surprised him again and asked, "So aren't you the guy who broke some track record this spring?"

He surprised himself by swiveling around and asking, "How did you know?"

"One of the dishwashers is from Pittsville, and he saw you in here."

"What's his name?" Adam was curious.

"Aaron something. I don't know his last name. I think he's in the kitchen. I'll let him know you're here and bring you your coffee."

Aaron Saltzman, a sophomore when Adam was a junior, came out in his paper hat and dirty apron. Adam last saw Aaron when he was buying fireworks last July.

"Hi, Ape!" Aaron smiled and waved respectfully from the kitchen entrance.

Adam waved back, forcing a smile after being called that name he despised. Then he was caught off guard again when the waitress brought his coffee and asked him why Aaron had called him Ape.

He answered back right away without thinking, "My legs are bowed and my arms are super long ... like an eighty-six-inch reach ... like an ape. It's a freak thing." Then he smiled and she laughed. It felt good to Adam to have fun banter with a relative stranger who had hardly spoken to him before. When she left the area, he looked at his smiling face in the mirror and liked what he saw, even though it wasn't a natural look for him.

Fasting and a buzz job with good coffee, he said to himself. He thought ahead to Saturday, a bigger day for him than any track meet.

Other World

Saturday at seven in the morning, Adam stood at the end of his driveway waiting for Clark to pick him up. Gop was lying on the driveway looking like a giant roll of dead sausage. Adam was looking toward Sycamore Street for the Bach family car to appear—a brown '68 four-door Buick. He wore the same new clothes he had on when he went to Union Station. At five in the morning he had scrubbed his face red. He had counted only eight visible zits right before his extra-long shower. Soon his smaller, confused stomach would have its first meal after six days with no solid food. He had never looked forward to breakfast as much as now.

Friday morning at the Pitt breakfast table, Adam had sipped his coffee while his dad read aloud a newspaper article about the Vietnam protest demonstrations planned for Saturday at several college campuses across the country.

"They bury stories like that on page nine! Tell me this paper ain't political!" Bill Pitt complained from behind his paper.

"You better just have fruit tomorrow," his mother had warned.

"I need protein more than fruit," Adam said.

"Meat! Eat meat!" his father declared from behind his paper.

"Mom cooks meat in shortening, and that's not good for my face," Adam replied in an angry tone.

"Oh, that's nonsense," his mother protested, defending her cooking.

The comment made Adam get up from his chair, yank the refrigerator door open, and pull out the container of used Crisco his mother stored in a mason jar. Extending the container of used grease toward her, he challenged her comment by telling her, "Why don't you smear a tablespoon of this on your face and see what it looks like tomorrow morning?"

Adam saw the Bach Buick headed toward him with Clark behind the wheel. He could see Helen's laughing face on the front passenger side; she, too, was wearing a dark purple T-shirt. Adam opened the back door on the driver's side and got in.

"We're twins, Adam!" Helen laughed as she turned back toward Adam, who blushed and forced an odd laugh that wasn't his. That made his face redder as he felt a pinch on his butt from his mother's Perry Como tape in his back pocket.

To Adam, the Bach car interior had the smell of order and cleanliness. The beige carpet on the floors had not a speck of dirt or litter. This was a nice change.

As they were driving out of town Helen turned back toward her classmate and asked, "You ready for school, Adam?"

"Yeah, I guess," he droned.

Clark laughed and said, "Not exactly excited about it, huh, Ape?"

Clark laughed at his passenger in his rear-view mirror. The urge to tell Clark not to call him "Ape" was stuck in Adam's throat and he couldn't move it out; so he stuffed it down to his starving belly and it swirled around inside his gut until he'd had enough. "Clark?"

"Yeah, Ape?" their eyes met in the mirror.

"Will you do me a favor?"

"Sure."

"Don't call me Ape."

"Sure … okay … it's a habit, I guess."

They nodded to each other in the mirror. Adam noticed his buzzed head and wondered why neither of them mentioned it to him.

Helen broke up the awkward moment by finding a tape in her purse and injecting the protest song "Ohio" into the cassette player. She called out, "Let's get ready for the protest rally!"

Adam was relieved for the diversion and listened to the lyrics that Neil Young had voiced for millions of Americans shocked and confused by the four students at Kent State killed by National Guardsmen.

Helen sang along, "Tin soldiers and Nixon coming / We're finally on our own ..."

We're finally on our own? Adam questioned inwardly. *Are we ever on our own when they can pull at and control our lives by sending us to war?*

"Soldiers are cutting us down / Should've been done long ago," Helen continued.

Yes, long ago, Adam agreed. *I should've left for Canada long ago ... when I saw this coming*, he continued telling his mind. *I fear what they can do to me so much that I've been cutting myself down ... as if I were the enemy. Is that why I'm ugly? Helen, do you see me as ugly? Please tell me the truth!* Adam screamed at his brain in the backseat of the clean Buick. He moved his fuzz-buzzed head, that he always knew was simian-sized for his body, to the song about that awful massacre that made his generation hate the war even more.

Helen rewound "Ohio" and played it again. This time Adam watched her sing as her brother took the turn onto I-29 south. Adam was thinking how lucky Bobby was to have Helen. *I would not go to Nam if my girlfriend was Helen Bach*, Adam thought. *I would stay at home and look at her perfect face that has no blemishes and not one flaw. Yes, how lucky Bobby is.*

As she continued singing the song, Adam could see how joyful and hopeful Helen's look and attitude were—not at all matching the pain and human pathos the lyrics projected as a national anthem to end the madness that was threatening to engulf them. Of course, Adam couldn't say a word about his observation.

Perhaps she's denying the awful truth about this war because Bobby will be a part of it soon ... part of this madness that puts so many young men and civilians in harm's way.

The song ended again and Clark stopped his sister's hand from rewinding it again. It made Adam think of what his dad said. "It's not the same for women. Oh, they'll worry and grieve their loss ... but they won't die like the men will. They'll go on and have their wounded lives forever. But they still don't have to fear their own death."

Clark ejected the tape, and he made his sister laugh by passing it over his head to Adam when she tried to get it back from him. Adam took the tape and was torn between honoring his driver's wishes and her pleadings for it.

"Don't give it to her, Ape! I mean, Adam! I can't take anymore of 'four dead in Ohio,'" he sang, which made Helen laugh and give up on the tape. Changing the subject he said, "So, Helen, tell Adam and me why you broke up with Bobby."

Adam was surprised both by the news and by Clark's blunt questioning.

"It was his idea," Helen explained. "He doesn't want me waiting for him and worrying about him when he's in Nam."

"That's his reason?" Clark asked her skeptically.

"Why do you say it like that, Clark? Just what are you insinuating?" Helen asked defensively.

"Because guys don't break up with a girl when they go off to boot camp or college or anywhere. That's *why*, Helen!" Clark said with such cynicism that it visibly hurt Helen's feelings about Bobby. Then Clark surprised his backseat passenger via the rear-view mirror and asked, "Am I right, Adam?"

Helen turned toward Adam, her bright blue eyes seriously interested in his opinion.

"I guess I can't say what Bobby is thinking or even know what his reason is. Goin' to Nam when he thought he'd be playin' football in Columbia ... that's screwed up."

Helen respected Adam's opinion. It made her see Bobby's situation in a whole new light and gave her insight into what he was going through. It helped cut through the confusion and pain

71

she felt about the breakup, but she had a few more things to sort out in her mind before she could lose her red-headed anger and her natural desire to get even.

Before long they left I-29 at the Lawrence exit and headed to the sprawling campus with at least twenty times the population of Pittsville. Clark followed his map and found Fields Hall—the two-story brownstone dorm building where he'd be living his freshman year. It was an L-shaped older building for males only. Clark would soon find out that most of the residents in his dorm were jocks on scholarship or upper-classmen from middle-class families.

Helen stayed near the family car that was parked in a loading zone. Clark and Adam carried in Clark's clothes from the trunk, and they left the lid open as a signal to the campus parking patrol that a student move-in was in progress.

Inside the dorm they found room 210 on the second floor. The halls were bustling with short-haired, big-muscled jocks in gym shorts, sandals and t-shirts. Adam found them to be glum-faced while moving about and getting situated in their rooms.

The door to Clark's room was wide open. Dennis, one of his two roommates, was in the room making up his lower bunk. He was a small-framed freshman with deep pock marks on his face, and he had a black brush-like moustache that matched his eyebrows. Affable Clark was cool the way he introduced himself and Adam to the young man from Wichita, who good-naturedly informed Clark that he had his choice of either top bunk bed since the two lower bunks were taken. They put Clark's bags on the upper bunk closest to the window, then Clark got directions to the Student Union and the nearest parking.

After Clark got his room key from the dorm manager on the first floor, they went back to the car. Helen was talking with a good-looking young man in a tattered t-shirt and faded jeans who was giving her easy directions to "the protest." The young man—obviously a jock—smiled his "see ya" and hustled into Fields Hall.

Helen laughed at her brother's knowing look that his sister was moving on after breaking up with Bobby. "What? I got good directions," she laughed.

Finally finding a parking space, they walked across campus to the Student Union Building. Inside the massive building they were impressed with the size of everything—especially the massive cafeteria-style dining hall. By that point Adam's stomach felt like it had shrunk to the size of a walnut after living for six days on lemon water, aspirin and coffee. He couldn't conceal his trembling hands when he picked up an empty tray and silverware in the food line. It was his depleted physical state that made him show the tremulous symptoms of fasting; although to a greater degree it was the coquettish way Helen was looking at the confident, more mature college boys who were returning her visual attention. Adam secretly admired their boldness and confidence because he knew he had no such power to attract girls.

Protein ... protein, Adam reminded himself when selecting a garden salad with hard-boiled eggs. He imagined what it would be like to be a freshman at the University of Kansas. *And the only way I would get here is on a track scholarship.* He remembered Coach Tubbs, the university's track coach, coming to his house earlier in the summer. He had told the confused man that he was ugly and wanted nothing to do with sports. *But even though now my zits are under double digits, I still feel this wall between me and everyone. And if any one of these people in this room could see me jump, they would talk about me here. But I would still have that damn wall that keeps me from flirting with girls I like. I look around this room with hundreds of people ... and they all ignore me. Even Helen and Clark are ignoring me. Yet I watch every little thing they do. I have to be the one who changes how I feel about myself. Now Adam! Now Ape!*

He felt the emotional fire rising up his throat as it had when he voiced his true feelings to the University of Kansas track coach. As he watched Clark and Helen pay for their breakfasts at the register, he heard the excited conversations of hundreds of students in the vast dining hall going on all around him. It reminded him of the buzz in the packed gym during a game when he was about to center jump, and how he'd always manage to sneak a look at Helen and see her face and red-gold hair. Then—as now—he wanted to yell, "HELEN! I'M GOING TO JUMP FOR YOU! WATCH

HOW HIGH I CAN JUMP WHEN I KNOW YOU ARE WATCHING ME!" *What can I say to her now?* he asked himself. *Do I get in her face and tell her not to support Bobby going off to war? Tell her now that it has to be the mothers, wives and girlfriends who tell their men that it is NOT right? That unless we are invaded, we are nothing but invaders?*

Just as Helen and Clark were walking away with their trays and Adam moved closer to the register, his face reddened at what he knew he was about to do.

"Clark!" Adam called out, which made Clark and Helen turn back in disbelief. "Did ya pay for mine?" Adam smiled at Clark's stupefied face, which let the Bachs know that Adam was just kidding. Then with his face flushing red at the register, he decided to use one of his dad's lines on the middle-aged woman cashier—a joke he'd heard his dad say a hundred times to cashiers in stores and restaurants. "Do you take cash?"

The cashier's loud laugh made Adam feel so good that he forgot his hunger. And, for the first time that he could remember, the obvious stares and snickering he got from strangers who saw his long, apelike arms didn't faze him a bit. His fatigued and bellbottomed bowed legs carried him with ease to the round dining table where Clark and Helen were seated.

Adam continued riding himself. *I have to keep this going. Don't shut down now.* That had always been his pattern in school and social situations.

Adam purposely sat in the chair facing all the strange faces in the crowded dining hall—a move he would never make before now. He could see that his friends were confused with his sudden personality change. The Bachs had no idea that Adam was taking his first bite of solid food in six days. He ate slowly, savoring every little bite of his boiled egg.

"Ketchup?" Helen asked Adam.

"Too much sugar in ketchup. Sugar makes my face break out," he admitted, hardly believing he had drawn attention to something he had been so embarrassed about.

They sat in awe of the atmosphere in the incredible Student Union Building where hundreds of young people of all races—

74

students from hundreds of small towns and big cities around the world—all seemed alive with colors and sounds and a palpable, exciting hope that one day they too would partake of what their families called "The American Dream."

Bite after slow bite, the self-proclaimed Freak from Pittsville was aware that if he didn't continue his out-of-character performance, he would be swallowed by his past and once again become invisible without a chance of being real or validated by peers like Helen and Clark. He envied his friends who were so lucky to be part of a good family with loving parents who would support them and give them good advice. Adam said to Clark, "It must be thrilling for you, Clark, to be going to school here in this other world. I mean, it's all so new and different, isn't it?"

Clark nodded in agreement while chewing his food and finally said, "That's why I could hardly believe you when you said you were done with track. It's like … here I am. I've got no chance for any kind of scholarship in any sport, and I'll just be another dorky freshman here with ten thousand other freshmen tryin' to keep my grades up so I don't end up in the army like Bobby …"

"Marines," Helen corrected her brother.

"Whatever. Bobby said you got a low number in the draft, too. But you could get a full ride to any college in the country and be a star for four years. And the way things are lookin', the war could be over by then. I just don't get it," Clark shrugged at his friend.

No way was Adam going to tell Clark why he quit track. Not with Helen right there. So he said nothing and finished his light breakfast while absently looking out the windows at the manicured campus grounds and stately buildings that would be Clark's home for the next four years.

"I might go to KU," Helen stated.

"Really?" Adam asked.

She nodded yes and was about to expand on her thought when a loud, long-haired, hippie-looking young man in a rage screamed and middle-finger-gestured with both hands to a table of young ROTC students in uniform who were having breakfast some fifty feet away, "WE DON'T WANT YOUR F—ING WAR!"

The room quieted and the obnoxious dissenter exited the dining hall right away. Adam's acutely heightened senses knew that the hippie was trying to make a point—as if winning a bet that he could muster enough nerve to do such a brazen thing—instead of really being some lunatic in a raging rant. The laughing faces of the rigid ROTC students showed that they weren't concerned by the brief incident. Adam immediately thought of his own buzzed head and hoped he wouldn't be taken for one of the ROTC students.

Breaking the uncomfortable silence at their table Helen said, "Isn't this the worst day to be in a military uniform on a campus demonstrating against the war? I mean, really, guys."

On their walk to the anti-war demonstration, they could hear Bob Dylan's song "The Times They Are A-Changin'" coming from speakers on the grounds of an open area with a large gathering of students scattered about in small groups. Most were sitting on blankets as if at a picnic. They could see all kinds of protest signs and banners carried by long-haired, barefoot students close to a cupola where a cluster of people were gathered to speak. On one white banner with green letters was a quote from Jimi Hendrix, "When the power of love overcomes the love of power, the world will know peace."

Now in the center of this growing crowd, Adam trailed Clark and Helen. Adam was becoming more aware that these college kids—some of them grown men and women—appeared uniformly to have an attractive shabbiness about them. Adam's fragile ego made him believe that his new clothes were too conservative and out of place. It was as if he were advertising that he was a rube from Pittsville. Adam was keeping himself stuck—ruled again by the same overwrought nervous system that made his skin boil and fester and erupt in a hundred places.

Across the whole country college students were burning draft cards and protesting universities furnishing grades to draft boards. The University of Kansas was not as radical as many schools, except back in the spring there was a massive demonstration on campus protesting military and Dow Chemical job fairs on campus. On that day sixteen students were arrested for throwing eggs at recruiters. Today's anti-war rally appeared sedate in comparison. The general atmosphere seemed to validate Clark's earlier statement that "these protest things are a good excuse to get high, get laid, and listen to some great rock. That's all."

"For What It's Worth" began to play from speakers as they sat down on the grass. Adam told Helen and Clark, "You know, I think this song is the ultimate protest song. I'm not surprised they're playing it."

Adam watched Helen singing along with the lyrics. "Paranoia strikes deep / Into your life it will creep / It starts when you're always afraid..." When the chorus came, Helen closed her eyes and seemed to get lost in the song. "I think it's time we stop, children, what's that sound, everybody look what's going down."

When Crosby, Stills, Nash & Young's song ended, the same ROTC-badgering hippie tried to get the radical anti-war slogan going. "One, two, three, four ... we don't want your f—ing war!"

Clark pointed at him and laughed to Adam and Helen, "Look. Nobody's joining in with him. Just proves what I've been saying all along." In the small, Midwestern town of Lawrence, Kansas, it was more of a peaceful gathering to protest a war that Nixon was already de-escalating somewhat, even though there were over 156,000 U.S. troops still in Vietnam.

A barefoot, dark-haired, handsome young man walking past their group smiled at Helen. Adam watched her smile back, which seemed to be invitation enough for the stranger to sit down next to her and strike up a conversation. He introduced himself to Helen as Robert, ignoring Adam and Clark as if they weren't there. Helen then introduced Clark and Adam to Robert simply as "my brother and his friend." Adam thought Robert was a steaming pile of arrogant talk. As the protest speakers were encouraging the crowd to write their congressman about getting our troops out of Vietnam, Robert and Helen stood up.

"I'll be back in a minute," Helen said to Clark, and she walked away with the handsome Robert.

"I guess she's over Bobby," Clark quipped to Adam with an impish grin.

Adam watched Helen walk away with Robert and then vanish behind the three-story limestone Science Building. For ten minutes Adam stared at the double-yellow daisies planted nearby, not hearing a word coming from the speakers crowded into the cupola around the only microphone. It wasn't jealousy that Adam was feeling; it was more like a feeling of terror that was overtaking him and was enhanced by a Joni Mitchell song that began blaring from the speakers, competing with his busy self-talk. *It doesn't matter what clothes I wear or the clever things I say ... or even how far I can jump. It's the good-looking guys that walk away with the girls. It's not her fault ... it's just the way we are.*

Meanwhile, Clark was muttering clock coordinates for chick sightings to his friend whenever he'd spot an attractive girl. "Two o'clock ... the blonde in the blue t-shirt. Wow!" or "Ten o'clock ... cute brunette in the red shorts."

As Joni Mitchell's song faded out, a hippie-looking young woman wearing rose-tinted sunglasses and a rainbow-colored bandana that fanned out her fuzzy hair began a tirade from the podium against "Nixon's war." She quoted the late Martin Luther King, Jr. from 1967, "If America's soul becomes totally poisoned, part of the autopsy must read 'Vietnam.'"

Clark started getting impatient for his sister to return. "Where in the world is she?" he asked, not really expecting an answer from Adam. "I don't want to sit here all day. I'd at least like to have some time to walk around the campus and check out the babes."

"Go ahead," Adam told him. "I'll wait here for Helen."

"You sure?"

"Yeah," Adam said. Helen had referred to her brother as a stoner many times in front of Adam, and Adam figured his friend was in search of more than just "babes."

Not much later a Joan Baez song started and Helen returned. Alone.

"Where's your friend?" Adam asked.

"Oh, he had to do something," she replied. She pulled out a pair of sunglasses from her pocket purse to hide the evidence that she had smoked a joint with Robert behind the Science Building.

"Where's Clark?" she asked Adam.

"He's walkin' around. He'll be back soon, I'm sure."

"Checkin' out girls, huh?" Helen snickered. Then she asked Adam, "So, Adam, have you ever smoked pot before?"

He lied when he nodded yes to impress her, willing to see where such a lie might lead.

Helen snapped open her pocket purse, pinched out a roach that Robert gave her, and handed it to Adam. "I don't have any matches, but you can smoke it behind that building," she pointed. When Adam started to walk away, she added, "Hey, Adam? Please don't tell Clark I was smoking weed." Adam promised he wouldn't. Helen watched him get matches from a student and head off in the direction of the same place she had smoked with Robert.

Adam walked among the crowd of passive "protestors," regretting he didn't bring his sunglasses to shield his spooked eyes from such a crowd. So he did what he was good at and became invisible—walking his short, fast-footed steps with his head down. He focused only on the path before him, passing the colorful pockets of gabbing strangers while the matches and the roach were sweaty from his fisted palm. Never had he smoked anything; yet here he was, off in another world and about to experience it alone after feeling marginalized by Helen.

Step after step he moved past strangers. Their voices were all brand new and intelligent-sounding to him. Their laughter and casual confidence was a mysterious blend of jasmine and accomplished youth, talented youth who made it this far because of superior minds that had a good chance of evading war and poverty. These were the ones who stood the best chance of capturing "The American Dream"—the elusive goal that screamed its unspoken promise of "a better life than your parents." It was a goal every young person was force-fed to achieve, yet it was completely unreachable for guys like Adam Pitt and Bobby Taggit. The unlucky ones with the low numbers.

Adam turned at the end of the Science Building, staying on the sidewalk to appear respectfully invisible while on his way to break a nationwide law. He felt like he was a world away from Pittsville, a place where the protesting wasn't as loud as the music from California. The tiny, illegal item palmed in his hand that was given to him by Helen was his country's symbol of free love, apathy and rebellion against the war and the hypocritical conservatives who support it and projected their past insanity onto the youth who were defenseless to stand against it.

Behind a dumpster in the alcove of a door marked "Emergency Exit," he faced the shadow of the Science Building's back door. He hunched over in his little pocket of fear to light the roach. He considered not inhaling and only pretending that he smoked it, but then he thought of Helen and glanced furtively behind him before hitting on it. He inhaled deeply and coughed from the harshness to his throat. His enervated state from fasting stoned him even quicker. After butting the roach into the wall, he tucked it inside his book of matches before stashing it in his back bellbottom pocket next to Perry Como.

A paranoid silliness was upon him as he walked back toward where he had left Helen sitting on the grass. Upon turning the corner of the building, he thought the crowd had grown considerably. The song "Ohio" was playing from the speakers, only much louder and with heightened clarity. "Gotta get down to it / Soldiers are cutting us down / Should have been done long ago …"

At first he thought Helen was gone, but then he saw Helen and Clark standing with a group singing along with the protest song as it was winding down: "This summer I hear the drumming / four dead in Ohio …"

Adam stood behind Helen, so close to her that he could smell the sweet fragrance of her strawberry shampoo. He playfully tapped Clark on the shoulder with his long reach and watched his friend turn to see Adam giggling in his pot stupor that included dry mouth. Helen turned around to see that Adam had tried her offering. She smiled into his eyes with her merry cornflower-blue eyes and noticed for the first time that Adam's eyes were a gray-green, an eye color she'd never seen before. But it was way too noisy to comment on such a thing.

That tiny moment of connecting meant more to Adam than all the records, blue ribbons, and adulation he'd ever received. Even though his legs were still weak from fasting, he felt like using

Clark's shoulders to leap-frog over him and land on the roof of the cupola. But in an instant his high from the pot turned south when handsome Robert returned and whispered words in Helen's ear that obviously tickled her, made her giggle, and caused her to move her body closer to this stranger as if she really liked him.

Now more than ever, Adam believed Clark was right in his observation that this gathering was not even close to a real demonstration that protested the war. It was more of a meeting place for attractive people like Helen and Robert to swap phone numbers and dates when they could meet again—things that Adam had never done before and was envious of.

After a couple more hours of listening to music and orations from ardent activists, Clark wanted to walk around the campus to find all the buildings where his classes would be. Smooth-talking Robert was trying his best to convince Helen to go with him. "C'mon, Helen. Let me show you my cool pad off-campus, and we can listen to some real music."

Clark was against the idea of his sister going off with a guy she'd just met. He didn't want her to be separated from them and expressed that to her wordlessly by shaking his head no when he overheard Robert's bold proposition. Robert finally left after getting Helen to write down her phone number for him. Adam and Clark were visibly bothered by Helen giving the confident college senior her number.

Helen saw their concerned faces and gave the boys a playful grin. "Oh, stop worrying, you two. I gave him a wrong number. Besides … I love Bobby."

The three of them walked around the sprawling campus, following a map of marked buildings until Clark felt pretty good about finding all his classes on Monday. Adam had a headache from the combined effects of the roach, the heat from the sun, and being dehydrated from not drinking enough water. Clark wanted to put away his clothes, make his bed and get settled into his new space. At the parked Buick, Helen hugged her brother goodbye.

"I hope you stay in track," he told Adam with a handshake, adding, "Ya know, it would be a lot of fun if you could go to school here and we could be roommates."

Adam didn't say anything about his plans for the future; he was tired of explaining himself. "Good luck, Clark," Adam smiled when opening the front passenger door to begin his ride home with Helen. Just the two of them.

Don't Tell Bobby

On their drive back from Lawrence, Helen was obviously concerned about her image with Adam, mostly because he was Bobby's friend.

"I didn't give Robert my phone number. I gave him some number I made up," she giggled.

Adam chuckled at the thought of smooth-talking Robert calling some wrong number.

"Please don't tell Bobby," she implored.

"Don't tell him what? I thought you two broke up."

"We did. I just don't want him to know I smoked pot with Robert."

Adam nodded, understanding her reason. "So when is Bobby headed for boot camp?"

"In early October."

"Why did you break up with him?" Adam asked, even though he knew it was a personal question.

"He broke up with me. He got the idea from his dad. So now he thinks it would be too hard on us with him going to Vietnam and being separated so long."

"Lots of couples stay together even though they're separated," Adam replied.

"I know. That's what I told him. He said he'd rather not have expectations or all that *drama* when he's in a war zone." She twisted the word "drama" to such a cynical degree that he could tell she was really hurt by Bobby.

"Well, I guess I can understand that," Adam bravely admitted.

After a long pause of awkward silence Helen confessed, "I really am in love with Bobby. If he weren't so hard-headed and stubborn, I believe we could stay together despite the distance between us and our time apart."

The time had come for Adam to act like he did in the Student Union cafeteria and lay it all out there. He believed it was most likely his only chance to be real with Helen Bach, the girl who inspired him to break records and jump out of the gym.

"Look, Helen … I know I'm too ugly to have a girlfriend … but I still know how Bobby feels. He's savin' you both a bunch of awful waiting."

She kept looking over at her passenger, her eyes going back and forth between the road and his profile, really taking in what he just said. She wanted to say something in the right way. "You're not ugly, Adam. How can you say such a negative thing about yourself? Kids our age are growing and changing …"

"For a second I thought you were gonna say that it's the inside that matters," Adam interrupted her.

"Well, it's true."

"No, it's not true, Helen. I'm not stupid. Girls go for the cute guys. Maybe when girls get older they start lookin' for the inside stuff, but not when they're young. Guys like me know that. Would you have given Robert any time if he was ugly?"

"You might have a point there," she burst into laughter, which made him do the same.

After a few moments of silence, Helen reached to turn on the car radio. That's when Adam removed the Perry Como tape from his back pocket and handed it to her.

"You brought it!" She inserted the tape into the car's tape player and played her favorite love song, "It's Impossible." She sang along to the song her mother played a thousand times around the house when she was growing up.

After she played the song a second time, her passenger quickly ejected the tape, making Helen laugh with him.

As they neared downtown Kansas City, Adam suggested, "Let's stop and have a late lunch at Union Station. I'll buy," he smiled.

Helen parked her parents' car in the Union Station lot and followed Adam around to the side of the massive train station. She wanted to stop and finish the roach she'd given Adam. He told her he didn't want any of it and shielded her from view while she finished it. Adam didn't have any interest in smoking any more of the illegal substance; he had spent too many years watching the effects of alcohol on his parents—their daily "manufactured low," he called it.

While walking to the front entrance to the station she again told Adam, "Don't tell Bobby."

Once inside the station, Helen stopped to marvel in gaping awe at the Grand Hall's ninety-five-foot ceiling. She told Adam she'd never been there before as her eyes took in the vastness of the national landmark that was busy with pedestrian traffic.

They sat on a bench where they could view the most people coming and going in front of them. Soldiers in uniform kept reminding Helen that Bobby was going off to boot camp in less than five weeks. Adam was under a spell that every young man experiences when he's with a girl that he knows is out of his league. He was succumbing to the dreaded feeling that he was becoming boring to her. An invisible wall of doubt loomed between them, just as it had in the cafeteria in Lawrence when he felt he just had to do or say something out of character in order to impress her.

Nothing good came to him. He sat there beside Helen Bach on the hard bench listening to his busy mind coming up with fearful, relentless reminders that he was running out of time with every passing second. She seemed to be lost in the manswarm of passengers arriving and departing. Then she stretched her bare, shapely legs and examined them as if she were ready for them to take her somewhere.

"You ready for lunch?" he asked.

"Yeah, I'm hungry." She yawned and stretched her arms above her head before standing.

As they walked toward Rudy's diner in the distance, Adam confessed to her, "I like to come here. It's a nice change from the reality of life with my parents."

"It's an incredible place," she said. "I'm amazed by all the people traveling through here on their way to somewhere … or saying goodbye to friends and family and lovers. And all the servicemen going off to war and being changed forever by it. Maybe Bobby will leave from here when he goes to boot camp in San Diego," she said wistfully.

"I think he said he was flying," Adam recalled Bobby telling him at the gas station. He thought it strange that Helen didn't know Bobby's travel itinerary.

"Oh, yeah, I think you're right. I remember now he did say he was flying. That was the day he told me he wanted to break up, and I guess I was too upset to hear anything else."

"Yeah," Adam understood. As they walked toward the diner, he pointed in the distance to the shoeshine stand outside the barber shop and told her that's where he got his buzz job. He felt her merry blue eyes looking at his head.

Out of nowhere Helen said, "I really can't believe you're not going to college when you can get a full scholarship to any school you want."

Adam debated inwardly whether or not to tell her the truth. The whole ugly truth. He decided not to tell her and changed the subject upon entering the brightly lit diner.

"I love the food here," he said and picked out a booth for them across from the counter stools at the fountain where he usually sat when he was alone or with Grover. The same friendly waitress was there who always seemed to wait on him.

"Chicken salad special with potato salad and a Coke?" the waitress smiled at Adam.

"Yes, but make that water with lemon instead of a Coke."

"I'll have the same thing with a Coke," Helen told her.

After the waitress left, Adam told Helen that sugar makes his face break out.

"Really? How'd you find that out?" she was curious.

"I fasted for six days."

"Really?"

He nodded yes. "I just got done with a six-day fast. In fact, today was my first day of eating solid food again. My mom fries everything in Crisco, and I've been having too much sugar. I asked the pharmacist, and he said too much sugar can cause acne ... so I stopped eating for a week."

"How did you do that Adam?"

"I just did it."

"That's amazing. Tell me what it was like."

"Well, for one thing my dreams were so strange. Usually I'll remember only one or two dreams a week ... and that's what was so strange. I'd have several dreams in one night, and every one of them would wake me up until I just had to get up."

"What kind of dreams?" she asked when the waitress brought their drinks.

"The one I remember the most was really scary. I was on this train, and I asked a boy where the train was goin'. He said 'Vietnam.' I remember running toward the back of the train, but I could never reach it. It was so real."

"Wow! I remember you said you got a real low number in the Draft Lottery like Bobby did."

"Fourteen."

"Yeah ... that is low. I've had bad dreams since Bobby and I broke up."

"Really?"

"I keep having the same dream where he doesn't come back from the war. And I can't tell him about it because we broke up. Even if we were together, I still couldn't tell him about it because it's something he doesn't want to hear."

The waitress arrived with their food and set their plates before them. Adam knew he had to eat slowly and take small bites.

Helen confronted Adam again and asked, "Adam, why aren't you going to college … at the very least to avoid the draft?"

Adam knew that kind of truth would be hard to explain because it was wrapped in feelings boys are trained to ignore and not waste their time thinking or talking about—especially to confident girls like Helen who liked confident guys who knew what they wanted. Finally he said, "I'm afraid of the attention. I'm ugly and I can't stand people staring at me like I'm some kinda freak in the circus."

A blush of fire covered his face like one giant inflamed pimple. Helen chewed her food without tasting it, staring at his red face and unsure of what to say upon hearing such self-deprecating words that kept his eyes averted in shame. When he finally looked at her, he could see that her eyes lost all their merry light. He whispered, "I don't want to be the 'Ape from Pittsville.' That's what I feel like when I'm being looked at for only my jumping ability. I know I'm ugly … and because I am, this overwhelming fire floods my whole body."

There! He finally said it the way he wanted to say it. The red fire on his face made him bend his head down from her view until she reached across the table and put her hand on top of his hand and squeezed it to tell him it was okay. His eyes closed and the dam behind his eyes released a liquid stream of shame he'd been holding back for too long. He raised his free hand to cover his eyes and said in a blurted whisper, "I'm ashamed of my parents … my life … everything. I can't be around strangers who ignore me face to face and then stare at me when I jump. I just can't do it anymore. And I don't want to die for a stupid war or be forced to kill for people who don't even know me or why we're there."

He kept his eyes shielded from Helen and hadn't noticed the waitress stopping by to check on their table, or Helen smiling as if saying "not now, please."

They continued eating in silence until Adam said, "Don't tell Bobby or Clark I said all that."

"I won't," she promised.

By the time they left the diner, Adam felt better than he had in a long time. Getting out his feelings had recharged his entire body and seemed to put out the fire that before would rage out of control from just a spark of shame.

A few doors down from the barber shop, Helen went into a cigar store to buy her dad a cigar while Adam waited in the station's Grand Hall. He could hardly stand still because he felt so alive and in sync with the manswarm all around him. *This must be what confidence feels like*, he thought.

For a brief moment he wished he were alone in that special place so he could walk straight into the wave of strangers off-boarding from three different trains that had just arrived from Minneapolis, Chicago and St. Louis. He felt exactly the way he'd felt before he jumped, when the eyes of the crowd were on him and he knew he was ready to explode into that invisible zone of space where memory is formed during held breath, thrust, and then the incredible feeling of relaxation after his bulging calf muscles in a long jump had pushed far enough to allow his legs to lay out and reach for that space where records live. And it was always made clear to him in his dreams right before a big track meet that the longer he remained relaxed after his take-off, the longer he would stay in the air. Now, after spilling his guts all over Helen, he felt the very same way he had in the air. He hurried with his apelike shuffle in his red-stringed black Converse high-tops toward the shoeshine stand, past the elderly shine man reading his paper, and into the barber shop to see for himself in the big mirrors—before it all vanished. Oblivious to the busy barbers and their customers, he stood looking at his reflection in the fluorescent-bright shop. It was there: his relaxed gray-green eyes, the healthy glow of his skin that tingled with aliveness the more he looked into the mirror, and his unwrinkled brow free of worry and self-doubt. He moved his face closer to the mirror and he looked into his febrile eyes. *Hold this*, he said to his reflection. Then he nodded and smiled at the barber before he hustled back into the Grand Hall.

Down a ways he could see Helen with a cigar fisted in her hand. As he approached her, he started feeling safe enough to ask her something impulsive. It was something his recent fasting was making him do, something he always wanted to do here in his favorite place on earth. "Helen, would you do me a favor?"

"Sure," she smiled, although distracted by more servicemen in uniform coming and going around them.

"Hold my hand while we walk through the station," he winced.

"Sure," she laughed.

He didn't have to explain, and yet he did explain as they walked hand in hand across the vast station. "I want to see how people look at me when I'm not alone, to see if there's a diff'rence."

"Oh, so I'm an experiment," she teased with such a sweet laugh that he was now free to see every detail before them just as pedestrian traffic really increased. He purposely led them against the flow of the manswarm, like a car going the wrong way on a jam-packed one-way street.

They left the station laughing and no longer holding hands. Their drive back to Pittsville went quickly because they talked about the upcoming school year and the funny things they knew about their classmates. Adam made fun of Steven Kaladi by saying, "That jerk is so rich, he wears a different pair of shoes every day of the week."

Walking up his driveway, Adam knew it was the end of the best day of his life. Helen was his friend, and he believed from then on Helen Bach would remain a good friend. He wished he had given her his mother's Perry Como tape. When she handed it to him he'd faltered, unable to give it to her.

Bobby will be gone to boot camp soon, and she's free now, he told himself as he stepped inside the house and into the stifling smells of second-hand cigarette smoke, fried pork, and Gop's dirty food bowl.

Except with Helen

The new school year began in Pittsville under a bright blue sky on a windless Indian summer day—the dry days of static electricity and dust when the nation's bread basket is about to turn into autumn. It was one of the few annual weather changes when seasonal colds and invigoration clash inside bodies still sluggish from the humid summer.

Adam, carrying only a notebook with a pen clipped to it, walked the six blocks to school in the same outfit he'd worn when he spent the day in Lawrence with Clark and Helen. Eight pounds lighter since fasting, he had managed to tell his parents that he'd appreciate no more smoking in the house until he'd left for school. And he would have only fruit or oatmeal or hard-boiled eggs for breakfast with no juice, only coffee. Plus, he would boil his own drinking water and never drink water from the tap again. Upon informing their gape-jawed faces of his requests, he told them, "I'm down to seven pimples now. I don't want to go back to the way things were."

As he was walking by Helen's house, for the first time he felt that he could be a track star from Pittsville who held two national records—even though now he was more resolute than ever about

91

being done with track and basketball. Ever since he gave up competing in sports, his bad dreams of being gawked at had stopped. He knew he had until November to break the news to the basketball coach, then in early spring he had to tell his track coach he was done with track. Yes, they are all good changes, yet he was well aware that the biggest test of all was coming up when he walked the halls after getting his new locker in the senior section. The combination padlock he'd used for the past two years was inside his back pocket and the combination memorized; but most of all he hoped his locker was close to Helen's locker.

He wondered if Helen would be walking to school this year since Bobby used to drive her and sometimes Clark to school in his black Mustang. A couple times last winter when it was really cold, Bobby stopped and gave Adam a ride. He remembered sitting in the back with Clark and smelling the sweet fragrance of Helen's perfume—a refreshing change from home.

I just have to accept that I'm stuck with my parents in their house until I graduate. But then what? Canada? he asked himself while passing house after familiar house, knowing every person who lived under each roof in the little town named after his family. Around him were clusters of kids of all ages wearing their new school clothes, on their way to one of the two schools that were separated by forty acres of Harold Dierdorf's cornfield.

For some inexplicable reason, Adam was getting the same waves and shout-outs from younger boys walking or driving by him in vehicles. "HI, APE! JUMP, APE!"
But now the attention wasn't bothering him like it had last spring.

Is that because of the fast? he wondered. *Or is it from spending last Saturday with Helen?*

For years Adam's parents had been telling him, "It's not what others say to you, it's how you handle it." But after any advice from them, he would bite his tongue—literally—and fight the wrath he felt for their shared weakness to smoke and drink and be lazy total losers.

Yet Adam loved his parents in the same way he loved God and hated religion. Anything with rules, like church dogma or forced biblical doctrine, he considered a manmade way to control and manipulate the masses. It was Adam's parents who broke away from the Methodist church after Grampa Pitt died and left most of his money to the First Methodist Church of Pittsville. The bitter paternal legacy blew into Adam's young brain in the form of spiteful, virulent words charged with sounds of hypocrisy spewed whether drunk or sober, Sundays or weekdays. It didn't matter.

Three blocks from school Adam stood facing the church, a building made from donated brick and mortar and sand that his grandfather had delivered personally. Yet Adam had never stepped inside its double doors. Until now. His prayers to God had increased during his fasting, as had his angst toward his ignorant parents. He blamed them for his yellow-snotted cowardice in every social encounter. Adam knew the rotting fuel churning inside his flat belly had to be diminished, or he would never make it through his senior year without killing both of them. This he believed more and more ever since returning from Lawrence and finding them both passed out in their recliners.

In one easy jump he made it from the sidewalk to the church's front doors without touching any of the five cement steps leading up to them. He knew this had to be the nicest church in town. There were only two others, each half its size. Inside the empty church he sat in the last row of pews staring at the incredible stained glass colors of Christ's likeness in the windows all the way from the back of the church up to the front and behind the pulpit.

Even though he was aware that Christ represents God to all Christians, Adam had never prayed to Jesus, "the Son of God." Just like he had in his prayers in his room, he directed his prayer behind his closed eyes to a God with no face or form or children that he knew of. *God, whoever You may be, please give me the skills I'll need to ride out this life I'm in ... and the power to change things when I can. I hate the life my parents live. I know they won't change, but can You change how I feel about them ... please?"*

His first visit inside a church took less than five minutes, and he did feel better. He felt as if he'd gotten away with something impulsive he tried, like fasting. Regardless, he did feel as if he was no longer inured to the way his body felt most of the time.

Walking toward the high school, he noticed that his steps were lighter somehow, and it made him wonder how far and how high he could jump when he felt this way. He smiled at the image of his mother swerving out of her buying routine to buy him the foods he wanted. Then two senior boys smoking in a parked car reminded him that tomorrow could be smoke-free at home. *I will say how pleasant the air is and how much I enjoyed breakfast,* he told himself. Perhaps by his own attitude he had the power to influence his parents to make a positive change also.

There they were—the five doors to the school's front entrance that led into those halls of shame and dread. All last year he picked a different door to enter every new morning of the week, then he'd change the sequence every week. His silly superstition made him giggle, and for the first time in memory he didn't pick a door. *I'm a senior now. This is my year.*

Once inside, it had to happen. He could sense a "sameness" in the way his peers and teachers had reacted to him ever since he'd broken records in track meets last spring.

"Adam!" Principal Brown extended his welcoming milksop right hand just inside the front doors while in the throes of greeting returning students, a ritual he performed every year. "Look forward to watching you break your records this year," the bespectacled boss smiled at his school's living legend.

By the time Adam got rid of his fake smile, he also got his right hand back from Principal Brown. But right away a freshman came up to him with an open notebook and a pen asking, "Ape, can I get your autograph?"

"No, I gave you one last year."

"Yeah, I know. But it's a new year and I want your senior-year autograph."

"Go away … and don't call me 'Ape.'"

Adam continued down the wide foyer, past the gym doors and the trophy cases. He found the long bulletin board where new locker assignments were listed by grade in alphabetical order, along with assigned classes and locations. He found Helen's name and saw that they had two classes together—Algebra II before lunch and Health the last period.

Just then one of his friendly classmates passing behind him called out, "Hey, Pitt! Nice buzz job!"

After writing down his new classes and his new locker number, he watched for Helen while making his way along the crowded hall that grew noisier with chatter and more colorful from all the new school clothes. He removed his padlock from his back pocket when he found his locker and dialed it open. Right after clicking it locked, he was startled when just a few lockers down he saw the back of Helen's red hair. She was putting her things inside her locker. Nervous, he felt like calling out her name, hoping her Bobby-blue eyes were happy to see him; except he'd have to yell to be heard above the din, and yelling wasn't part of his character. Unless he was yelling at his parents.

Helen was talking to another senior girl about Bobby, explaining the whole situation about their breakup with such animated fervor that Adam walked away not wanting to impose or compete with an ex-boyfriend—a heart-sore named Bobby Taggit.

For a change, Adam felt like walking the halls before the bell rang. For all of his junior year he had avoided these halls of shame by arriving at school just when the bell rang. Over the summer he had pondered this issue and decided he would walk alone and start acting like he was a star athlete who held two national high school track and field records. It was a big part of his vow to not fear the little things. He alone had allowed his mind to hurt him in big ways his entire junior year. But his vow was frangible because he was stuck with his own personality. He truly believed that everyone who knew him would never see him any other way. No matter what.

Being labeled a shy person by other girls would be the most difficult of things he wanted to change. Not only had he been responsible for so many of these weak first impressions, he also had created a perception of himself that he believed was unanimous among his peers as being socially inept—except with Helen. Now he believed that Helen Bach was his only chance to vanquish the cowardly feelings that he knew had to be precancerous to a young man's soul. The very essence of himself knew he had been afraid to live and far removed from the triumphant song of victory that his heart needed to feel in order to stay clear of that spiraling cesspool of addiction that he saw his parents drowning in day after day his entire life.

His new black Converse high tops with red strings felt like tethered bricks as he shuffled along the buffed hallway clockwise on the right side as if in traffic on the streets of Pittsville. Just as he had last school year, Adam had that same feeling of being stuck in his own self-judgmental prison without any connection to his peers. And it was growing in intensity, reminding him why he quit all athletic competition.

There was just enough time to finish one more lap and come around again to Helen's locker. *I hope she's still there,* he thought.

Step after step Adam thought of what he would say to her. Nothing clever came to him; so instead of continuing on to her locker, he ducked into his first period classroom and sat at a desk at the back of the room just as he always did at the start of every new school year. He vascillated about whether to move up to a desk in the middle of the row in order to be in a more sociable location, but he sat there. Stuck. He was paralyzed by his fear and unable to make a simple yet audacious move that would force him to be more "out there" and break the vicious cycle that once again threatened to hold him back.

If I stay here ... I can at least think of Helen more, he reasoned, even though she was not in this first period class with him.

Reggie

In early October Bobby flew off to boot camp in San Diego. Meanwhile, Helen started walking the halls more and more with Steven Kaladi, the rich kid and wannabe-jock that nobody liked. Except Helen. To Adam's great pleasure, it seemed like the whole school thought even less of Kaladi when he started hanging out more and more with "Bobby's girl." And even though Helen was free to date, it bothered Adam that she was dating the guy he hated most in the whole world. Adam was convinced that Helen only went to lunch with Kaladi in his new truck—the one he had been given from his father's dealership—to get back at Bobby for not saying goodbye to her before leaving for boot camp.

Adam spent his Saturdays in downtown Kansas City. He would go to the YMCA and shoot baskets all by himself at one of the six hoops that he usually had all to himself if he got there when they first opened. He would spend an hour shooting and rebounding quickly, getting a good cardio workout. Then he would hit the weight room to lift for a while before taking a long swim.

He'd been sticking to his healthier fruit and vegetable diet and staying away from greasy fried foods and tap water. His daily pimple count was down to five—another record for Adam Pitt.

Even his parents noticed their son's improved appearance and made their kitchen a permanent smoke-free zone. In turn, the Pitt living room became a smoking ashtray that Adam avoided by holding his breath whenever passing through.

Adam liked going to the Y because it replaced his old pattern of working out with weights and shooting baskets in the school gym once or twice a week. Because of not wanting to be approached by any coaches for the coming basketball and track seasons, he didn't want his workouts to be a matter of public spectacle.

One particular Saturday in October, Adam drove his parents' car to the Y. He looked forward to at least one day a week of rigorous exercise so he could eliminate toxins from his body and protect his face from flare-ups. While shooting baskets alone at one end of the creaky basketball court, Adam saw a lanky, dark-skinned, six-foot-two, smiling kid with black-framed glasses strapped to his small head. His round head appeared smaller only because his shoulders were so broad. He wore black gym trunks and a white t-shirt. He was shod with black high-top Converse with black strings over black nylon socks, and he had a black wristband around his right shooting hand. He dribbled a ball over to Adam and rebounded Adam's missed fifteen-foot jumper as if he were a fluid cat that wanted to play.

"Shoot 'til ya miss?" the young man asked Adam politely.

"Okay," Adam agreed, which meant that the other would rebound for the shooter until the shooter missed.

This guy doesn't miss, Adam complained to himself as swish after swish sizzled the twine. After the incredible shooter made sixteen twenty-foot jumpers in a row, Adam started talking to him to see if he could throw off his shot. "What's your name?"

"Reggie," he smiled upon swishing in number seventeen.

"My name's Adam," he said as Reggie moved along and stayed beyond the line of the twenty-foot arc.

"I don't need a rebounder," Reggie grinned, motioning for Adam to let the ball go after he made his next shot.

That day Adam witnessed the most incredible yet simple shooting exhibition he'd ever seen on any basketball court. Not only did Reggie swish through every shot as he moved along the arc, he also made the ball return to him whether he remained in the same spot or moved left or right. Adam just stood back, marveling at the flick of Reggie's wrist combined with the reverse spin on the ball created by his long fingers. Then the swishing ball would always bounce back to Reggie in diminishing bounces that followed and reached him at about knee height wherever he moved to take his next shot.

"Incredible! How do you do that?" Adam admired.

"Practice," Reggie smiled.

Finally after the twenty-third swish, Adam stepped up and caught the ball after it zipped through the net.

"I'll betcha a Coke that you don't make the next shot," Adam said with confidence.

Reggie laughed and said, "You gonna block it?"

"That's right," Adam smiled.

Reggie knew he could elevate his shot so that it rained straight down right next to the top of the backboard. *Ain't no way that white boy can block it,* he thought smugly to himself. "For a Coke, right?" Reggie confirmed.

"Uh-huh," Adam replied.

Standing under the basket, Adam saw the higher trajectory of Reggie's shot and timed his jump perfectly to easily swipe the ball away from its certain path into the net. To Reggie, it seemed like Adam had blocked the ball near the top of the backboard. The stunned shooter stood there looking at the white boy with the long arms until he asked Adam how he could jump like that.

"Practice," Adam grinned.

Reggie was getting more curious about this guy. "Can you touch the top of the backboard?"

Adam nodded yes.

"Man, you are unreal. How can you jump that high?"

"I took a mail-order exercise course and increased my jumping ability. But I can't shoot worth a darn," Adam confessed.

Reggie laughed and said, "Lots a guys can shoot, but not many can jump like you. If I could jump like you … man, I wouldn't be goin' to no Vietnam. I know that much."

"You got drafted?"

"I enlisted in the army."

"When do you leave for boot camp?"

"January eighth."

"Really?"

"Uh-huh. My eighteenth birthday is comin' up soon, and my momma won't sign for me to go. She wants me to do it on my own. She says she don't want no part of sendin' me to war."

"Did you graduate?"

"Nope. Dropped out last year. No good jobs out there for me. I can go to any school I want on the G.I. Bill when I get out. Got no use for school now. Don't know what I want to go to school for." Reggie started dribbling the ball and swished a twenty-foot jumper.

"Did you play high school ball in K.C.?" Adam asked.

"Just pick-up games here and there."

Adam was confused why a guy who could shoot like that didn't play high school ball.

Reggie removed his glasses and adjusted the black strap after cleaning his lenses with the bottom of his shirt. "You want your Coke now?" he called out to Adam.

Adam wanted to hit the weight room and then go for his swim. "Maybe a little later," he nodded to Reggie.

It was well over an hour later when Adam left the Y. Reggie was in sweats waiting on the front steps. He handed Adam a can of Coke.

"Thanks," Adam was surprised.

Reggie started to walk away carrying his gym bag over his shoulder.

"You want a ride?" Adam asked.

"I like to walk. See ya."

"Thanks for the Coke."

On Adam's drive over to Union Station, he couldn't help thinking about Reggie and how he was just another brave young man headed for war because he had no other options. *That damn war is suckin' us all in.*

100

Instead of going inside to Union Station's Grand Hall, Adam walked around to the other side of the building where the trains arrived and departed. That was where they cleaned some of them on Saturday to make them ready for their weekly runs Monday through Friday. Smiling porters on a smoke break recognized the Kid from Pittsville who was friends with Grover, and they nodded at him while smoking and joking about "that white boy's jumping ability."

Adam slowed his walk in order to get in touch with his thrilling feelings of expectancy of one day boarding one of these cream-yellow passenger cars with brown trim and being taken to a place far away and safe from war. He dreaded the impending choice coming his way, yet he knew it was a choice that could save his life.

I guess I'd rather be ugly than dead, he reminded himself in the midst of the great train smells of oil and fuel. He was bolstered by wistful presentiments of new places and new faces that would welcome him and not punish him with looks of priggish patriotism or judgments of his cowardice.

Unless he saw Grover from the platform, he didn't think he should board the train. Grover always ushered him onto the Wichita Express, his weekday run that was now being vigorously cleaned by the railroad's maintenance men who worked as independent contractors at $4.50 an hour on the weekends. These men were young Kansas City men and middle-aged veterans who enjoyed this part-time work on Saturdays.

Adam stood outside the dining car waiting to see if he could spot Grover and be invited to walk through the lavish car with the white linen-covered tables and the expensive silverware placed inside the perfectly folded matching linen napkins. This was Grover's crew, and sometimes he was just too busy to visit.

Adam walked into Union Station. The activity inside the Grand Hall echoed distant sounds of closing doors, footsteps and shouting voices—sounds of lives in motion and a life Adam could only experience when he was there.

One long counterclockwise lap around the massive station, then he was outside via one of the front doors and headed for his

101

parents' car with a carry-out cup of ice from Rudy's—and on his way to enjoying that Coke he'd won from Reggie.

Bothered

By Thanksgiving morning, the grim jail of winter was blowing across Pittsville in horizontal sheets of stinging white stuff that made Adam turn away from the wind and walk backwards on Sycamore Street. *By far the nicest street in town,* Adam thought.

Clark was home for the holiday. He had called Adam Wednesday evening and invited him over Thanksgiving morning to catch up on college life in Lawrence and to "check out some good weed."

Adam's gray hooded parka was taking the biting blasts of stinging snow when Adam looked up to the power line and saw that his retired red track shoes were still draped over the line frozen stiff, reminding him that he had made the right decision. Basketball season was underway. Earlier in the month he had curtly informed the head coach, "I'm not going out for basketball." He was proud of himself for speaking those words and then walking away, as if he had nothing else to say and nothing he wanted to hear. Best of all, he felt no guilt about his decision or any need to explain himself. Ever since he'd fasted over the summer, he'd noticed that he felt more confident around teachers, coaches, or any adult.

If only I could feel more confident around Helen, he complained to himself until he saw Steven Kaladi's new black truck parked in front of the Bach house. He'd seen Helen riding in it enough times since they started dating. *I still can't figure out why Helen would waste her time with that idiot!* Adam grumbled inwardly.

Adam's excitement at seeing Clark and Helen turned to disdain at the thought of having to see Kaladi's smug, arrogant face. He thought about turning back and letting the white wind blow him back home, but he didn't. *Things like this I have to do,* he convinced himself.

He stood in front of the Bach front porch door where two huge carved pumpkins were still standing on either side of the porch steps. Before knocking, he realized that he wasn't jealous of Kaladi. It was more like a feeling of terror since Kaladi was good at embarrassing people when he wanted to. Besides that, Adam liked Helen and Bobby, and he believed that they should be together.

"Hey! Get in here!" Clark barked as he threw open the front door.

Adam left his coat on the porch coatrack before brushing his feet on the bristled doormat that spelled "Welcome."

The peaceful, orderly Bach family home was another universe for Adam Pitt. The roaring fireplace drew attention to the family photos on the mantel. Warm, comfortable furnishings—all orderly, fresh and clean—sat atop area rugs and were positioned in just the right places on the dark oak flooring. All of the friendly Bach faces greeted him above the Thanksgiving Day Parade on the color television.

On the couch Kaladi had his arm around Helen. He was obviously relaxed and genuinely friendly when he greeted Adam with "Hi, Ape!"

"Happy Thanksgiving, Adam," Helen smiled as Henry and Carol waved and smiled at Adam from the kitchen. Helen patted the sofa for Adam to come sit beside her. And he did.

Clark stood in front of Adam wanting to give him a fast-talking update on college life. "Adam, you wouldn't believe how different college is from high school," the freshmen glowed with eyes as big as blue quarters.

"Yeah, it's diff'rent 'cause he's got a girl!" Kaladi teased.

"Tareeesah!" Kaladi cackled his annoying laugh. It reminded Clark of the time last year when Kaladi intentionally fouled him when going in for a lay-up in a basketball scrimmage.

"You met a girl?" Adam stayed positive.

"Yeah, she's from Leavenworth," Clark said.

"From or *out of* Leavenworth, Clark?" Kaladi and even Helen laughed.

Clark motioned for Adam to get up and follow him to the front porch.

"I know what you're going to do," Helen teased her brother.

"Don't you worry about what I'm doin'," her brother grinned while looking slyly to see if his parents were still in the kitchen.

"Oh, Clark," Kaladi sniped out of the corner of his mouth, "he's gonna have a doobie with Ape Man."

"Shut up, you moron," Clark scowled at the rich jock.

Kaladi laughed harder and gently pulled Helen closer to him with his muscular arm that was resting over both her shoulders. Then Helen's new boyfriend dipped his handsome face into Helen's red hair and announced to everyone, "Oh, my God, you smell sweet!"

Helen slapped his thigh, pushed him away and got up from the couch.

"Where you goin'?" he asked her possessively.

"I'm going with Clark out to the shed."

"Well, I'm gettin' my butt outta here." Kaladi looked at his expensive wristwatch, "I told my parents I'd be home by now."

Adam followed Clark out to the front porch where they donned their coats, exiting fast. Clark was afraid he'd cause a scene with Kaladi if he didn't get outside. They walked toward the backyard along the west side of the house, a route taken because his parents couldn't see them from any kitchen window. They walked on the frozen dead grass to the old shed at the back of the Bach lot—a secluded place nobody would want to visit on a cold day, especially with company due any minute.

Out of the howling wind, Clark latched and locked the shed door behind Adam.

"I can't stand Kaladi," Clark scowled. "I don't know what Helen sees in that bigmouth. He's the total opposite of Bobby."

Adam agreed, saying, "Yeah … and Bobby would kick his butt if he wasn't in boot camp."

"No kiddin'," Clark agreed while removing a thin joint from his jacket pocket. "I know she's with Kaladi just to make Bobby mad. She knows that if Bobby finds out she's datin' Kaladi, she'll hear about it directly from Bobby."

"'Cause Bobby can't stand him either."

"Exactly," Clark nodded and lit his joint, inhaled, and passed it to Adam, who hadn't smoked since he went to Lawrence with Helen and Clark.

Adam turned down the joint and Clark laughed. "You in training, Ape?"

"Maybe."

Being called Ape by Clark didn't bother Adam now; however, it did bother him when Steven Kaladi had called him "Ape". If Helen hadn't been there, Adam knew he would've said something about it to Kaladi, if only to test his vow to himself to always let certain idiots know when they bothered him.

Helen knocked purposefully on the shed door and said, "Let me in, Clark."

Clark stopped Adam from unlatching the door, wanting to tease his sister a bit. "Who is it?" Clark called out with a wink to Adam.

"Clark, open up! It's freezing out here!"

Clark shouted into the crack of the latched door, "Is your stupid boyfriend gone?"

"Yes," she whined, knowing full well that her brother didn't like Steven.

When Clark finally unlatched the shed door, she entered the shed like a storm and punched her brother on his arm.

"Ouch!" he complained and kept the joint out of his sister's reach.

Adam thought they were acting like a couple of ten-year-olds not wanting to share.

"Why are you acting like such a jerk, Clark?" Helen demanded.

"Because I can't stand that asshole you allow in our house! You know you're just waiting for Bobby to come back after boot camp so he can see you with the one guy he'd most hate to see you with. That's so uncool, Helen."

It was Clark's tacit smile at her that made her cover her mouth to conceal her smile.

"He's not comin' here for Thanksgiving dinner, is he?"

Clark kept his unlit joint out of her reach until she said, "No, he's not."

Clark lit the joint and handed it to her. After she took a quick hit she passed it over to Adam, who passed again without explaining.

"How's college life treatin' ya?" Adam asked his friend.

"It's great. One of my roommates is a jerk, but I really started likin' it there when I met Teresa."

"You said she's from Leavenworth?"

"Right," Clark nodded, "and we hit it off right away in our political science class."

"They sit across from each other," Helen teased.

"Shut up," Clark butted his joint and returned it to his coat pocket.

"So does Teresa smoke weed?" Helen asked her brother.

"No way. She thinks it's for weak and stupid people."

"Does she know you're weak and stupid?" Helen laughed.

"No, I mean … this is probably only the third or fourth time I've smoked since I met her."

It was too cold for Helen in the shed, so she left after complaining about it.

"So did ya hear about the basketball game last weekend in Pittsville against Leavenworth?" Adam asked Clark.

Clark shook his head no.

"Yeah, Kaladi blew two free-throws at the end of the game."

"So Pittsville lost?"

"Yeah. They were two points down when Kaladi got fouled and missed a ten-foot jumper with three seconds left. After he missed the first free-throw, Coach called time-out. Everybody in the gym knew what Kaladi was gonna do …"

"So he missed it on purpose," Clark said.

"Yeah, but he fires the ball into the backboard so it can come back to him and he can be the hero and take the last shot to win the game, right?" Adam started laughing, which made Clark laugh. "Well, one of the Leavenworth players slams the ball back toward Kaladi and it nails Kaladi right in the nuts when the buzzer goes off."

"Oh, crap! That's so funny. I wish I had seen that," Clark laughed.

"So numb nuts is writhing on the floor in agony while everybody's leavin'. Even the coaches didn't help him. They just left him on the floor," Adam said above Clark's laughter. "But then Helen went over to him and I saw that she was even laughin' … or tryin' hard not to."

"She was cheerleadin'?" Clark asked.

"Yeah," Adam nodded, "it was funny to see her turn away so Kaladi didn't see her laughin'."

Clark changed the subject when he told Adam that he was driving his parents' car to Leavenworth Friday morning to visit Teresa. "I can see if she has a girlfriend if you want to go with," Clark mentioned hopefully to his friend.

"Okay," Adam said, not wanting to break another vow to himself to change his life by doing new and different things.

On Adam's walk home after an incredible turkey dinner with the Bachs, it bothered him that his family was not even close to being a real family who celebrated holidays together. His parents had gone to a buffet at Marv's Tap in Kansas City. If it hadn't been for Clark's invitation to have Thanksgiving dinner with the Bachs, Adam would've gone with his folks to that smoky bar for a third Thanksgiving in a row. And he would've missed out on his possible blind date on Friday.

Yes, things were looking up for Adam Pitt. For the first time in his teen years he was close to being pimple-free. Only one thing really bothered him now. He was stuck on Helen Bach being with Kaladi. In every possible way.

Clark's River

The next morning Clark picked up Adam at his house, and twenty minutes later they were in Leavenworth. Teresa's parents had money. Her father owned several grain elevators in Kansas. Clark was more impressed than Adam with the size and apparent opulence of Teresa's house. Adam was the third-generation only child of a once-wealthy family who lost it all to alcoholism before Adam was even born. Clark's family was rich in genuine love and closeness, yet he had never experienced the wealth of Adam's grandfather.

Adam waited in the car while Clark anxiously rang the front doorbell and was soon invited inside by Teresa. Adam was into his head about their conversation on the way to Leavenworth when Clark confessed to Adam that he'd never gone "all the way" with a girl before. "Nope ... haven't crossed that river yet. But maybe I will with Teresa. Have you ever crossed that river?"

"Not yet. I'm too ugly," Adam replied in all seriousness.

Clark laughed but was unsure whether Adam was kidding or not. Finally Clark had to ask his quiet passenger, "Do you really think you're ugly?"

"I know I am." Adam was dead serious.

110

Adam's blunt response shocked Clark and caused him to say with a cynical snorting of irony, "I've never heard anyone say that before."

Adam kept his eyes fixed out the front windshield, but he could sense that Clark was looking at his profile. Adam believed Clark was studying his face as if wanting to find something positive about Adam's looks. But Clark said nothing.

"I can't believe you feel that way about yourself, Ape ... I mean, Adam."

"I've always felt that way. That's why I have no business going to college ... at least as long as I feel ugly. Haven't you ever felt ugly?"

"Oh, shit! I missed my turn!"

After getting back on track Clark asked Adam, "So is that why you aren't going out for track this spring?"

"That's a big part of it. I don't feel so good around people. Like that time we went to Lawrence and I teased you about buying my meal in the Student Union. I could've never done that if you and Helen weren't there. That's the only reason I'm here today. I have to do impulsive stuff like this, or I'll end up like my parents ... isolated hermits ... drunks with no life."

"If you'd go to KU, I'd be there and Helen might go there. I know you could get a full-ride easy on the track team. That way you'd avoid the draft and goin' to Nam like Bobby."

Adam's shook his head as if trying to shake away the idea, and he stared absently at the Kansas countryside. Finally he confessed, "Track meets freak me out. Sometimes I think I jump so far because I'm scared shitless around all those strangers looking at me."

"But they're not lookin' at you because you're ugly. They're lookin' at you because you're a record-breakin' wild thang."

Adam decided not to tell Clark that he thought about Helen every time he competed in track and basketball, but that he was too big of a coward to ever ask her out. All because he felt ugly. Unworthy. Stuck.

111

"Well, this friend of Teresa's is Lee Ann. And who knows … you might really like her," Clark said almost in response to Adam's thoughts.

"Yeah, but will she like me? I doubt it," Adam said as they arrived in Leavenworth, a big prison town and one scary place for two virgin boys from Pittsville.

Clark had been inside Teresa's house for forty-five minutes while Adam waited gutlessly in the cold car, so frozen by the bitter-cold temperatures and his own fears that he was unable to get out and see why Clark was taking so long. Adam just stayed in the car shivering from the cold and from the awful feelings of rejection he knew were coming his way. Finally, Clark came out of the house alone.

"Sorry I was so long." Backing out of the driveway, Clark was acting like he was leaving the scene of a crime.

"What happened?" Adam had to ask.

"Remember when I said I hadn't crossed that river?"

"Yeah."

"Well … now I have," Clark laughed while driving away and pounding the top of his parents' steering wheel with his palm.

"You did? Really?" Adam was stunned.

Clark nodded with a smug grin on his face. Every single time Adam center-jumped and out-jumped the opponent, he slapped the ball to his favorite guard, Clark Bach, who always wore that same grin. And his sister Helen, the girl who motivated him to jump, cheered both of them on.

Clark had started plenty of conversations about his friend, "the record-breakin' wild thang from Pittsville," to KU athletes all over his dorm. To Clark's amazement, everyone there had already heard of Adam, the high school kid who held two records. He always managed to work Adam into every chat about where he was from. "Adam Pitt … the long jumper … he's from Pittsville, too."

But now Clark Bach had shot past Adam, leaping into life and leaving him stuck in a place he no longer shared with his friend.

"She was home alone, Ape. She wanted to give me a tour of her house. And when we got up to her bedroom, she put on her

Carol King album … and we smoked the rest of that joint in her bathroom."

"I thought you said she doesn't smoke."

"Hey, I didn't think she did a lot of things," Clark laughed. "Then we sat on her bed and she showed me some pictures in a photo album. Next thing I knew I was roundin' first base headed for second … then to third. Before the album was over … I crossed that river, Adam."

Adam could only nod in disbelief while dark feelings of green envy took over. He watched the passing leafless branches of trees as they drove through the opulent part of Leavenworth. Some would sway at him as if taunting him, reminding him of dreaded premonitions—like his nineteenth birthday in just a few days and that he would have to register with the draft board. Just the thought of being drafted and still a virgin made him roll down the window after turning off the car's heater that was stifling him.

"You okay?" Clark asked with genuine concern.

"Yeah … it's too hot in here. I need some air."

"Hey … uh … I'm sorry 'bout bein' inside Teresa's house so long. I just couldn't get away, ya know?"

"Yeah, I know. And her friend Lee Ann wasn't there?"

"No. Teresa was there alone."

Adam only nodded. "So, that's it? We're goin' home?" Adam was curious.

"Yeah, I guess so. Teresa told me Lee Ann couldn't make it. I didn't want you to feel like a third wheel. And after crossin' that river … I pretty much wanted to get outta there myself before her parents came home."

Adam nodded that he understood. "Do you know why Lee Ann couldn't make it?" he asked.

"I don't know. Teresa just said that she couldn't make it."

Back in Missouri Adam asked Clark, "So do you think Helen's crossed that river with Kaladi?"

"I can't say for sure, but I don't think so. I think she's waitin' for Bobby to get back from boot camp. She knows Bobby wouldn't want anything to do with her if she did it with anybody … especially Kaladi."

"Yeah," Adam agreed, now feeling inspired by Clark's reasoning regarding his sister's relationship with Kaladi. "So does having sex change things between you and Teresa?"

"I guess. I don't know, though. I mean, I'm still stunned by it all and how fast it happened. It was strange that right afterwards there didn't seem to be any special connection or anything said about how this changes anything. All she said was she'd see me in class Monday and seemed to be glad I was goin'.'"

Back in Pittsville, Clark stopped at Taggit's Gas Station to fill up the car on his parents' charge account. Jimmy Taggit told Clark that Bobby would be home for Christmas leave on the 17th, and that he was shipping out for advanced training at Pendleton on the 28th.

Yes, the ex-Marine was full of pride, telling Clark, "In his letter he said he's in the best shape of his life and real anxious to serve his country."

Passive Adam and Clark were unmoved by hearing the patriotic remarks made by their friend Bobby, who was known to be an animal on the football field, punishing everyone he tackled.

Driving away from the gas station, Adam had the strange feeling that Mr. T. was terribly anxious about his son coming home from boot camp. Adam saw the same anxiousness in Mr. T. when he would sit in the bleachers and watch his son play linebacker through his binoculars. Adam couldn't help but stare at the muscular mechanic's dark blue, green and red tattooed forearms. The faded letters of USMC were on one arm, and the other arm had a red snake coiled around a dark sword.

As Clark pulled into the Pitt driveway to drop off Adam in front of his house on that dreary November day when Clark had crossed his first river, Adam asked Clark if Helen was home.

"I have no idea," Clark shrugged his thin shoulders. His mind was on Teresa and how it would be between them on Monday.

114

Welcome Home, Bobby

L
ate Friday morning, December 17th, snow fell in big flakes that slowly floated down on a rare windless day. The Kansas City airport was located seven miles north of downtown Kansas City—a real easy drive from Pittsville. Jimmy and Evelyn Taggit were there to pick up Bobby on Christmas leave after his graduation from boot camp.

The drive to the airport in Bobby's black '65 Mustang had been somewhat unsettling for Jimmy Taggit. Evelyn, who was riding as a passenger in the vehicle Bobby requested his father pick him up in, had found one of her son's tapes and randomly played "For What It's Worth" by Buffalo Springfield, an anthem for anti-war protestors. When she wanted to eject the tape about halfway through the song, Jimmy wouldn't let her. He wanted to hear the song all the way through—partly just to hear the kind of music his son would enjoy and partly to digest the words being sung. He really stayed open all the way through the song, listening and trying hard to see the war's insanity that the song was trying to portray. "Everybody look what's goin' down." When the song was over, nothing was said by Bobby's parents.

They stood near the arrival door at the plane's off-boarding ramp when they saw Bobby in his immaculate USMC dress uniform. His mother's comment to her husband, "He looks taller," made the ex-Marine improve his posture, seeing clearly that his son was in the best shape of his life. The senior Taggit flashed back on his own graduation from basic training when he too arrived home and his parents were waiting for him on the platform of Union Station.

The Taggit family went home to Pittsville after stopping for brunch at Denny's off of I-29. Then they stopped by Grandma T's house in Pittsville for dessert so she could see how handsome her only grandson looked in uniform. Once they were home, Bobby found himself alone, unpacking his sea bag in his room. He was looking forward to going to the home basketball game that night that his father had told him about. When his mother told him that Helen was dating Steven Kaladi, Bobby just nodded. His clear, unemotional eyes indicated to his parents that the news about his ex-girlfriend didn't mean much of anything to him one way or the other.

Clark was due home for Christmas break Saturday morning. Adam and Clark had made plans to go over to the Taggit Gas Station together to look up Bobby as soon as Clark returned home from Lawrence. But Adam had a feeling he'd see Bobby, his old teammate, at the game Friday night—the last game before the long holiday break. No way was Adam going to miss seeing Helen cheering for Kaladi with Tag at the game.

The early evening stayed windless and the snow had stopped falling. It was only the second basketball game Adam would go to his senior year, and probably his last. The last time he went, he was a target for loud-mouthed fans cheering for him and yelling at him to get into the game. He always detested that kind of blatant attention. Vivid memories of being laughed at for his freakish jumping ability had been creeping back into his dreams. Three nights earlier he had been awakened by the relentless chanting of fans, "WE WANT APE! WE WANT APE!" He woke up recalling the insidious images of the lower classmen who revered him and yet were imitating primates while he was on the bench or warming up on the court before each half. To Adam it was a circus; it was awful.

Dressed for the game, Adam walked away from the upstairs bathroom mirror feeling satisfied after finding a mere three visible pimples. Passing the dark living room, he stopped in the entryway and waved goodbye to his parents' bloated faces atop atrophied bodies that were reposed in their matching recliners ten feet from Walter Cronkite.

"Have a good game!" his mother called out, raising her glass of scotch and water as if she were toasting his upcoming game. Adam left the house hearing his father correcting her, "He's NOT playin'! He didn't go out for basketball this year, for Pete's sake! He's just goin' to the game!"

Outside in the fresh air, the early darkness of December was illuminated by the ankle-deep snow that glared white under the city's dim street lights. His breath was a snorting fog, but he liked the way the cold air felt going in and out of his nostrils as he made fresh tracks down his long driveway that he'd have to shovel in the morning.

He stayed on the sidewalk on his side of the street where no feet had trod since the snow stopped falling earlier in the evening. Vehicles moved cautiously past him headed for the game. Rare feelings of gladness to be alive came over Adam and forced his throat to swallow a sudden urge to laugh out loud—to celebrate that he was going to be out in public of his own volition. This wasn't a game he had to go to; nobody had even asked him to go. And now, as on his walks to school, he liked to play a little game he called My Timing—something he'd started doing around the time his pimple count was consistently below double digits.

Reaching Elm Street he stopped on the corner and stood there waiting, even though no traffic was in sight. He counted to himself his age, nineteen, and then crossed the street. He believed that by stopping on his own terms, he had subsequently changed the spot where he would sit on the hometown side of court in the bleachers, along with who would sit near him. This conscious way of controlling his reality was a way he figured he could be responsible for his life and stop blaming God, his parents, and everyone else for the way his dark reality and negative feelings were beating him up and wearing him down.

"My timing," he exhaled into the cold air. Again he stopped on the sidewalk, waiting for as long as he wanted, until it was time to continue on. He refused to be moved by his fear or self-consciousness and just stood there observing others passing by. He would move only when he was ready to move, and that would be when fear was not present. This way he could not and would not blame others for what might happen that night, because now he was not being run by his mind's fears that had made his life an unbearable misery.

He paid the fifty-cent admission price inside the high school's front doors and walked down the hallway to store his coat inside his locker. There were just a few seconds remaining in the sophomore game, which meant that the varsity cheerleaders weren't on the floor yet. He wanted to get a seat high up, in the top row of the bleachers close to where Helen would be with the other cheerleaders. And he wanted to be able to find Bobby in the packed gym.

Just as he was leaving his locker, he heard the final buzzer in the early game and made his way down the long hallway—a confining corridor of passing students and parents on their way to the bathroom or outside to grab a smoke before the varsity game.

Inside the brightly lit gymnasium, three underclassmen were dusting the hardwood court with their thirty-six-inch dust mops in preparation for the varsity game. It was a full house with both courtside bleachers crowded, as well as the bleachers on the stage.

Adam found a place to sit at the top row directly in front of Helen and her cheerleading squad. They were already performing a routine with their red-and-white pompons that matched their outfits. Helen looked especially beautiful, as if she knew someone special might be watching her tonight. Everyone in town heard that Bobby had returned home from boot camp. It was obvious to Adam that many in the crowded gym were looking for Bobby and watching for Helen's reaction as jersey number 1 worn by Steven

Kaladi emerged from the locker room to lead his team onto the court in their home red uniforms with white trim. As cocky Kaladi led his team in warm-up drills, Adam could see Bobby—a handsome Marine in dress uniform with his hat in his hand. He was shaking hands with people and taking a seat in the middle of the bleachers at the other end of the court as Helen was in the throes of a routine. Meanwhile, a teammate shooting warm-up jump shots let Kaladi know that Bobby was in the bleachers. Steven followed his teammate's eyes and saw his girlfriend's ex-boyfriend chatting with friendly well-wishers seated around him. About that time, Helen heard the news that Bobby was there. During a routine cheer, Adam could see Helen discreetly looking down to the other end of the bleachers trying to spot Bobby in the crowd. Anyone who knew Helen Bach could tell that she was a bit flustered and into her head about Bobby being there. It was all so exciting to Adam. His hands were perspiring, more than not from his idea of leaving his seat to go over and say hi to Bobby. Adam decided to stay put for the time being.

Bobby could see Helen at the other end of the court. He felt bad about not writing her after getting her honest yet hurtful letter four weeks into boot camp. He remembered the sting of her words, "Since you decided you don't want me anymore, I have decided to start dating Steven Kaladi. I'm going to homecoming with Steven and ..." Bobby didn't read any further and tore up the letter. He was hurt by the memories of his first homecoming with Helen his senior year—the night of their "first time."

Bobby Taggit and Steven Kaladi had a negative history. In football practices and scrimmages, Tag would forearm the big-mouthed halfback every chance he could, oftentimes knocking the rich kid on his back. One winter day Kaladi finger-printed "F U" in bold letters on Tag's snow-covered Mustang after basketball practice. The next day in gym class during dodge ball, Bobby literally knocked out Kaladi after firing a fast ball into his face from twenty feet away. What really bothered Bobby the most about Helen dating Kaladi was that Helen knew he didn't like Kaladi.

As the confident senior guard Steven Kaladi dribbled the ball down the court, Bobby thought of the grueling ten weeks he'd managed to endure and how right now he was in the best physical shape of his life. It would have been nice to spend some time with Helen on his leave before heading to Pendleton. He wanted to at least warn her about that jerk—a spoiled brat whom Bobby felt would only use Helen and end up hurting her somehow, even though he was certain she was trying to hurt him by dating Kaladi in the first place.

At halftime Bobby thought about leaving as the cheerleaders were doing their routine in the middle of the court, but then he saw Ape waving to him from atop the bleachers at the other end of the court and decided to go talk to him. Walking with perfect posture, carrying his hat and the pride of a Marine in uniform, he smiled at Helen and she smiled back. Bobby could feel the eyes of the town on him as he waved and smiled back at spectators calling out to him, "HEY, BOBBY!"; "WELCOME HOME, BOBBY!"

Adam could see Helen watching her ex-boyfriend as Bobby was climbing the bleachers after motioning to Adam that he was coming up to talk to him. They shook hands.

"Ape, how are ya?" Bobby sat down next to his friend.

"I'm fine, Bobby. How are you?"

"Oh, I'm doin' great. Ready to ship off to Pendleton ... then Nam."

"Wow ..." was all Adam could say about that.

"How come you're not out there out-jumpin' every damn one of 'em? Savin' yourself for track, huh?"

"I'm done with all sports ..."

"What? Are you crazy? You could get a full ride to any college in the country. You want to end up in Nam like me?"

"No. And I don't want to go to college."

"Why not?"

As the teams were coming back onto the court for the second half, Bobby's eyes were on Helen cheering with the other girls. That's when Bobby changed the subject and said, "I could stand about any guy with Helen but that asshole Kaladi."

"Yeah, that's what Clark said."

"How's Clark doin' in Lawrence?"

"He's doin' great. He's got a girlfriend now."

"Really? Clark Bach has a girlfriend?" Bobby said incredulously and laughed hard.

"So, how was boot camp?"

"Oh, God, Ape ... the first couple weeks were tough, I thought I'd never make it. But then I got this survive-or-die attitude. They know how to make you fight for your life."

"Your dad was a Marine, wasn't he?" Adam asked.

"Yeah. He was in some real deep shit when he was in the Corps."

Adam saw Helen looking up at Bobby every chance she got after the second half started.

"Clark's comin' home tomorrow. He's gonna stop by and see ya," Adam said.

"It'll be good to see Clark. I'm glad my breaking up with Helen didn't ruin our friendship. The three of us go way back."

"I know."

"Come by the station while I'm back. Tomorrow if ya can. I'll be hangin' out there with my dad. Good seein' ya, Ape. See ya soon."

"Okay, Bobby."

Adam watched Bobby leaving the gym. Helen was watching him too. That was the exact moment when Adam could see for certain that Helen was only dating Kaladi to get back at Bobby for dumping her. Adam felt like leaving too, the game seeming meaningless after seeing Bobby leave the gym.

Outside fresh snow had fallen. Bobby's tracks were visible in front of the school and trailing off in the direction of the Taggit house. Adam decided he'd go to the Y in Kansas City in the morning instead of going with Clark to see Bobby. Adam made up his mind that he didn't want to be around Clark and Bobby because Bobby might want to talk to Clark privately about Helen. And Clark's new girlfriend was not a subject Adam cared to listen to. Again.

On Adam's walk home he thought of Bobby's path and how his obscure steps through the snow in dinky Pittsville were leading

Bobby to war. Then he thought about Clark in college with a girlfriend named Teresa. These were things Adam knew he wasn't ready for. Adam stopped walking on the snow-covered sidewalk and looked back at his own fresh tracks that he could see under the street light. "That's my path," he said to himself out loud. He heard the distant blaring horn of a passing freight train heading north to the land that was far away from the paths his friends had taken. Bobby's path leads to war and possible death. Clark's path leads to another kind of death Adam would have to endure for four long years—starting all over as a freshman. It was another setback that was like the one he had to endure when he flunked the fourth grade.

"I should've graduated with Bobby and Clark," he muttered and returned to his path home. He thought of Bobby in the fourth grade and how now this grown Marine was one of the few, like Clark, who never taunted or made fun of him in or out of school after he was put back a year.

His mind shifted to Clark's path, a path that if taken by Adam would force him to live with and around strangers. He would endure a new crop of judgmental faces that would put his very soul through another sort of death, just as his freshman year in Pittsville had. He didn't get to tell Bobby that college would be an invisible death he alone would see a thousand times a day each time he was ignored or whenever they openly laughed at his freakish long arms and apelike bowed legs.

"No way," he mumbled in clouds of December breath that stayed above the sidewalk on his path home—a place he had to leave soon.

Stop! In The Neighborhood

Early Saturday morning Adam drove his parents' car to the Y in Kansas City. Before leaving Pittsville he filled up at Taggit's and told Bobby, "Let Clark know I"ll be in K.C. most of the day."

Bobby had a plan for later and told Ape, "We'll get some beer and go to Packy's tonight. We'll pick ya up about seven."

"Okay," Adam nodded, knowing that Clark would bring some weed with him along with more stories about his crazy girlfriend.

At the Y Reggie was swishing thirty-foot jump-shots like gangbusters—all without chasing a rebound. When Reggie saw Adam, right away he wanted to win his Coke back.

"I'll hit ten straight without a rebounder!"

"For a Coke?"

"Yeah," Reggie nodded, then swished ten jumpers without moving a step. Then they played HORSE a few times. Of course, Reggie managed to not get an H.

"I don't know why you're not playin' for some school on a scholarship," Adam told his new friend.

"I know why," Reggie smiled.

123

"Why?"

"'Cause I'm in the army in January."

"That's right. So you're headed for Nam."

Reggie nodded yes and missed his first shot.

After working out at the Y it was snowing hard and piling up fast on the downtown streets. Adam told Reggie, "Hey, I'll give ya a ride home after we stop at Union Station to have a Coke."

On the slow drive to the station, Adam played the car radio. The Supremes were singing "Stop! In The Name of Love" and Reggie sang along. After the song was over Adam confessed, "I always thought the words were 'Stop! In the Neighborhood.'"

Reggie laughed hard at this white guy's confusion and the irony of experiencing the same thing to certain lyrics in songs. "I know whatcha mean. Like, if I don't know the words to a song … I'll just make up my own," Reggie laughed.

When Adam wanted to go around to the back of the station where the trains were being cleaned, Reggie took the lead and said, "Follow me."

They walked to a fenced-off area where no vehicles were allowed.

"Where you goin'?" Adam asked as they crossed the snow-covered cement lot.

"To see Grover," Reggie answered, his long athletic strides further apart than Adam's.

"You know Grover, the crew chief on the Wichita Express?" Adam asked.

"Known him my whole life. He's my neighbor," Reggie said.

"I know Grover!" Adam exclaimed, adding, "He gives me pie and Cokes."

"We'll just have our Cokes here, then," Reggie grinned back at Adam.

"He never charges me," Adam said.

"Yeah, but tip him like you paid for it. He might as well make a buck instead of somebody else."

Adam agreed, thinking how smart and quick Reggie was. Then Reggie literally stopped in his tracks. "I have to get Grover a Christmas present," he said suddenly.

Adam followed Reggie all the way to the station's front entrance and over to a little gift shop. All the while both of them marveled at how the other knew Grover Cleveland. While Reggie shopped for a gift under five dollars in the shop, Adam waited outside in the Grand Hall. Reggie bought a letter opener for $4.95 and was glad it came in a box that he could gift wrap at home.

Heading over to Grover's office Reggie told Adam, "I got him a letter opener ... to open my letters from Nam. He said he'd write me if I write him," Reggie chuckled.

Adam felt he shouldn't mention his feelings about Nam, so he followed Reggie to the platform area where the trains were being cleaned and serviced.

Reggie knew that Grover Alexander Cleveland was close to seventy-three years old and had lived in Kansas City his whole life, spending a third of his life on the silver-metaled, sixteen-car Wichita Express that ran from Kansas City to Wichita and back every Monday through Friday. And he knew that today, Saturday, was cleaning day. He also knew that Grover started working at Union Station when he was twelve years old, toting baggage for tips and shining shoes.

Reggie told Adam while on his shortcut to Grover's office, "Grover was born in 1899, and he tells everybody that he's gonna live to see the next century. That way he can say he was alive in three different centuries."

Reginald "Reggie" Baldwin first met Grover as a neighbor. Grover lived three houses up from Reggie's house just a mile from Union Station in the older section of south-central downtown Kansas City.

To Adam, this "other side" of the trains was another world to him—a private sort of place for railroad employees that the public never saw. On Saturdays Grover was the boss. He had his cubbyhole office at the back of the kitchen car that was linked to the two dining cars, where Reggie stopped at the bottom of the steps. Only employees were allowed on any of these cars on Saturdays, a rule Reggie learned long ago when he would come here as a boy to be around the fun-loving clean-up crews that his pal Grover supervised.

Adam could see he was the only white person around. And for the first time since coming to Union Station, he felt out of place—an outsider. Yet nothing had happened or changed except his approach was different from any other time he had been coming to visit Grover on the trains. Then Grover's inimitable laugh came booming out from the kitchen car passageway, and Adam realized that one day he would board a train like this that would take him safely to Canada to escape his dead-end future in Missouri.

He followed Reggie's lead by waiting with him outside the back iron steps of the kitchen car. To Adam, Grover looked like a tall panda with his round face and belly and bulging brown eyes that had dark half-circles magnified by his glasses.

Soon the crew chief waddled into their view, his big feet sore from a gout flare-up. "Reginald, my man! And who's that red-headed boy with you? Why, it's Adam Pitt from Pittsville! My Lord, come on up here," he gestured. His big grin was genuine and inviting to them.

Upon scraping the snow from their shoes on the grated stainless steel floor that worked like sandpaper, the boys followed Grover a short way along the kitchen car's passageway and took a quick left into Grover's dinky office that was equipped with a bathroom. There was just enough room for Reggie and Adam to sit on the folding chairs across from Grover's desk, a desk that was way too small for a man his size. The newspaper clipping about Adam breaking two national high school track and field records was laminated under Grover's glass-top desk.

"You're that guy!" Reggie exclaimed to Adam when he realized that this was the white dude who long jumped over twenty-six feet.

Reggie's realization tickled Grover immensely, along with taciturn Adam's reply, "Yeah, that's me."

126

From his swivel chair the affable crew chief bent down to inspect the contents of his tiny refrigerator, asking, "You want a Coke, Reg?"

"Please."

"You too, Pittsville?"

"Yes, please."

They thanked him in unison when Grover opened and handed them each a cold bottle of Coke before reposing in his chair with his big hands holding the back of his head. His big brown bovine eyes were animated and friendly-looking behind his glasses.

"Now what's goin' on with you gentlemen?"

"We were shootin' hoops at the Y," Reggie said.

"You mean *you* were shootin' hoops at the Y," Adam injected dryly, which made Reggie and Grover laugh.

"Ya know what they call this man in the neighborhood?" Grover asked Adam.

Adam shook his head no.

"Swissshhhh," Grover exaggerated the last two letters of the word.

Adam agreed with a nod, adding, "I've never seen anyone shoot like this guy."

"I've NEV—ER seen anybody, especially a white boy, who can jump like he does," Reggie pointed to Adam.

"And, Swish, you do know the facts about Mr. Pittsville sittin' right next to ya, there?"

Reggie shook his head no.

"So you don't know that this JUNIOR … listen now … holds TWO NATIONAL high school records in the long jump, AND," Grover paused to extend two fingers from the hand that was still holding the back of his head, "a SECOND NATIONAL record in the triple jump?"

Reggie looked over at Adam and craned his head back in disbelief upon hearing these singular facts about the guy sitting next to him in Grover's office.

"How far'd you jump?" Reggie asked.

"Twenty-six-two," Adam answered.

"No! You jumped TWENTY-SIX FEET AND TWO INCHES?"

"He sure did!" Grover laughed. "He sure did. I read it in the paper last spring! Front page on the sports page! It's all right here," Grover pointed to the article under glass on his desk.

Adam had been dreading this moment, for Grover was the one person he knew would be disappointed in hearing his decision.

"Grover, I'm not going to compete in track this spring … or go to college." Maybe it was because Reggie was there, and that's why he told Grover.

The old Red Cap leaned forward in his chair and out of the blue asked Adam what his Draft Lottery number was.

"Fourteen,"

"Fourteen," Grover repeated, his bulging eyes looking at Adam as if he really wanted to understand why. Again Grover repeated Adam's lottery number, this time looking at Reggie, who Grover knew was leaving for boot camp soon. But Grover's finger pointed at Reggie when Grover said, "You hear this? If you could jump like he can and could go to any college in the country … and if your lottery number was fourteen … what would you do?"

Reggie shrugged and said, "Some people aren't cut out for college. Like me. I dropped out of high school and reduced my options."

Grover sat back in his chair nodding that he understood what Reggie said. Then Grover turned his eyes on Adam and asked, "What you gonna do?"

Adam took a big drink of his Coke, wiped his mouth and shrugged his shoulders, not wanting to tell Reggie or Grover he was going to Canada.

In a compassionate tone, Grover told Adam he could make his own destiny by going to school. Reggie nodded in agreement and said, "He's right about that."

Adam pretended to agree with them, yet he was confused why the opinions of these two people carried so much weight with him. These were just two casual friends he'd made in the city. Why should their opinions matter to him at all? But they did. The opinions of his parents, Clark, Bobby, teachers or coaches didn't mean nearly as much to him as these relative strangers sitting with him in this little office on the Wichita Express.

Rage and Ice

Packy's was an old fishing shack on the Missouri side of the Missouri River where underage Pittsville boys had been going to drink beer for generations. Clark had picked up Adam and then Bobby around seven that night in his aqua-blue '67 Nova—an early Christmas gift from his parents. Bobby was wearing civilian clothes, riding shotgun, and wishing he'd brought his music to play in Clark's tape player. Adam rode alone in the back with two unopened six-packs of Schlitz beer that Bobby's old man let him steal from the gas station. The by-the-books ex-Marine would never sell beer to his underage son or his friends.

They didn't want to go inside the dirty shack because it was too cold; instead, they stayed in Clark's car drinking beer until it was all gone. Tag gulped down eight of the beers while his lightweight buddies sipped just two cans apiece over the span of some three hours. Bobby did most of the talking, mostly about the Corps and what he'd learned about himself after graduating from such an intense experience on Worm Island. Both of Tag's friends were glad to hear that Bobby had six months of training in Pendleton before going to Nam.

The only college student of the trio said, "Maybe Nixon will end the war before you have to go."

"Negative ... won't happen," Bobby shook his crew-cut head after slamming back the last beer. They gathered up the beer cans and dumped them in Packy's. Some homeless drifter always picked them up and cashed them in somewhere down the road. After they got back in the car Clark said to Bobby, "You know, Tag, opposition to the war is growing and ..."

Bobby cut him off with curt and raw drunken slurs. "Aw, that's a bunch of B.S., Bach. You college guys don't have a clue."

It didn't take long for Bobby to start talking about what was really bothering him, directing his words to Clark, "I never thought Helen would go for Kaladi. There's not one good thing about that asshole. What does she see in him anyway?"

Clark shook his head indicating he didn't know and didn't want to talk about his sister.

Adam kept his mouth shut. Now that Bobby's words were fueled by alcohol, it reminded him how he consciously tuned out his parents whenever they'd been drinking and wanted to talk to him. Except here he was, trapped in a car and couldn't just leave to get away like he could at home.

After more angry diatribes about Helen dating Kaladi, Clark finally had to tell his friend, "Bobby, I can't control who dates my sister. She's made it clear it's *her* life and *her* business."

Bobby finished gulping down his eighth beer, crushed the aluminum can in his palm, and said, "Let's get somethin' to eat."

Clark drove them to the Sinclair truck stop a few miles west of Pittsville off of I-29. Clark and Adam each had a burger and basket of fries while the hungry Marine ate three cheeseburgers and two baskets of fries.

Just when it was looking like Bobby was starting to sober up after his big meal, Helen and her boyfriend walked into the crowded dining area. They were laughing and didn't see that the trio was watching them get seated in an adjoining dining room. Adam could see right away Bobby looked like he had a bad taste in his mouth. Peace-loving Clark and Adam sat across from Bobby, who was still watching Helen and Kaladi in the distant dining area.

Clark tried to break the ice by saying, "Small world, huh?"

"Yeah," Adam agreed. He and Clark sensed that their friend wasn't going to sit still for long, and they were right.

Bobby got up from their table, picked up their check, and stomped toward the register to pay the tab. Clark and Adam followed him. At the register Adam and Clark could see that Helen saw them. Kaladi's back was to them, but Helen must have said something to Kaladi because he got up from the table and started walking toward the register area with his right hand extended to welcome Bobby back home. Instead of accepting Kaladi's welcoming gesture, Bobby popped him hard on the jaw and knocked him out cold. Bobby watched Helen come running to the aid of Kaladi, who was coming out of cold storage and starting to flutter his eyes after Tag's sucker punch.

Adam and Clark hurried Bobby out of the restaurant and into the car before the manager had a chance to call the cops. Helen protected Clark and Bobby by getting her boyfriend off the premises before the cops got there.

"God, Bobby, you might've killed Kaladi," Clark told Bobby as he drove his Nova toward Pittsville.

"I think I broke my hand," Bobby grinned while holding his red and swollen right fist up in the air for Adam to see from the back seat.

"You really nailed Kaladi," Adam laughed.

"Yeah ... AND IT FELT REALLY GOOD!" Bobby laughed.

"Not funny!" Clark chimed in. "What if he's dead?"

"He's not dead," Adam injected. "I saw him movin' as we were leavin'."

"I'm more concerned about my hand. If it's broken, it'll set me back in trainin' and I'll end up doin' shitty latrine and mess duty."

"You better get some ice on that hand," Clark advised.

They pulled into the town's only convenience store where Clark bought a ten-pound bag of ice for Bobby's hand.

"You really think it's broken?" Adam asked while leaning forward to see Bobby's hand.

"I sure hope not, Ape."

"Maybe you should go to Outpatients in K.C.," Clark suggested.

"No way. It'll be fine. No hospitals. My mom's a nurse ... she'll know if it's broke or not."

"Can you move your fingers?" Adam asked.

"I can move one," Bobby laughed after lifting the ice off his hand and extending his middle finger.

Helen's Answer

Six days later on a cold Christmas Eve late morning, Carol Bach answered the knock at her front door. She was surprised to see Bobby Taggit standing on her porch steps, his hands inside his coat pockets and looking very contrite when he said, "Merry Christmas … Can I please talk to Helen?"

She opened the door without hesitation and saw his right hand that was badly bruised from the Kaladi incident. From the chilly porch Bobby noticed the blinking lights on the tree just inside the front room window.

Carol Bach took a long look at the handsome Marine after wishing him Merry Christmas. "How are you, Bobby?" she asked, genuinely glad to see him.

"Fine, thanks," he stood there humbly with his wool cap in hand.

"Come on in," she smiled.

Henry Bach was reading the paper in his recliner and closed it upon seeing the respectful young man covering his bruised hand with his cap. Henry and Bobby were exchanging pleasantries when Bobby noticed Clark and Helen wrapping gifts at the dining room table.

Clark came into the front room with his stunned sister. Bobby's eyes were on Helen, unblinking and tinged with contrition. Then Helen felt it—a strange feeling most people have felt, a sense that this was the last time she'd ever see Bobby again. She saw the way he always bit his lower lip with his crooked tooth, the same tooth she saw and loved about him when they were in grade school.

Clark and his mother ushered Henry Bach into the kitchen to give Bobby and Helen some privacy, it was too cold for them to talk on the front porch. Bobby went and stood by the Christmas tree and she came over to him. The scent of pine was strong around them, and the colors of the wrapped presents at their feet changed with the blinking lights. Immediately, they fell into a convulsing hug, both aware that time was in short supply.

He talked slow into her neck as they held each other. "Sorry 'bout punchin' Kaladi. When I saw you with him ... I snapped."

She buried her crying face into his muscular shoulder that smelled of oil and gas from working in his dad's station.

He continued, "When I saw you at the game cheerin' for that jerk ... I just wanted to puke my guts out and leave this town. On my walk home in the snow I kept seeing you with him ... and I was beatin' myself up for losin' you to a creep that doesn't deserve you."

Helen kept crying and kissing his neck relieved to be back in his arms but dreading his future. He would only be in town a few more days, and she knew full well this could be the last time she would ever be in the arms of the Bobby Taggit she loved.

"Helen, I know I blew it. But I want to be with you alone just one more time before I go. We don't have to do anything you don't want to do. I won't hurt you ... but I have to be alone with you before I go back."

He shut his sorry mouth and held her in front of the blinking Christmas tree. Right at her feet was the green-and-red wrapped gift with the tag that read "To: Steven/From: Helen." It was a bottle of English Leather cologne, a scent that Helen loved because Bobby would sometimes wear it when they went out.

Helen grabbed her coat and told her mother, "I'm going for a ride with Bobby. I'll be back in a little bit."

As Helen left the house Clark told his parents, "They'll be back together when she gets back."

Henry Bach didn't care one way or the other and went back to his paper he had left folded on his recliner. Clark and his mother stayed in the kitchen voicing their opinions about Helen and Bobby. "I'd rather see her with Bobby than Kaladi any day," Clark declared.

"I just hope she doesn't get herself messed up," Carol sighed as she made another pot of coffee.

"You mean 'pregnant,'" Clark smiled.

His mother's look of concern told him he was right.

Bobby and Helen sat in his warm idling Mustang parked in front of the Bach house. He talked more than he had his whole time in boot camp about his experiences there on Worm Island.

"I went there still numb from breaking up with you. It was easy for me to tap into that killer instinct. They know how to bring it out of you, believe me. When they were breaking me down, I got so angry at times … more than I ever did in football. Helen, I'll tell ya … I've never been so confused or conflicted about serving my country as I am right now. It's like … I'd be the first one to fight any country stupid enough to invade us … but I just don't know about goin' so far away from home to kill somebody who hates me because I've invaded his country."

She reached over and touched his face before lifting his injured hand and kissing his fingers near his bruises.

Bobby said, "When I first got home, I told my parents about how I tapped into my killer instinct and became this bad-ass m— f—er. And before I could go on and tell 'em what I told you, I saw this ugly look in their eyes. Maybe it was pride or somethin', I don't know. But they looked so happy to hear I could kill now. I couldn't go on and tell 'em how I really felt. So I kept quiet and felt this empty kind of feeling like I just had dinner with two strangers who had no idea who I was or what I was goin' through."

"Bobby, I wish I could say anything to help you … but all I can do is hope and pray the war ends soon … before you have to go. I wish you would just go to Canada like some of them are doing. Could you?"

Bobby shook his head absently while seeing in his mind the faces of his shamed parents and how he couldn't do that to them.

"Let's go for a drive," he said.

She nodded yes.

Parked at their favorite parking spot, Bobby's car radio was playing The Moments singing "Love on a Two-Way Street." Much more than passionate kissing was Helen's answer to Bobby's question, "Do you still love me?"

By the time Helen got out of Bobby's cramped Mustang and hurried into the warm Bach living room, she knew in her heart that Steven Kaladi was in her past and that he wouldn't be getting the Christmas present she removed from the base of their tree. Her family waited patiently for Helen to tell them what her brother had already predicted. Finally, Clark asked her if she was back with Bobby. Her blushing smile and "shut up, Clark" confirmed Clark's words to his mother as they watched her leave the house with Kaladi's wrapped present.

On her walk she removed the gift tag from the wrapped gift before dipping her chin into the buttoned front of her winter coat and allowing herself to feel the thrilling rush of being in love with Bobby again. She thought back to the conversation she and Bobby had just before making love in his Mustang. He told her, "Ape scared me the night I punched Kaladi. He told me I was stupid for letting you go, and that I would never find another girl like you. It got me to thinking just how much I've allowed my parents to influence me. When Adam said that, I knew he was right. I really don't want to lose you, Helen."

Down the sidewalk she went, turning the corner onto Pitt Street and walking fast to the old Pitt House that was devoid of any Christmas lights or decorations. The Pitt driveway needed shoveling, so it took her a while before her cold feet stepped onto the front porch. When she knocked, she saw Bill Pitt's scowling face peering out from behind the slit of his door he was reluctant to open.

"Is Adam home?" she shivered, holding the gift in both gloved hands in front of her.

He opened his door and she stepped into the blue haze of second-hand smoke. It reminded her of all the smoky bars and cafes she tried to stay away from. Helen could easily hear Bill Pitt's labored breathing as he groaned and wheezed while climbing the stairs to Adam's room. His weak legs were covered by baggy jeans that revealed no form to his lazy body that routinely had been sitting in a recliner for twelve hours a day. His wife remained seated in her recliner, and Helen waved and courtesy-smiled to her without going into the source of the smoke wafting from the matching aluminum ashtrays on matching TV trays between the matching recliners. Helen thought it was odd that the dog lying between the recliners hadn't barked or even moved an inch when a stranger knocked and came into the front entryway.

Soon Helen heard the quick steps of Adam's feet coming down the attic stairs after his dad told him he had a visitor. He nearly ran over his dad on the way downstairs. It was the first time Adam could recall having a visitor. He was breathing hard from excitement when he found himself suddenly standing five feet from Helen and she handed him Kaladi's wrapped present.

"I didn't have time to put a tag on it … so I just walked over to give it to you."

Before he could even blush, she was gone after planting a quick peck on his cheek and wishing him a Merry Christmas.

He followed her to the open front door and called out to her in fogging words, "Merry Christmas!"

She waved back at him, and he watched her retrace her deep footsteps down their unshoveled driveway. As soon as he closed the door, his parents wanted to know about the present.

"Whatcha got there?" his mother called out from her recliner after blowing out a stream of smoke toward their cream-yellow ceiling that used to be eggshell-white.

Adam stepped into the TV room. Above the laugh track of an "I Love Lucy" rerun he said to his parents, who were both reposed back in their recliners, "It's a Christmas present from Helen Bach."

Bill made his best incredulous, sourpuss face that asked, "What? You got a gift from a girl?"

"What is it?" his Penny was curious, her face matching her husband's frozen-negative scowl.

"How would I know ... it's wrapped!" Adam scowled back at his parents.

"Open it!" his dad insisted.

Adam balked before saying, "It's not Christmas."

Adam's hesitation and the spooked look on his face made them both more aggressive. "Open the gawd-damn present!" Bill blared.

"Yeah, it's Christmas Eve! What's the diff'rence?" Penny flicked her wrist at him as if it was no big deal.

He peeled off the red-and-green wrapping slowly as if it were a precious thing. Even Gop raised his sausage-shaped head and for a moment seemed to lose his pathetic look of umbrage as his beady black eyes watched the careful unwrapping that revealed the boxed bottle of English Leather.

"Fancy," his mother nodded positively with pursed lips that seemed to be saying *not bad ... not bad.* Penny lowered her recliner's footstool and said, "Let me smell it."

He carried the cologne over to her in the dark TV room with both hands as if it were a valuable thing too precious to be dropped. The three males in the room watched her open the box then unscrew the wooden block top. Then she dipped the end of her pointed nose close to the bottle's opening and lightly whiffed in the fragrance.

"Oh, yeah ... yummy," she moaned. "You want a dab?" she offered her sourpuss sidekick, who made her cackle when he made his twisted-mouth scowl.

She handed the open bottle back to her son who, in turn, sniffed the most popular men's fragrance on the planet.

"Good, huh?" she smiled up at Adam. "Boy, the girls're gonna love you," Penny cackled and coughed.

Up in his room Adam sat on his twin bed, still holding Helen's gift and flattening out the green-and-red wrapping beside him. *Tomorrow's too late,* he reasoned while in the busy mind of a

139

boy's rush when he knows that a girl he likes also likes him. *Why else would she come over in this weather?* he reasoned while getting up and turning his attention to the incredible blanketing whiteness on the other side of his frosted window. He tried to see the footsteps she left on the driveway.

He went over to his stack of cassette tapes and riffled through them until he found his mother's old tape of Perry Como's hits that included Helen's favorite song "It's Impossible." Perry was soon sealed perfectly inside the same wrapping and taped with the same original tape. Instead of making her a gift tag or writing on it, he simply dabbed a little English Leather on the paper.

Should I deliver it now ... so soon after she was here? He paced back and forth the length of the attic holding the wrapped gift for Helen in both of his hands. He was in a state of intense pensiveness, acutely aware that timing was everything—just like when he broke his records.

Feeling exactly as if he was about to launch himself at a track meet, he stopped his pacing and stared at the standing row of encyclopedias at the foot of his bed, books that had given him national records and a passing grade for every class he'd taken ever since flunking the fourth grade. The academic aspect of things pertaining to the delivery of his gift came to him—words like "timing" and "Christmas gifts" and "girls." But nothing at all came to him on the visceral gut level that could help him make the right move at the right time. He looked down to his stockinged feet and realized he was stuck, unable to move or make any decision one way or the other. To Adam, this was no different than the impending move he would have to make in order to avoid certain death—one way or another.

Could I even make that move to save my life? he directed his thoughts to the books that had gotten him the fame and attention that scared him to death. *Could you get me Helen?* he asked, knowing that if he delivered the gift to Helen he feared the kind of bad timing that would send him back to his room rejected and blushing about it for months in agonizing regret and isolation.

Just as the encyclopedia salesman had changed Adam's life by flipping a coin, Adam removed a nickel from his pocket and flipped it onto his bed. *Heads I go ... tails I stay.*

He followed her smaller footprints all the way to Sycamore, then down the sidewalk leading to the Bach house. As always, when he reached the spot where he could best see his record-breaking track shoes dangling from the power line, he stopped to look up at them. As soon as he saw them hanging from the line covered in snow with hardly any red visible, he heard a loud voice moaning up ahead. The voice was coming from a parked vehicle in front of Helen's house. The engine was running with the exhaust clouding the back of the vehicle, and the view was obscured by trunks of older oak trees along the sidewalk. It was a male's voice that was in obvious pain, his words unintelligible.

Adam stayed hidden behind the tree trunks, moving closer in a line that made him invisible to anyone in that vehicle. One tree closer and he could hear Helen's voice sounding contrite when she said, "I'm sorry ... I don't know what else to say, Steven."

Adam could see that it was one of Kaladi's new trucks with dealer plates, and he could identify that it was Kaladi's voice, even though it was altered by the punch he received in the jaw from Bobby.

Inside the truck Helen was feeling sorry for breaking up with Kaladi on Christmas Eve and for the obvious pain in his eyes from his jaw injury.

Another tree closer and Adam heard Kaladi moaning, pleading for Helen to change her mind.

"No! It's over, Steven! I've made up my mind and I won't ever change my mind!"

What sounded like more pathetic pleading from Kaladi ended with Helen getting out of the truck and high-stepping through the snow toward her house. After a while Kaladi drove off in a rage of spitting snow, his tires spinning and his back end fishtailing down the frozen street as if taking Helen's rejection out on his truck.

Adam removed the wrapped gift from his coat pocket and stared down at it in his gloved hand. He decided not to deliver it in person since she'd just broken up with Kaladi. *It's too soon after that,* he reasoned. He figured that if he put Perry in the Bach mailbox, she wouldn't get the gift until the next mail day two days after Christmas. *Too late,* he thought. *Under the doormat on the front porch? No. Someone could step on it and break it.*

He pulled out his ski mask and put it on, telling himself he had to be quick and invisible. He took off toward the Bach house making incredible leaps as if he were competing in the triple jump. In no time he was at the Bach front door where he left Helen's gift just inside the front screen door on the porch floor where he hoped someone would find it before Christmas. With his mission accomplished, he quick-walked away from the house using every other snow hole until he hit the sidewalk and was out of view from anyone inside the Bach house.

Turning the corner onto Pitt Street he could breathe again. All the way home his mind played with him. *She dumped Kaladi* and *"It's Impossible."* He couldn't remember any of his steps to his back door or of removing his shoes and leaving them on the two-week-old disintegrating newspaper just inside the kitchen.

Once again on his bed, still breathing hard from his quick delivery, his mind made him wonder what Bobby would think when he found out Helen broke up with Kaladi and started dating Ape. *Would he punch me too?* Adam wondered.

To get his mind off Helen and Bobby and Kaladi, Adam reached down and pulled out his W encyclopedia and found Winnipeg, Canada, the largest city straight north of Pittsville. Grover talked about the weekly Burlington Northern passenger train he used to work on and how it departed Union Station every Wednesday on its run to Omaha, Sioux City, Sioux Falls, Fargo, and Winnipeg.

Facedown on his bed with the black-and-white Winnipeg skyline of the 1950s six inches from his cold face, Adam thought the sprawling town seemed much bigger than Kansas City even though the populations were pretty close. His father had read to him from the paper that Winnipeg was a haven for young American men who had fled there to evade the draft. Before rereading the pages of facts, history and information on the

Canadian city, Adam paused to think whether or not he would go north if Helen's answer to Perry was positive.

An hour later at the Bach house, it was Clark who saw the tiny wrapped gift on the front porch floor. He took it in the front room and showed his family the wrapped gift. "There's no name on it, though," he said puzzled.

At first Helen thought it might be from Bobby—or even Steven Kaladi—until she recognized her wrapping paper. "Oh … I think I know who it's from," she said.

"Who?" Clark was curious.

"Adam."

"Ape?"

She explained to her brother and parents, "I gave Adam Steven's gift … and so I guess he felt he had to give me a gift."

"Open it," her brother insisted playfully.

"On Christmas Eve?"

"We always open one gift on Christmas Eve. I'm curious what Ape gave you."

She unwrapped the gift carefully and smiled at the Perry Como tape. "Oh, my God!" she squeeled and showed her family the gift, telling them that she loved Perry Como.

"What did Bobby give you?" Clark was teasing his sister, knowing that she would get his meaning.

She couldn't keep a straight face and punched her laughing brother's arm. Their parents were openly delighted that Helen had dumped Steven and was back with Bobby.

Later that night Helen told her mother that Bobby asked her to wait for him while he was in Vietnam. When his time was over, they'd get married as soon as he was discharged.

"So you're engaged?" Carol Bach asked her daughter.

"Not exactly," Helen winced.

"Did you tell Bobby you'd wait for him?"

Helen nodded yes, looking happier than she'd been in months.

I Hate Goodbyes

Tuesday morning Adam was clearing snow and scraping ice from his parents' car as it idled in the Pitt driveway. He was headed for the Y in Kansas City to say goodbye to Reggie before he left for army boot camp. Clark drove up and called out from his stopped car, "I'm goin' over to Taggit's Station to say goodbye to Bobby! He's goin' back today! Stop by there!"

"Okay," Adam waved.

Adam didn't really have much experience saying goodbye. And even though Helen liked him enough to give him a Christmas present, he was very curious to know if Bobby knew that Helen had broken up with Kaladi or that she had given Adam the gift.

How do you say goodbye to someone you've known your whole life ... and he's headed for war while I'm here safe from it all and wanting his girlfriend to run off to Canada with me before they draft me?

There were dozens of vehicles parked around Taggit's Gas Station, the place where Bobby's friends and relatives had gathered to say goodbye before he flew back to California for more training at Camp Pendleton before being deployed overseas.

Adam parked beside Clark's car next to the feed store and walked over to the gas station. On this short walk, Adam thought of that morning at the breakfast table when his father read out loud to him the names, ages, and hometowns of two rural Missouri soldiers recently killed in action in Vietnam. Adam was well aware that his father was telling him about the casualties because he wanted his son to go to Canada.

Now he thought of Bobby and how scared he must be. It was possible Bobby might be seeing the people and places he cared about for the very last time. And he thought of how war would change Bobby forever.

I'm not gonna let 'em do that to me, Adam vowed to himself.

Most of the people inside Taggit's were older men and some friends Bobby went to school with. A few teachers and coaches were there in the warm station drinking good coffee or pop and eating some of the delicious cookies and treats Evelyn Taggit and her mother made for this special occasion. The two-stall shop doors were closed and a space heater was on, making the Marine-clean APCO station warm and cozy despite the chilly seventeen-degree temperature outside. Laughter and all kinds of blandishments about how good Bobby looked and the bright future he would have when he returned home safely filled the crowded station's waiting area.

Nobody dared protest the war around Taggit's Gas Station. Its owner was a decorated two-tour Marine, and his son was about to serve the Corps in Southeast Asia. Adam observed the proud Jimmy Taggit standing next to his son. He knew that beneath the long sleeves of his flannel shirt, Mr. T's muscled arms from forearms to biceps were covered with green and red tattoos he'd gotten when he served in the Second World War. He was talking with friends, customers and locals who wanted to wish his son a safe return, supporting him on this proud day of honor for the Taggit family.

Behind the register area seated around the bookkeeper's desk were Helen and Carol Bach. Adam saw them chatting with Mrs. T. A sudden sense of foreboding told him something embarrassing was coming. And he was right.

Bobby, the bruising gone from his right hand, entered the room from the shop and went right over to Adam. "Ape! Thanks for comin' by, buddy!"

That's when Helen came over and put her arms around Bobby's waist, making it obvious that they were back together.

"Adam, thank you for the Perry Como tape!" Helen gushed with genuine appreciation.

Adam nodded, unable to stop the crimson red from reaching his pale face. His uncontrollable blushing was heating the areas of his neck and face where he had dabbed on English Leather. Unable to smell anything but that cologne, Adam feared he was stinking up the entire place.

"I'm on my way downtown and wanted to wish you good luck. I'll see ya when ya get back," Adam stammered.

"Thanks, Ape," Bobby leaned over to Adam and gave him a hug.

I hate goodbyes, Adam complained to himself while hurrying to his parents' car. It was clear to Adam that Helen had broken up with Kaladi in order to be with Bobby. *Why didn't I realize that before?* he admonished himself.

Reggie wasn't at the Y. After a quick shoot-around by himself the self-deprecating Freak from Pittsville drove over to Union Station hoping to catch Reggie there visiting Grover, but Grover had the day off. Adam thought about driving over to Reggie's house, and then possibly both of them could walk over to Grover's house. Instead, dejected Adam decided to drive back home, convincing himself that Reggie and Grover were probably enjoying the holidays with their families.

Besides ... I really do hate goodbyes, Adam reminded himself after his recent awkward moments with Bobby and Helen.

Arrogant Winter

A dam's journal entry for January 21, 1972:
I hate this arrogant winter.
    *That's what my mother said at breakfast this
morning after she slipped on the side doorstep when
going outside to clean up the garbage can that Gop
had gotten into and made a big mess. I don't
complain about the weather like my parents do.
They're stupid to complain about something out of
their control. I keep learning how to live by not
wanting to live like they do. I learn so much from
them.*

Adam had started making journal entries at a more consistent
rate, since he wanted fewer confrontations at home and a good
grade on an upcoming English final that required keeping a
journal.

At least now Helen would stop in the halls at school or stand
by Adam's locker and talk to him. She only talked about Bobby
and Clark—mostly Bobby and what he had written in his most
recent letter to her. Even Adam was stopping her to chat with her,
diving into the very core of his self-consciousness. Just like he had

to take whatever the "arrogant winter" blew his way, so he had to take whatever came of his conversations with the object of his affections. Including blushing. But this time he was proactive instead of reactive, knowing that what he was doing was for his own good.

Journaling had become habitual for Adam. Most days when he got home from school he would race up to his room, tear open his journal, and write something. His entry for January 24, 1972, read:

> *I stopped to talk to Helen in the lunchroom and even sat down next to her. She told me that Bobby was working harder than he ever had in his life at Camp Pendleton, and that he was really into going to Nam to serve his country. That sure makes me feel like a spineless coward for what I'm going to do.*

February hit Pittsville like a white tornado, blowing snow and grayness into every snot-snorting day and leaving many of its residents with a dull, obdurate feeling that nothing was going to get better. Ever.

On the first Saturday in February, Adam went to Union Station after shooting baskets alone for an hour at the Y. Even though the weather was still arrogant—having its way by making visibility close to zero—he strained his way to Union Station and Grover.

Grover was glad to see Adam. A retired Red Cap and old friend of Grover's, O. C. Smith, was seated on one of the two guest chairs in Grover's dinky office. Grover offered to make his two guests some hot chocolate and went off into the kitchen car. Adam stood at the office door in the narrow passageway waiting for his hot chocolate and making small-talk with Mr. Smith. The elderly gentleman was razor thin, his posture so straight and rigid it appeared to Adam as if the old man's raspberry-colored crushed-velvet vest was attached to the back of the chair. Becoming a consistent journalist, Adam had developed a keen sense of observation, noting things he would write down later in his journal. He made a mental note of what he would enter later that night:

*2/6/72 – Met Grover's friend O. C. when I visited
Grover at Union Station today. Funny man. He
sang to Grover when sipping his hot chocolate,
telling Grover in made-up lyrics how much he loved
that "yummy for his tummy."*
After O. C. left Grover's office, Grover told Adam with great
joy on his face, "I got a nice letter from Reggie. He says he's doin'
jus' fine. Says he put on fifteen pounds eatin' three squares a day,"
Grover laughed. Adam could see in Grover's "big eye" a Reggie
memory coming as he leaned back in his swivel chair with his mug
of hot chocolate in his fist.

"Well, I'll tell ya ... that boy would walk past my house in the
wintertime and every time he would look up at our house and see
either me or my wife lookin' at him from a window. And every
time ... I don't care what window it was ... he'd see us. Then one
of us would wave him inside, and we'd give him a cup of hot
chocolate with marshmellas. He loved those little marshmellas,"
Grover laughed and leaned back farther just a notch, as if the
memory of Reggie had physically taken him back like some
delayed force or big wind that he had seen coming in the distant
trees and finally reached him.

All the while the Kid from Pittsville was feeling safe and
secure with the bright and alive railroad man who knew all the
right moves to get safely to Canada by rail.

I can't ask him now. I can't ask him now.

His drive back home seemed endless because of the white-out
conditions that dropped his speedometer to eight miles per hour for
three hours with zero visibility. By the time he got home, he had a
headache from straining to see and keep his parents' car on the
road. For most of his arduous drive back home, his mother's words
kept coming into his mind. "This is another arrogant winter!" She
made the same complaint year after year. He also thought about the
newspaper article his father read out loud to them that very same
morning. "An average winter in America kills thirty-six thousand
people every year ... ten times the average number of U.S.
servicemen killed in Vietnam every year."

Don't Ask ... Tell

More than ever Adam resented that whole year that was taken away from him when he had to repeat the fourth grade. Instead of having the better part of a year after he graduated to be free of school and free to work at a job he wanted, he was likely to be drafted sometime during the summer after he graduated.

Track season started in March, and Adam finally had to tell the coaches and at least a hundred students that he wasn't going out for track his senior year. Yet scholarship offers kept pouring in, and the college recruiters continued calling on the kid from Pittsville whose remarkable records could be unbreakable for many years to come at the high school level.

The spring weather continued pulling at Adam to make his escape to Canada. *Before I graduate ... before I'm drafted.* Throughout March, though, Adam suspended his Saturdays at the Y and his Union Station visits to see Grover. He wanted to take a break from his routine because he didn't want to see Reggie when he returned home on leave after boot camp, or be tempted to press Grover for details about his best route and timetable for his train ride north.

❖ ❖ ❖

One late March day at his school locker, Helen invited Adam
to go along with her to pick up Clark in Lawrence to bring him
home for spring break since his car was in the shop for repairs. But
Adam declined, telling Helen he had plans when he didn't. After
being so wrong about her when she gave him a gift for Christmas
and seeing her back with Bobby, he didn't want to be around her
and the constant reminder that they could only be friends.

The rainy Saturday morning Helen was to go and pick up Clark
at school, she made an early stop at the Pitt House with the engine
running and the windshield wipers swaying in slow-motion. Adam
was drawn to his open front window upon hearing Perry singing in
his driveway.

Quickly he dressed and ran outside. The cold rain was stinging
his neck, making him hunch over and run for the front passenger
door.

Helen turned off Perry as soon as Adam slammed the door
shut. "Hi," she blinked lazily. Adam could tell she had been
crying. She was fumbling with a wad of tissues on her lap. Adam
knew bad news was coming when he asked her, "What's wrong?"

She kept her face averted from his eyes and said, "I'm
pregnant."

"Are you sure?"

She nodded yes, adding, "The worst part is, I'm not sure who
the father is."

"Bobby or … Kaladi?"

She nodded yes again and said, "I don't know what I'm going
to do. I love Bobby and I can't tell him it might not be his baby,"
she cried.

Adam drove Helen to Lawrence, envying Kaladi for having
been with Helen.

As Clark drove them home from Lawrence, Helen shared her
news with him. Helen had said a blood test could be done on the
baby to determine whether Kaladi or Bobby was the father. "But I

152

don't think it'll matter," Helen said through her tears. "Bobby would never marry me if the baby was not his. And if Bobby found out I had sex with Steven ... I don't think even if Bobby was the father he'd want to marry me.

"Why not?" Clark asked.

"Because ... I lied to him and said I never had sex with Kaladi."

"Why would you even have sex with that piece of shit?" Clark asked his sister.

"I was drunk and upset with Bobby because he came to that basketball game and walked right past me and never even said a word to me."

All the way back to Pittsville, Clark kept pressing his sister about Kaladi. "Are you ever going to tell him it could be his baby? You know, he's going to see you showing soon."

"I don't know!" Helen almost screamed.

"You've got to tell Mom and Dad," Clark stated quietly.

"I know."

"Are you sure you're pregnant?" Clark repeated.

After Clark dropped Adam off in front of the Pitt House, Adam went upstairs to make his journal entry.

3/19/72 – Helen's pregnant. Kaladi or Bobby? I
hope it's Bobby, and so do Helen and Clark. I drove
Helen to pick up Clark in Lawrence. Clark drove us
back. Helen told her brother she's pregnant. Clark
was cool. Helen cried a lot. I really hope Kaladi's
not the father.

Upon closing his journal, he realized he probably wouldn't be around to find out who the father of Helen's baby was.

Helen had told Adam on their way to Lawrence that Bobby's most recent letter said he would be coming home in July for two weeks after his training at Pendleton and before shipping off to Nam. But Bobby wouldn't know that she'd be seven months pregnant until he saw her.

Kaladi's Blood

Helen missed school on Monday so Clark could drive her and their mother to the family doctor in Kansas City. When Helen and Carol went into the doctor's examination room, Clark was aware that his sister had told their parents that Bobby was the father of her baby. On his own, Clark approached one of the nurses and asked her if he could have a private conversation with her about his sister's condition.

Behind the closed door of another examination room, the serious University of Kansas freshman wanted to know the truth from a professional regarding the awful situation his sister was in. "My sister doesn't know who her baby's father is. It's one of two guys. Can she find out from a blood test while she's still pregnant, or does she have to wait until the baby's born?"

"After the baby's born a blood test can tell," the friendly young nurse replied.

"And blood has to be drawn from both guys and the baby?" Clark asked.

"That's the ideal way," she nodded.

"What if the two guys have the same blood type?"

154

"Many factors are tested to determine paternity. The lab will know exactly which man is the father," she smiled confidently. Clark nodded, thanking the nurse for the information before exiting the examination room with her.

The doctor confirmed that Helen was pregnant. After speaking with the nurse, Clark knew there was no sense in getting a sample of Kaladi's blood anytime before the baby was born. Besides that, Kaladi would do the math and assume he could be the father of Helen's baby when he found out she was pregnant. And since Adam detested Kaladi as much as Clark did, the Pitt house was a good place for Clark to consult with an ally about the trouble that arrogant ass would make for his sister when he found out she was pregnant.

Clark nervously paced the floor of the attic atop the Pitt house, his skinny neck twitching and jerking with all the anxious thoughts he was unloading on Adam. "Helen told my parents that she's not gonna let Bobby know she's pregnant till he comes back home on leave. You know Kaladi'll think it's his kid even if Helen tells him it's Bobby's kid. And you know Kaladi'll tell Bobby that he's the real father. Then Bobby will find out from Helen it could be Kaladi's kid and YOU KNOW for sure that Bobby won't have anything to do with Helen or the baby!"

Adam sat on his bed with his hands clasped between his legs, agreeing with his friend. Then Adam asked Clark something that made Clark stop his pacing. "What if it turns out to be Kaladi's kid?"

Clark blinked a few times, staring past Adam. His thoughts were logical, as if working on a math problem, until he finished his internal quizzing and stated absently, "Kaladi can't be around when Bobby comes home on leave."

Adam played the mind game with Clark and said, "When Bobby comes home and finds out she's pregnant … he'll want to marry her right away … as long as he thinks it's his kid."

"Right … but Helen will just have to put marriage off …"

"Since it could be Kaladi's kid."

"Exactly."

"Would she do that?" Adam asked.

"She'll have to," Clark's tone turned to irritation, knowing his sister would have to be smart and do the right thing for Bobby's sake. He plopped himself down on the bed beside Adam and dropped his head in his hands, moaning in frustration. Just then an idea came to him. "Wait a minute … Kaladi's stupid … right?"

"Right," Adam replied tentatively.

"What if I went to Kaladi and told him the truth … that Helen's pregnant. But what if I told him the doctor needed a sample of Kaladi's urine to determine if he's the father. I call that pretty little nurse in advance … tell her I need to talk to her in private again. I bring in Kaladi and he gives her a urine sample. She leaves for a couple of minutes, then comes back in and tells Kaladi the news that he's not the father. Even though you and I know it takes a blood test to determine paternity, Kaladi's just dumb enough to buy the urine story."

Adam nodded, agreeing that Clark could fool Kaladi.

"Then when Bobby comes home on leave, Helen can stall him about getting married. Meanwhile, Kaladi doesn't blow it for them because he already thinks he's not the father."

"Sounds good," Adam nodded, adding, "When're ya gonna do this urine thing with Kaladi?"

"I don't know. I have to think this out. Timing is everything."

"Yeah," Adam agreed.

The Good, the Bad, and the Honest

Again, Adam rode with Helen in the Bach car Sunday when Clark drove back to Lawrence at the end of his spring break. By the time Clark parked in his dorm parking lot, Helen was clear about keeping her pregnancy a secret for as long as she could, even though she knew it wouldn't be long before she would start showing and everyone who saw her would know. She liked her brother's nascent plan to fool Kaladi in her doctor's office in order to keep him from causing big problems when Bobby came home; however, she suggested a smarter version of the ruse concerning Kaladi's paternity test when she told her brother that she thought Steven should provide his urine sample at the doctor's office as an anonymous paternity donor.

Adam and Clark agreed with Helen, and they all had a good laugh imagining Kaladi handing over his urine sample to determine paternity.

"Oh, God ... please be Bobby's," she patted her belly on the face-chilling spring day as they rolled into Lawrence.

Studious Clark went straight to his room to study for finals that were more than six weeks away. He was worried because his grades had been slipping some, probably because of all the time he had been spending with Teresa. An increasing number of students on campus were burning their draft cards in protest of the university furnishing grades to draft boards. Clark knew he didn't have the guts to burn his draft card, flee to Canada, or join the service like Bobby did. Even though his Draft Lottery number was considerably high—286—like most young men his age he feared the politicians would continue escalating the war, and it was just a matter of time before he was sucked into it.

Helen wanted Adam to walk around the campus with her in order to get some exercise for herself and her three-month-old passenger. The weather was still too cool for anti-war protestors. Compared to their visit there last summer, Adam found the campus during spring break was more to his liking. There were far fewer students around, no blaring music, and plenty of open space.

Helen was glad to be away from her brother's badgering and redundant talk about her situation. Adam was a refreshing change from Clark. He was pleasant to be around and had only positive, observant comments, which kept her mind from trailing off to negative thoughts about her future with Bobby.

Adam did his best to keep Helen positive by pointing out things that proved that spring had arrived for good. "Look at the green buds," he pointed at the line of elm and maple trees up ahead of them on the sprawling campus. "And the grass is starting to turn green all over this place."

"I wish you would accept a track scholarship here … or anywhere, Adam," she said wistfully, unable to get him to look at her.

"No," he answered while keeping his eyes on the ground, "I'm done with school. The last thing I want to do is start all over as a freshman and go through that nightmare again."

"What about a small college somewhere … at least so they won't draft you?"

He changed the subject by pointing to a black squirrel peeking at them from behind a tree trunk. "There you go, Helen. A nice little pet for you. I think he likes you."

"You can't blow me off that easy, Adam. What about going to a trade school in Kansas City?"

"Look, Helen … I'm ugly. Maybe not as ugly as some people, but if you're not cute or really good looking … I mean, look at my parents. They're ugly. And I'm from them. I was doomed from the beginning. Nice people who aren't ugly—like you and Clark—try to talk me out of feeling that way. I can't feel this way about myself and be around all those normal people who would totally ignore me if I wasn't a track star. I won't do that to myself, Helen. So please don't ask me about that anymore."

After an awkward pause she asked him, "But what are you going to do since your Draft Lottery number is so low?"

He kept his promise to himself that he would never tell anyone about his plans. Not even his parents. "Maybe the war will be over and they'll stop the draft," he answered.

"Do you really believe that?"

"I don't know what I'm going do. I'll let you know when I know," his eyes now were pretending to be observing the nature around them.

Realizing she was fighting a losing battle, she changed the topic to her favorite subject. "When Bobby gets out of the service, his dad told him he can take over the station if he wants."

"Really? Does he want to do that?"

"He thinks he might give that a try. When he gets out he wants us to drive all over the country and really see it … for at least a month … just going place to place and seeing if we'd like to live somewhere else."

"So you'll take the baby with you?"

"I don't know. Maybe his folks or mine could take turns watching the baby. That way we could be alone."

"Like a long honeymoon?"

"Yeah," she faked a smile and broke down when she asked: "What if it's not Bobby's baby, Adam? What will I do?"

"You got a fifty-fifty chance. It's like flippin' a coin. But you gotta stay positive. I believe my mother was way too negative when she was carrying me."

"How do you know that?"

159

"She's always negative. She told me she drank alcohol and smoked the whole time she was pregnant."

"That's awful."

"I know. But at least it made me not like alcohol or cigarettes. I can't stand second-hand smoke, and I think I'm allergic to alcohol. Be honest, Helen. Doesn't your family think my family is weird? I mean, I know I'm weird … but aren't my parents known to be total losers 'cause they don't work and they drink their lives away?"

She thought about her answer before saying, "Your parents are loners and want to be left alone. I think the name Pitt around here has a mysterious and infamous quality to it. Your grandpa had sort of a celebrity status in this town, and it is named after him. And now that your jumping records have set you apart from everyone else in Pittsvile, your family is once again the most famous family in Pittsville. Maybe they just can't handle all the attention … real or imagined."

Adam was surprised but satisfied with her comment, hearing for the first time what somebody besides himself thought about his family.

Adam drove them home after stopping to get Helen a hot fudge sundae at the Leavenworth Dairy Queen. Adam figured the ice cream must have cheered her up, because when she played her Perry Como tape on the ride home, she sang along with him instead of crying.

Grover's Light

One Saturday in mid-April, Adam drove his parents to Kansas City. As he was backing them out of their driveway, he noticed in the rearview mirror that his mother was growing a neck flap like his father's. Right away Adam was tempted to say something about having her flap removed, but then he looked over at his father's hairy yellow flap that was half-curled against his purple collar. Seeing their neck flaps combined with two cigarettes lit at once made him gag until he could roll down his window and take in deep breaths of fresh spring air that smelled like wet rocks after a cold rain.

Adam had bet his mind that nobody would say a word between Pittsville and Marv's Tap. His mind won the bet when his mother yelled from the backseat as soon as he got onto I-29, "Roll up that damn window! I'm freezin' my ass off back here!"

The young designated driver dropped them off at Marv's Tap with orders to pick them up at six. Adam was filled with an overwhelming feeling of freedom as soon as they slammed their doors shut and turned to walk briskly toward the familiar burgundy-stained door without so much as a friendly wave or smile goodbye. Their treatment of Adam was demoralizing, which made being away from them all the sweeter.

Adam decided to skip the Y that morning and head straight to Grover's office. When he got there, Grover wasn't in his office or on the train; he was at Rudy's having lunch. Upon entering the station's casual diner, he immediately noticed Grover seated on a stool chatting with customers and waitresses listening with rapt attention. From forty feet away, Adam stopped to watch the way his friend told a story. His hands and voice combined like a symphony to convey his thoughts. His hands, massive paws, were like the black and tan brushes of a painter revealing shapes and time and the pace of his story. And his liquid raspy voice emanated from a face lit by giant white teeth and round eyes bulging with an obvious gratitude to be alive.

Adam made copious mental notes whenever he was around Grover, for many times Adam would see something remarkable that Grover said or did that he wanted to put on the pages of his journal that day. Grover had given him the lighter side of life that he craved and always compared to the darkness his parents were addicted to. *Both sides are interesting to observe,* he'd written months earlier, *except Grover's light is incredibly more fun to be around.*

It was in Rudy's where they had lunch together one Saturday that Adam recalled Grover's reaction when he told the old Red Cap about his parents. He had complained, "Their lives are so useless. Their dull eyes and sagging faces show the same expression day after day … no matter what is going on around them."

Grover laughed, tilting his bald head back as if commanding his laugh to leave his throat and send loud expressions of joy and aliveness to the entire universe. That laugh brought more peace to Adam's world than any words that had ever been spoken to him. He knew Grover had seen hardship in his life, yet he could still laugh as if life were a wonderful and precious thing.

More than once Adam had written in his journal:

Today I needed to be around Grover's laugh.
Grover's light brightens me and stays with me all
day. He's the only adult I look forward to seeing.
All my negatives vanish when I'm about to visit
Grover.

Standing in the diner watching Grover's animated joy added
peace to the feeling of freedom he had felt when he dropped off his
parents. Grover turned and saw Adam standing there and said,
"Hey, Adam from Pittsville! Come on over and have a seat. Been
thinking about you a lot lately."

Adam walked over to where Grover was sitting and sat down
beside him. Grover said to the waitress, "Set my friend Adam up
with a chicken salad special and a Coke."

"Nah ... that's all right. I'm not really that hungry today. I just
wanted to hang out with you for a while since I brought the folks to
K.C. today." The truth was, Adam was hungry. He just didn't
have a dime to his name, and he didn't want Grover to know that.

"Uh-huh. Right," he said to Adam, rolling his eyes. Then he
turned back to the waitress and said, "Go ahead and get him his
meal."

Adam sat down on the stool next to Grover. Within minutes the
old man's big brown eyes watched with delight as the kid from
Pittsville wolfed down his meal.

"For a guy who's not hungry ... you shore do eat, uh-huh,"
Grover laughed. Then the old porter switched the conversation to
Reggie. "Reggie was home about a month ago on his leave after
boot camp. My, my, my ... you shoulda seen that boy! He came
down to the train to see me. I bet he put on at least twenty pounds
of lean muscle ... and he shore looked sharp in that uniform. He
sat there so straight and proud with his hat on his lap and his shoes
so shiny black I could see the light from my desk lamp shinin' on
'em!" he laughed and roared with joy. "He told me he got the
highest points in his company for marksmanship. And when I says,
'Reggie, I didn't know you could shoot,' he says, 'I didn't neither
'til they put that rifle in my hand.' Aw, Lord, we laughed!" Grover
laughed with his entire being, causing even passive Adam to
chuckle.

When they finished eating, Grover told Adam he wanted him to read a letter he'd received from Reggie earlier in the week from Fort Hood where he was being trained for duty in Vietnam. On their way back to Grover's office, they walked past the middle of the vast station and saw a group of young servicemen from all the military branches seated on pew-like benches awaiting a train's arrival. Grover stopped and whispered to Adam, "Those men in uniform over there, they're honor guard. They all wait for the same train from San Francisco that carries the coffins of servicemen killed in the war. These men load the coffins into government vehicles and escort them home to their families."

Adam nodded with spooked eyes. "When does the train arrive from San Francisco?" he asked

Grover looked at his watch and said, "Two forty-seven."

"Can I see them when they unload the coffins?" Adam asked solemnly.

"No sir. They don't let the public watch that," Grover said as they continued on to Grover's office.

The exterior of the Wichita Express was being pressure-washed when Grover and his guest boarded the kitchen car that held Grover's tiny office. Right away Grover removed Reggie's letter from his desk's top drawer and opened it before sliding it over to Adam and adjusting his desk lamp so Adam could read the letter under the light.

"Read it out loud," Grover requested.

"*Dear Grover,*

I have some time to write ya a quick letter in this busy world of the U.S. Army. They won't let me talk about any details of my training here, but I'll just say it's the toughest physical and mental thing I ever experienced. I thought being a little brother at home was tough, but all the brothers are tough here.

It was good spending time together on my leave. And that punkin pie Mrs. C. made me I managed to eat in one sitting the day I took it home. Momma put whip cream on it with a whole bag of them little

*marshmellas I like. I know I gained 10 pounds when
I was home, and I also know that the Army worked
it off me in 3 days, I swear. Can't say when I'm
leavin' for Nam, but I think it'll be sooner than
later. You take good care of yourself Grover, a hug
for Mrs. C., and tell that freak from Pittsville to
keep jumpin' his way out of this war.*
                        Love, Reggie."

Adam looked up from Reggie's letter and saw the perfectly
satisfied face of Grover nodding and saying, "Uh-huh. That was a
real nice letter." He watched the old baggage handler fold the
letter gingerly and return it into the envelope before putting it back
into the desk drawer in the spot where he kept his most valuable
things.

Adam had decided that morning that this was going to be the
visit when he talked to Grover about his run to Canada to avoid
being drafted. Adam was anxious to learn the best train and
timetable for crossing the border without detection. But he couldn't
bring himself to ask Grover about it now—not when the light of
pride glowed so brightly in those big brown eyes after reading
Reggie's letter.

"Were you ever in the service, Grover?" Adam asked.

"No sir. I reckon since I was forty when the Second War came,
they left me on the job here. And I was too young and too black for
the First War," he laughed. "Back when I was your age, the
military was no place for a man of color. Too many friends told me
it was like slavery, the jobs they make a Negro man do. Things no
white man would do ... no sir," Grover slowly shook his head
wistfully as if to say that was not for him.

No Sense ... No Feeling

The last week in April Steven Kaladi overheard two girls in Health class talking about Helen Bach being four months pregnant. Right after school Helen's ex-boyfriend drove his truck over to the Bach house knowing that Helen would be walking up to her front door minutes after his arrival. Loretta Lynn was singing "One's On the Way" on Kaladi's truck radio when he saw her walking toward him on the sidewalk. He didn't like the way her body appeared to stiffen with apprehension when she saw him parked in front of her house.

He got out of his truck and leaned against his front grille with his arms folded in front of his chest, appearing to Helen like she owed him an explanation about her pregnancy since she was starting to show. She had been rehearsing this very moment in her mind for many weeks, so much so that she felt like she'd been through this exact scene with him before. Clark's urine test ruse was her only chance to keep him from spoiling her life with Bobby.

She stopped six feet from him on the sidewalk and looked into his eyes confidently when she said, "I'm pregnant with Bobby's baby."

"How do you know it's not mine? We had sex the night before he sucker-punched me."

"Look, Steven, you can go to my doctor's office and be tested to know for sure that ..."

"I'm not goin' to no doctor. I'll know when the baby's born if it's mine or not ... and so will you! Have Bobby get tested. If it's not his ... then ... I guess it's mine ... right?"

Helen was caught off guard and totally surprised by his response. She folded her arms in front of her chest and matched his implacable attitude.

"So you're gonna marry Bobby?" he went on.

"Yes."

"Even if it's my kid?"

"It's not your baby, Steven."

"You don't know that for sure. So why would you marry Taggit if it could be my kid? I just don't get that, Helen. It's not fair to me or Bobby."

"I wouldn't marry you if it was yours."

"Then why would you have sex with me?"

"Because."

"Because why?"

"Because I wanted to hurt Bobby, that's why!" Helen yelled in her anger and shame.

The truth stunned Kaladi because it was true. He could only nod and look at her with his tongue pressing against the inside wall of his cheek. "That's cold, Helen," he said at last.

She knew he was right. It made no sense to her then or now. That's why she had no compassion for Steven about how he must feel, even if it was only a wounded ego. All she wanted was for him to go away and let her live her life with Bobby.

Just when she thought the worst was over with Kaladi he asked, "Does Bobby even know you're pregnant?"

He could see the answer in her eyes and in her hesitation. His busy mind made him point at her and vow, "You won't raise my kid with Taggit. No way that's gonna happen. And you and your perfect little family," he jerked his head in the direction of her house behind her, "won't have anything to say about it."

Helen watched him drive away, burning rubber and racing his truck's engine like the spoiled rich brat she always knew he was.

That scene with Steven was the beginning of Helen's worst fear realized and the end of Clark's plan to remove Kaladi as a threat to having a life with Bobby. With tears stinging her eyes, she turned from the street and opened the mailbox to find a letter from Bobby.

Alone in the house she hurried to her room to read the letter on her bed with the door closed for assured privacy.

Hi Baby,

I'm in my barracks with a chance to write you and my folks a quick letter. They don't give us much free time for letter writing. There's so much to learn with literally so many obstacle courses and inspections to pass. And they always seem to get harder and harder to pass. But I'm passing every test with flying colors, just like I did in football. I want you to know that I see us having a life together when I come back from Nam. I can hardly stand to think about the next time I'll see you in July before I ship out. I'm never letting you go again, Helen. I promise.

I love you, Bobby.

Three more times she pored over his short letter, each time crying a bit more than the last time until she stopped herself with the thought that she might be harming her baby. Her thought patterns had to be changed—and fast—because Kaladi had destroyed the plan that would keep Bobby in her life. She needed to talk to Clark about her dilemma, but she knew he was either studying for finals or in class. *I know ... I can talk to Adam,* she thought.

On her walk to Adam's house she tried to come up with a new plan, a new way to keep Kaladi from ruining everything. Nothing was coming to her except a headache, and with that more guilt-ridden mind-talk about the harm her worrying was doing to her baby.

As she walked up the Pitt driveway, she could see Gop licking his scrotum on the grass near the front steps. She went to the side door and knocked. Penny Pitt opened the door after looking through the glass and recognizing the Bach girl, Adam's friend. "Hi, Mrs. Pitt. Is Adam home?" Helen smiled. Penny invited Helen in. "Adam's upstairs in his room. You can go on up there if you want."

The strong smell of vinegar permeated the air from an open gallon jar of pickled pig's feet on the counter near the refrigerator. The odor and sight of the pig's feet instantly repulsed Helen and forced her to breathe through her mouth. Bill Pitt was in his recliner reading the paper as his burning cigarette wafted rising smoke plumes from his ashtray. He lowered his paper and nodded at Helen as she passed by on her way through the kitchen. Helen courtesy-smiled at him as Penny escorted her to the bottom of the antique walnut stairs.

Each step she climbed made Led Zeppelin's "Whole Lotta Love" louder as she followed the sound up the poorly lit flight of stairs. The stairwell was as dark as a moonless night as she climbed them. Feeling her way up the stairs along the wall, she closed in on the slat of light coming from Adam's door. It was cracked open just enough for her to see him on the bed lying on his stomach; he was obviously writing something important. The music was so loud that she decided to stand next to the door in the unlit, creaky, dark, musty stairway and wait a bit for the song to wind down before knocking. Finally, when she knew the song was about over, she knocked on the door without peering in.

Adam's response was angry since he assumed the knock was coming from his mom or dad. "WHAT?" he screamed.

"Adam … it's Helen!" she replied politely, yet loud enough to be heard over the music.

Adam bolted off his bed and turned off Zeppelin, thinking he'd heard Helen's voice but not quite trusting his ears over the loud music. His quick footsteps moved toward the door and what he thought he heard. Helen took a step backward so Adam wouldn't know she had looked into his room. But in the narrow space at the top of the stairwell, she misjudged the distance from Adam's door

169

to the top step and fell backward down the dark stairway, turning to her side in midair without mitigating the force of her long fall in total darkness down the attic steps.

Adam heard the terrible sound of the thump on the other side of his bedroom door. His first assumption was that one of his parents had fallen from a drunken stumble, which had happened a few times over the years. Upon yanking open his door he saw an unfamiliar body lying at the bottom of the dark attic steps.

"Adam!" his mother called out from the kitchen after hearing the fall.

He saw the limp body of Helen lying face down in a curled heap of twisted limbs. Her legs were motionless and angled up the bottom steps. Adam flew down the stairs and knelt next to her head. He leaned down close to her face, he called her name, but he got no response.

"Call an ambulance!" he yelled at his mother's concerned face that had turned ashen white.

"What happened?" Penny asked with a look of horror on her face.

"She fell! Call an ambulance! Hurry up!"

Adam flicked on the hall light, but that bulb was burnt out too. He was having a hard time seeing if she was still breathing. That's when it dawned on him that she was pregnant and that there was more than one life to worry about.

"An ambulance is on the way!" his mother called out to Adam just when Bill lumbered over to Adam and knelt beside him to check on Helen's injuries. Adam felt he had to tell his dad that Helen was pregnant.

"Oh, God," his father moaned, "this is all I need. I'll be sued into the poorhouse."

Adam was repulsed by his father's selfishness. "What are you talking about? She's hurt real bad and she has a baby, and you're talking about that crap! What's wrong with you?" Adam scowled at his father's blanched face and hot breath that reeked of cigarettes, coffee, and pig's feet soaked in vinegar.

Helen's motionless upper body lay atop a bristled floor mat at the bottom of the attic stairs. Bill thought it best for them to drag

170

her closer to the top of the staircase by pulling the floor mat over there so the paramedics could get to her quicker and have better light.

By the time the wailing ambulance arrived, Helen had opened her fluttering eyelids and looked into the frightened eyes of Adam and his father staring down at her. Adam knelt down to her face as the sounds of heavy footsteps came in the front door.

"Helen, can you hear me?" Adam asked her.

She nodded yes, she was unable to move at all or speak.

"The ambulance is here," Adam reassured her as he moved away so the paramedics could take over.

"What happened?" the female paramedic asked as a burly male paramedic began strapping Helen to a board and prepared to move her onto a stretcher.

"She fell down the steps," Adam pointed behind them to the dark attic stairs.

"How did she get over here?" the woman pointed.

"We slid her on the floor mat. We didn't lift her at all," Bill Pitt explained in a blatant defensive tone that reminded Adam of the unquenchable laziness and irresponsibility his father drowned in every day of his miserable life. Myriad little household details went largely ignored by the unemployed goldbricker, like replacing light bulbs around the house to keep it from looking so neglected and shabby and friggin' dark.

As the paramedics lifted Helen carefully onto the stretcher, Adam told them that she was pregnant. Adam stayed with her until she was put into the ambulance, then he followed it on foot as it backed out of his driveway. Then, as instructed by the paramedics, he walked toward the Bach house to tell Helen's parents what happened. It was the most dreaded three-minute walk he'd ever taken. It was even worse than standing on his take-off spot on the long jump runway when everyone at the track meet was watching his every move. He had to ignore the curious neighbors standing outside, searching for answers to why the ambulance was at the Pitt House.

On the power line he again saw his old faded-red track shoes dangling from where he had tossed them, reminding him of how

Helen had been his inspiration for every leap he'd ever made. *She and her baby could be dying ... or dead by now,* he feared as he cut across the Bachs' green front lawn in a hurry to get the awful news delivered.

He knocked hard on the Bachs' front porch door, impatiently going inside to the porch when there was no answer. He knocked on the front room door and saw nobody home through the glass. The door was unlocked, so he opened it and called out, "ANYBODY HOME?" He stepped inside, not even caring that it was uncharacteristically bold of him, and went all the way into the kitchen and opened the basement door. Again, he called down the steps, "ANYBODY HERE?" and again he got no response. From the kitchen window he could see that there were no vehicles parked by the garage. He looked feverishly for phone numbers where her parents worked but found none.

He went to Helen's bedroom and stood in the doorway, his eyes scanning the room for something she may want or need at the hospital. There on her bed was an open letter from Bobby. He read it fast and put it back where he found it. Then he saw Perry's cassette tape on her nightstand beside her little cassette player.

His walk back home was full of busy thoughts about calling Helen's parents at their work, but he wasn't sure where they worked. As his panic began to lift, Adam remembered Clark had given him his phone number at the dorm where he could be reached, so he started to run for the phone number he knew he had written down somewhere in his room.

On the sidewalk he saw a growing number of neighbors curious about the ambulance that had left the Pitt House with red flashers on. Adam ignored their bug-eyed faces that pretended to care about what happened; he despised their rat-like eyes that just had to know what happened. He ran past them all, protective of Helen's fall and her secret baby as he hustled to his side door. Gop lay on the same spot on the grass where Helen had seen him earlier.

"Did you tell them?" Penny anxiously asked her son as soon as he entered the kitchen. His father was putting the jar of pigs' feet back into the refrigerator.

172

"Nobody was home. I'm going to call Clark and have him call his parents."

His mother followed him to the staircase and called up to him before he reached the top of the stairs with his easy, gazelle-like leaps, "Don't you think we should all go to the hospital?"

"Yeah, I guess. I've gotta find Clark's number."

Adam quickly called Clark at his dorm hallway phone.

"Oh, my God! Will she be okay?" Clark's voice seemed to be pleading for a positive answer.

"I think so," Adam said confidently to Helen's concerned brother. "Her eyes were open and blinking." But deep in his heart he prayed as never before that his words wouldn't turn out to be a lie.

"Thanks, Adam. I'll call my parents, and I'll meet you at the hospital."

Everybody arrived at the hospital within minutes of each other. Clark walked in less than a minute behind Adam and his parents, and Henry and Carol Bach arrived about ten minutes after Clark. The Pitts took a seat in the waiting area, while the Bachs went into the ICU to see Helen. It was close to an hour later that the Bachs came into the waiting area and stood in front of the sorry-looking Pitt trio.

"What exactly happened?" Henry Bach directed his inquiry at all three of them after talking with the doctor about his daughter's condition.

Bill and Penny Pitt let their son answer for them. "Helen came up to my room and she fell down the attic steps."

"It was an accident," Bill added.

"And just what was she doing in your room?" Henry asked in an austere tone that told the Pitt family he was a father who meant business.

Adam stammered back, "She d-didn't make it to my room. Sh-she was outside my door and f-fell down the steps before I got to my door."

"It's not like Helen to just fall down steps," Carol Bach joined her husband in fault-finding.

"Well, she did!" Penny Pitt fired back.

Adam asked Clark, "How is Helen doing?"

"We don't know yet. They said they'd let us know soon."

"What about the baby?" Adam asked Clark discreetly.

"They don't know yet," Clark answered, his body fatigued from negative thoughts about Bobby, Kaladi, and a thousand what-ifs.

God's Will

Early in May, Helen was at home and had fully recovered physically from her fall. But the emotional toll from the loss of her baby was another matter. She told her brother, "Spiritually, I feel like I've had the life sucked right out of me. I can't sit around the house anymore. I've got to get back to school. That'll help me pull out of this bad case of the blues."

Helen insisted on not knowing her baby's gender and never considered blood work to determine paternity. Since Helen was fully insured by her family's health plan, Henry Bach made a deal with Bill Pitt: No litigation as long as the Pitts never mentioned a word about Helen's pregnancy.

Clark reassured Helen she wouldn't have to worry about Kaladi. "That ex-moron-boyfriend of yours could never prove you were pregnant. If he ever brings it up, it'll just be his word against yours. Nobody listens to that bigmouth anyway."

"But what if he tells Bobby I was pregnant when Bobby comes home on leave?"

"I don't think he will. He'll be too afraid of getting his lights punched out again."

In the last few weeks of the school year Kaladi stopped twice at Helen's locker. "What happened to our baby?" he asked her each time.

Each time she curtly replied, "I wasn't pregnant," then she walked away.

In Lawrence Clark had been studying hard and taking his finals. He was worried about the guilt his sister was feeling over losing her baby, and he had called her several times to impress on her that the accident was God's will and that she should put it behind her and move on with her life with Bobby.

Twice during the last week of school, Pittsville's varsity track coach pulled Adam out of a class in order to meet with college track scouts from the University of Nebraska in Lincoln and the University of Iowa in Iowa City. Each scout offered the high school record-holder a full scholarship with part-time job perks and a furnished studio apartment off campus if that would close the deal. Each man walked away confused, especially after reminding the star athlete that his Draft Lottery number was too low to refuse such an offer.

"Sorry, I'm not interested," was Adam's stoic reply.

Usually, whenever Adam was approached by a college scout, he would let his parents know—but not the last two offers he got in May. They were getting more and more anxious about their son being drafted as graduation neared in early June. His father seemed to be reading more news about the war every morning from the newspaper and emphasizing the casualties with a critical eye observing his son's reaction.

As the last school day of Adam's life neared, he was walking home and spotted Kaladi's truck parked about fifty yards back and across the street from the Bach house. He had parked there intentionally so he could see Helen walking home without being noticed by her.

Except for Kaladi being here, it's a perfect spring day, Adam thought to himself.

Invisibility was easy for Adam. He ducked behind an oak tree and stayed out of view from Kaladi as he waited for Helen. For ten minutes they waited. Just when Adam thought about going home, he could see Helen approaching on the sidewalk and that she was unaware that she was being watched by himself and Kaladi. To Adam she appeared happy and not at all tormented by her thoughts about the past or a future to be feared.

Helen checked the mail and there was nothing from Bobby. She continued to the front door of her house, still unaware she was being watched by two classmates—one from afar who became her friend, and the other a mistake she made by going too far for all the wrong reasons. The week before, Helen had received a letter from Bobby telling her that his leave had been delayed until late July. He wrote, "Nixon is pushing for peace by putting more boots on the ground later." She was concerned about Bobby's tone in his letters. He seemed to be getting more and more turned off about going to Southeast Asia. Helen was glad his leave was delayed. It gave her hope that the war would wind down and troop withdrawals would mean that Bobby would be spared the horrific combat she was seeing every night on the news.

From Adam's vantage point, he could see that Kaladi looked weird. His blank stare was creepy behind his dirty windshield, reminding Adam of the disgusting bathroom scene Kaladi had staged in grade school. Adam remained crouched behind the tree and waited for Kaladi to get out of his truck and approach Helen. He was ready to sprint just like he did down the long jump runway, except this time he would run across the street and onto the Bach front yard where he would time his incredible leap perfectly twenty feet from his target, descending with his legs scissored around Kaladi's neck until Kaladi was on the ground with Adam's powerful legs squeezing the life out of him. *C'mon, you loud-mouthed chicken. Get out of that truck,* Adam's impatient thoughts prodded.

But he didn't. Kaladi just sat there behind the wheel of his big toy with the same stupid look he had on his face when he exited the boys' bathroom after impishly leaving the toilet bowl of excrement for someone to see. They both watched Helen disappear into her house.

I saw it, Kaladi. And you will never again have or harm Helen Bach ... you stupid idiot, he growled within and waited until Kaladi's truck disappeared around the corner before continuing on his walk home. Adam knew he could never have Helen Bach for his own. Her heart belonged to another. But Adam knew it was his family's fault that Helen had been hurt, and he vowed not to let that happen again. Until Bobby was back for good, Adam would do everything he could to protect Helen.

Adam felt an unexplainable surge of pride welling in his gut. This was yet another big step for him in overcoming his negative past and taking a proactive stance on his future. Protecting Helen benefited no one but Helen and Bobby, yet Adam was empowered by his decision to be that secret protector. More and more, Adam was leaving behind his helpless state as a victim of his parents' lousy choices and moving forward to making a difference in his own life and in the lives of people he cared about. Maybe that was God's will for Adam's existence.

Summer Plans—And Some Are Not

It was one of those glistening-green pre-summer days on the first Saturday afternoon in June. As Adam received his long-awaited diploma from his principal, he heard the voice of his three-drink-minimum, violet-flushed-faced father hooting and hollering from the audience.

His mother was there too, sitting beside her husband on a folding chair. In a rare moment of maternal concern, she was applauding and wondering just when her son was leaving for Canada—and if she'd ever see him again once he left. After their son walked off the stage, Bill and Penny got up and left the packed gym as planned.

Instead of returning to his seat on the gym floor with his classmates, he went to his locker and dialed open the combination lock which he then put in the pocket of the jacket that was hanging in his locker. He quickly removed his cap and gown and left them hanging inside his empty locker as instructed. Now he could set in motion the entry he made in his journal the night before:

Tomorrow I will leave school feeling free and
positive about my future. Grover has to be told
tomorrow. That's the first step of my plan. I must do

*it and know that he will try to talk me out of it. Now
I know I should've dropped out and left for Canada
last summer before I even registered for the stupid
draft. I could've just been a drifter who dropped out
of sight, long forgotten by now. That was my dumb
mistake.*

He slammed his locker shut and walked down the long, empty
hallway for the last time. Fisted in one hand was his kelly-green
spring jacket; in the other hand was his diploma. When he reached
the boys' bathroom, he pushed open the door and walked into a
stall that he locked behind him before stepping up to the toilet
bowl. His eyes were fixed on the bowl of water as his hand
crumbled the stiff cardstock paper of his diploma until it was the
compacted ball of garbage he believed it was ever since he was put
back a year and had to repeat the fourth grade. For a moment he
thought of all the endless hours of wasted time in classes he'd
endured, and all the kids who had made fun of him for flunking
that year. Kaladi teased him more about flunking a grade than
anybody. And when Kaladi left that disgusting mess in the toilet
and made that awful comment in the bathroom—that dumb kids
like Adam who flunk end up cleaning up other peoples' shit—the
visual of that memory was too much to forgive. Yet more than any
one thing or any one person, Adam hated the way most of the
students ignored him—until he started breaking records. He was
angry about his useless past, bitter about his useless parents, and
fearful about his useless future.

Adam ceremoniously dropped his "ball of achievement" into
the bowl of water and watched it slowly sink before flushing it into
the Pittsville sewer.

Exiting the bathroom with his jacket on, he felt better because
of what he had just done with his diploma. It was not at all part of
his plan that day. It was radical and unconventional and it just
happened. And Adam had complete control of the situation.

As he walked past the applause in the gym, he asked himself
why he didn't stay and graduate with this class. He knew the
answer. She was seated three rows in front of him, the back of her
lush, curled, red hair so easy to find. *She was the only reason I*

stayed...the only reason I'm not in Canada now, he told himself. He could still smell the English Leather he'd dabbed on his jacket collar before leaving the house that morning.

Outside, his parents were waiting in their idling car in front of the school. Alone in the back, Adam fake-smiled at their congratulatory statements—all the while nursing his deep resentment toward them for being sick and spineless alcoholics his entire life. *Yuck,* he cringed inwardly at their obvious elation to be headed for their favorite watering hole in downtown Kansas City. Marv's Tap is where they would celebrate his graduation while he walked to the station to see Grover.

Exactly what he'd say to the old man he wasn't sure. All he really knew was that Grover was the only person in the world who could talk him out of his plan. And that scared him. Every recent visit with Grover, he'd seen those big brown eyes lit with so much pride over Reggie. Whenever Grover read his letters or talked about the neighbor boy, it was always with palpable loving reverence. Yes, Grover could talk him out of going north if only because Grover Cleveland was the only person he knew who really had genuine faith. He prayed daily either by himself or with his beloved wife and away from the churches and hypocrites that Adam believed kept America stupid and blind to the invisible realities of truth and love and fairness. These were new concepts and feelings Adam had never experienced until Grover came into his life. Yes, Adam Pitt loved Grover, and that's why his upcoming walk to Union Station scared him to silence as they drove to Kansas City on his graduation day.

It wasn't long before he watched his parents going into the bar. They looked like kids excited about recess. He needed the good, long walk over to Grover's office. For the first time that day he noticed how the weather was perfect. He was away from his parents and released from a school he believed had imprisoned him for fourteen years.

As he moved along the concrete jungle of Kansas City on his powerful bowed legs, past the giant buildings that never failed to energize him, he thought of the reason he hadn't sent Grover an invitation or an announcement about attending his graduation.

Never in his entire life, except during home football and basketball games, had he seen any person of any color other than white in Pittsville. He was certain his father would not appreciate meeting his railroad friend. All those negative racist comments he heard his father make over the years permeated his mind. *I would never put Grover through that,* Adam had told himself several times. That was the reason he didn't invite him to his graduation.

The city blocks were going by too fast because he dreaded telling Grover about his plan, and then dragging him into it as an accomplice by seeking the railroad man's help with the best timetable and train that would carry him safely into Canada. Clear images of his friend's grave disappointment in him were making his belly ache and his palms sweat, just like they had whenever he was competing in a track meet and his team needed him to win his events in order to win or place in the meet.

He removed his jacket as he walked and visualized sitting across from Grover's desk and laying out his whole plan. He pictured Grover's face listening intently and complying with his desire to avoid the draft. That was all he envisioned—all the way to the station—just as he'd done each time he soared into the record books. This time he was acutely aware that he was trying to save his life by avoiding serving his country. *To keep my name out of the paper,* he cynically told himself.

Three blocks from Grover he saw why he could never take a track scholarship. It stopped him cold. It was his reflection. He put his face close to the storefront window of an auto specialty shop that had a chrome mirror on display.

Only four or five pimples could be seen on the face of the high school graduate that he now confirmed could only be an invisible freshman if he went on to college instead of Canada. *I'm not putting myself in that position,* he said matter-of-factly to the reflection of his jaded eyes that of late were dull and tired-looking. He was being brutally honest to his image in the chrome mirror. He was angry with his image for never really laughing loud as others his age did. Adam had even heard Kaladi laughing loud and clear after Helen had dumped him. *The dark age is over,* he told his image and continued his walk to Grover's office.

Because it was such a nice day, Adam went around back to the trains instead of cutting through the station—the same route Reggie liked to take. Soon he could see that the train's passenger cars and engines were glistening clean from a spring rainfall that had passed through the Kansas City area earlier.

For the first time that he could remember, Grover's office door was closed. Even when he went to lunch, he'd normally leave his door open. Something was wrong because he never missed work. Grover was proud of that. Adam knocked lightly on the narrow aluminum door. No answer. He turned the doorknob and the door was locked.

Down the skinny passageway in the same kitchen car he could hear a vacuum running and walked toward the sound. He found a young man who turned off his machine in order to hear Adam. "Is Grover workin' today?" Adam asked.

"He's at a funeral," the young man said.

"Who died?"

The young man shrugged his shoulders and went back to work. *Maybe Grover's wife died,* Adam thought as he left the train. He hurried into Grand Hall hoping someone in Rudy's might know something. The day Adam gave Reggie a ride home, Reggie had told him as they drove past Grover's house that Mrs. C. has very high blood pressure.

Heading for Rudy's, an awful fear in his gut came over him when he heard Buffalo Springfield singing "For What It's Worth." It was coming from a young man's portable cassette player: "Paranoia strikes deep / Into your life it will creep / It starts when you're always afraid…"

That's when it hit Adam, the paranoia of who Grover was really saying goodbye to. That song was the same song played on the University of Kansas campus when the students were protesting the war. Adam quickened his pace, now headed for the front of the barber shop at the shoeshine stand where there was always a newspaper. He'd been avoiding his father's ritualistic morning reading aloud of the war's local casualties.

Shine Man was working on a pair of shoes when Adam stood in front of an empty elevated chair riffling through the newspaper in a furious search to find the obituaries.

It took his breath away when he saw the smiling army boot camp photo and the write up: "PFC Reginald 'Reggie' Baldwin of Kansas City, Missouri, was killed in action on May 25th after recently being deployed to Vietnam."

He walked away from the shoeshine stand after tearing Reggie's obituary out of the paper. *Reggie, how could this happen?* his busy mind kept asking until he realized he was walking in the wrong direction if he was going to the Ebenezer Baptist Church listed in the obituary, which Adam remembered was not far from Reggie's house. The church had to be less than a couple of miles from Union Station. He looked at the big clock on the station wall and believed he could still make it to the funeral that had already started.

Conscious-stricken

Adam hurried east in a conscious-stricken fog until he was in Grover and Reggie's neighborhood. Reggie's obituary was still in his pocket, but he didn't want to look at it again. Unless he had to. An elderly man walking on the sidewalk gave Adam directions to get to the church just four blocks away.

Adam sprinted toward the church for fear of missing his friend's funeral. But when the church was in view, he slowed back to a walk and noticed a pair of black high-top tennis shoes draped over a power line.

Reggie wore shoes like that. Could they be his? Adam recalled Reggie's incredible jump shot.

There were dozens of vehicles in the crowded church parking lot. Reggie's service was obviously still in progress, and the black hearse and its driver were waiting for Reggie's coffin.

Up the four cracked concrete steps, and Adam was inside the brownstone church that was over a century old. A gray-haired minister in a purple robe was concluding the service. Adam sat down in the last row of pews at the back of the church. Just as the choir started to sing "Rock of Ages," Adam could see the back of Grover's head up front in the second-row pew next to the aisle. He appeared to be seated next to his wife. Up at the front of the church was Reggie's closed coffin draped with an American flag. Seated off to the side of Reggie's coffin were six young army pallbearers—an honor guard in dress uniform waiting to carry one of their own fallen comrades to the hearse outside.

Upon completion of the song, the army pallbearers took their positions around the coffin. The flag was folded, and one of the soldiers gave it to Reggie's mother seated in the first row in front of Grover and his wife. It was heart-wrenchingly awful to see the slump-backed grief of Reggie's mother when she and her family followed the honor guard as they carried her youngest son out of the church.

The people seated in the pews up front exited the church first. As Grover escorted his wife out of the church, he spotted Adam seated in the back row next to the aisle and motioned for him to leave the church with them. Once outside, Grover told Adam he wanted him to ride along with him to the cemetery after he dropped his wife at home.

Adam rode alone in the back of Grover's black '67 Lincoln. Mrs. C. was friendly to Adam and talked softly about the nice service. "You know, that sweet boy was only in Vietnam for eleven days when he was killed," she said quietly.

Grover explained to Adam, "Reggie's mama told us her son was killed by mortar fire on the base outside of Saigon. It happened at night. Maybe he was asleep," Grover said hopefully, and his wife nodded her agreement.

During the short drive to the Cleveland house, Adam could see the sadness in Grover's eyes in his rearview mirror and in his body language. He helped his wife out of the car and escorted her up the steps to their front door. They were an elderly couple dressed in black, and they'd been hurt by this devastating loss. *This is no time to talk to Grover about Canada,* Adam thought to himself. *Or is it the perfect time?* he wondered while getting out of the Lincoln's back seat and into the front passenger seat. He could smell Mrs. C.'s perfume and Grover's Old Spice that he only wore during his Wichita Express runs and on special occasions.

When Grover got behind the wheel he talked as he drove. He repeated with more animation, "He'd only been there for *eleven* days!" Grover emphasized the word "eleven" by tilting his head toward his passenger and flashing his huge magnified right eyeball behind his silver-framed glasses.

"What's mortar fire?" Adam had to ask.

Grover explained that Reggie's barracks was hit by artillery shells at night. "That's what the army told his mother," Grover shook his head sadly, adding, "It had to be a closed coffin."

While leaving the cemetery in Grover's car after the burial service, Adam was getting anxious about time and getting back to Marv's, where the car was parked. "Grover, I came to see you at your office today to tell you I want to go to Canada before I'm drafted. For a long time I've wanted to ask you for the best route by rail I should take to go to Winnipeg. And now, after what happened to Reggie, I was thinkin' I could leave sometime in July after I make some money at our fireworks stand."

Grover drove in silence. Finally, he looked over at his passenger with his big brown eye bulging and said, "I remember this one winter night on a Sunday, they was calling for six inches of snow to fall overnight. I knew the next morning I'd have some shovelin' to do in order to get the car out of the garage so my wife and I could get to work. Well, I got up early that morning, and when I looked outside … the whole driveway, sidewalk AND all the steps were shoveled. I knew Reggie done that 'cause he'd shoveled for me before and I paid him five dollars. And that boy … oh, you shoulda seen his eyes light up when I gave him that five spot. He was fulla joy. So that Monday after school he came by the house … but it had snowed again all day just as much as the night before!" Grover laughed, his palm feigning a smack on his steering wheel. "So he comes up to the front door in deep snow with his shovel standin' beside him, and all the work he did that mornin' long gone. And I says, 'You better come in and have some hot chocolate before you get started.' So he liked that!" Grover laughed. "And when he was sittin' at the table sippin' his hot chocolate with marshmellas, my wife comes over and hands him a ten-dollar bill and tells him it's for his great shoveling job from that morning and that afternoon, and that we was both grateful to him. And that boy …" Grover's voice broke and tears welled in the corners of his eyes, showing Adam how much he loved Reggie.

Adam pointed out his parents' car in the tavern parking lot, and Grover parked right next to it. He cut off his engine and turned in the driver's seat to face his passenger. "There's only one passenger train that goes to Winnipeg from Kansas City. That would be the 10:27. It leaves the station every Wednesday morning at 10:27. It stops in Omaha, Sioux City, Sioux Falls and Fargo. They don't check for passports at the border, but you should have a driver's license in case they do."

They shook hands and Adam got out of the Lincoln and watched his friend drive away.

Before going inside the bar to let his parents know he was outside waiting to drive them home, he was still in his conscious-stricken fog recalling Reggie's flag-draped coffin under the green canvas pavilion at the cemetery. Adam thought about how glad he was that he didn't tell Reggie about his plan to go north. But then guilt overcame him for not trying harder to convince Reggie that he should try to get a basketball scholarship.

Walking toward Marv's back entrance, he knew that he had to save money from the fireworks stand. *Then I can leave on the 10:27 from the station … on a Wednesday.*

By the time he'd driven his "happy" parents back home, it dawned on Adam that he'd never told his parents about his friends Grover or Reggie. That aspect of his relationship with his parents saddened him. It made him go up to his room and crank up the volume on the Black Sabbath song "Paranoid" while lying on his bed near the end of his graduation day. *The worst day of my life,* he mused.

The Letter

E very single person in Adam Pitt's universe was growing increasingly paranoid with every passing day in June. Even old Gop seemed stressed out with diarrhea from his greasy diet and the upcoming holiday that everyone in the Pitt House knew could be their last one together as a family—messed up as they were.

Adam had most of June to get the fireworks operation ready for the Pitts' biggest and only holiday of the year. And it appeared it would be the last season for the small business because of the town's new stricter zoning laws. Each passing day seemed to be a little hotter than the day before. And just like every June for the past five years, Adam blasted his music from his portable cassette player. Lately it had been Zeppelin, Buffalo Springfield, and Black Sabbath. This would be Adam's ultimate Independence Day—the one holiday that would finance his trip to Canada. After that he was on his own. But that didn't bother him.

The week his parents pulled their fireworks trailer to Tennessee to restock for the upcoming holiday was the perfect time for Adam to finalize his plans to go north. Every day he would go over every detail of his plan, just as he had done when he was about to jump into the record books. He had his suitcase packed with all the clothes he would take with him to Canada, and it was hidden in a closet in his attic bedroom.

Will they take away my records? he wondered while dumping all his track ribbons into the trash can in his room. All the while he told himself, *It's not too late to stop this. You can buy yourself a year by taking a track scholarship and purposely failing to place in any meets.* But his response was always the same. *That would be stealing. And I'd still have to go to classes and compete for good enough grades to keep me in school. I can't do that anymore.*

Adam opened his encyclopedia to a map of North America and saw just how far he would be going from Missouri. He knew that a permanent sense of regret was coming his way and would always be with him once he arrived in Canada. And he wondered again why he couldn't just hide out in the Ozarks or get lost in the manswarm of St. Louis. *But why bother?* he asked himself with cynical resignation, *there's nothing for me here. I can start over up there, and at least not end up like Reggie ... shut up forever in some closed coffin covered by a flag that got me killed for something that doesn't matter one bit to anyone. And it never will.*

The nights alone in his parents' house kept driving Adam out into the streets of Pittsville. The darkly-lit rooms and saturated smells generated by their unhealthy habits seemed to be more intensely noticeable when they were gone. For Adam, each evening walk brought deeper clarity and an imminent sense that his departure time for real freedom was nearing.

Adam walked around town more, prowling the streets at night as if getting a last look at the only town he'd ever known. Having pored over all fifty states and the Canadian provinces in his encyclopedias, he really felt like he had already been to all those black-and-white cities and towns that filled a thousand pages. He had also studied all the wars his country had fought in, knowing that soon he would be labeled a sniveling coward by all in the little town that was named after his family. That thought sickened him.

One night Adam passed by the Bach house. He knew that soon Helen would be back in Bobby's arms doing her best to hold onto their fleeting time together before her soldier went off to war. From the sidewalk he could see the yellow Black-eyed Susans Helen had planted in the spring near the front porch steps, their green stems shining in the Missouri moonlight. And he could almost see and certainly feel an invisible harmony that exuded from a house where alcoholism and unemployment were absent. It made him question how one man could live in a home like this and another could only envy it from afar.

Moving along Sycamore Street he came upon his weather-beaten track shoes that dangled from the line above him. They reminded him that he'd already made a name for himself—and that it meant nothing to him now. Just as Vietnam meant nothing to him, he refused to let patriotism and honor send him to an early grave.

He walked past his house on Pitt Street and tried to see all the things around him now. Things Reggie would never have again— like the sound of his footsteps free to move where he wanted them to go, and the rushing wind moving into his eardrums, and the distant horn blast of an approaching freight train reminding him of his freedom to plan and leave this place that had never once felt like home to Adam. Reggie really never had the freedom to choose and decide whether war was something he wanted to participate in. *But I do have a choice,* Adam declared to himself.

He continued his walk toward the town's railroad tracks, even though the fast-moving freight train would be long gone by the time he reached the tracks.

Once he was standing between the tracks, he looked around the obscure Midwest town that had raised him to this point in time. All things in view were strangely familiar to him, yet the things he saw held no emotional ties to keep him there. Nostalgia was not at all part of who Adam Pitt was. For his memory, there had never been a considerable or consistent period of events strung together in time to make for the stuff of dreams or the cherished memories of a safe home. There was no safe place for Adam to be a normal person in Pittsville. He had to be invisible because this was his grandfather's town, and he was the only grandson of the town's biggest employer who out of the blue closed down his business and left the lion's share of his money to a church and a pittance to a worthless alcoholic son who never amounted to anything but a lazy, self-centered drunk.

At least I broke some records they'll never forget, Adam scoffed inwardly as he made his bowed legs head back for the house he'd always been ashamed of.

Adam returned home and once again rehashed his plan to head north. He decided it would be a good idea for him to stash his birth certificate someplace in his suitcase just in case he needed it down the road. He remembered years ago his mother had told him she put his birth certificate in Grandpa Pitt's old roll top desk that was in the living room. As Adam searched through the drawers that were filled with mostly junk that reeked of cigarette smoke and fried food, he wondered what his late grandfather would think of the desk if he saw it now. He remembered the day his parents had ransacked it in a drunken rage, throwing away every ledger, document and record related to Pitt Gravel—all the while cursing the selfish old man who thought the church was more important than his only son. The majestic old piece of furniture that had at one time been the heart and soul of Pitt Gravel was now covered with nicks, scratches, and water rings from highball glasses left sitting on it during the humid summer months. His parents had done to the desk what they had done to every other thing in their lives that had any value—they trashed it.

Opening a little cubbyhole drawer in the top part of the desk, Adam found several important documents. On top was his birth certificate, and underneath it were the birth certificates of his parents. Beneath that was their marriage license. On the very bottom of the green-felt-lined drawer was an envelope with To My Son scripted on the front. Inside the envelope was a letter to Adam's father and a copy of Grandpa Pitt's will. Adam opened the letter and read the last words ever written by Lawrence Garfield Pitt:

> *Dear Son:*
> *I know my time is near. There are many areas in my life where I have been a great success, but just as many where I have been a great failure. The*

192

greatest success of my life was having you as a son, the greatest failure of my life was not investing in you the way I should have.

I don't know how much of your childhood you remember—or even care to remember. You were only three when your mother died. When I left for Europe to fight in the war, it scared your mother something awful that I might never come back again. That's when she started drinking. She kept it hidden from her parents and friends, and nobody ever knew how bad her problem was. Until we were married, even I didn't know how bad her drinking was. No matter how much I begged and pleaded with her, she never could put down the bottle. That old demon had ahold of her good, and he wouldn't let her go.

The day she died, a part of me died with her. I loved her so much. She was my light and my life. Your Aunt Hennie tried to convince me that I still had a piece of her in you, but I couldn't bring myself to accept that. I poured myself into my business day and night because it was the only thing I felt I could control. It was the only thing that kept me from despairing. Knowing most of the town's men relied on me to feed and shelter their families gave me a sense of pride and purpose that I had lost when I lost your mother. I agreed to pay your Aunt Hennie a weekly salary to look after you and give you what I couldn't bring myself to give you.

As the years passed and my pain diminished, I began to regret my decision to turn you over to Aunt Hennie. I wanted a relationship with you, but I didn't know where to start. A couple of times I wanted to talk to you, but you were busy with school sports or your friends or church activities. I figured at some point we'd be able to make up for lost time, but that just never seemed to happen.

193

Around the time you graduated from high school, I started hearing rumors around town about how you were drinking heavily. My heart was gripped with fear when I thought about you following in your mother's path. That was the time I finally confronted you and told you I was concerned about you and that I wanted us to have a better relationship. You laughed at me. When I offered you a job at Pitt Gravel, you got angry with me and told me you'd rather starve to death than take one dime from some sperm donor who never had the time of day for his son.

Your words cut me to the quick. They pierced my heart like a bullet. I knew you believed they were the truth. I tried to explain that it wasn't like that at all, but you wouldn't listen. You were angry and you walked out of my life. I tried a couple more times to reach out to you, but you refused my attempts. I can't say I blame you. In an effort to earn your love and respect, I decided to pay you a small weekly stipend so you could have your freedom. I was hoping that when you got done sowing your wild oats, you would realize you could come to work at Pitt Gravel and earn a very handsome salary. But that was not the case. You were content to live on my handouts.

When I found out you had met Penny and were planning to get married, at first I was very happy. I figured you certainly would want to come to work at the gravel company so you could provide for your family. But again, that was not the case. I learned that Penny was a heavy drinker also. On your wedding day I realized I was not ever going to get through to you, so I quit trying.

When I was diagnosed with tuberculosis and was past the point of any treatment that would work, I decided to close my business. The Good

194

*Book says that "pride goeth before the fall." I
guess that's true of me. I'm a proud man and I
didn't want the people of Pittsville to watch me die
away. I also did not want to spend my last days
watching you squander my life's work. I left for
California to live out my last days in peace and
solitude.*

*I was Pittsville's greatest business success, but I
was also Pittsville's greatest failure as a father. I
know I let you down, and I will regret that to my
dying day. Worst of all, I have watched you adopt
self-destructive habits that I couldn't do anything to
stop. I have watched your wife do the same thing.
But where I failed as a living father, maybe I'll
succeed as a dead one.*

*As I said, I know my time is near. I love you very
much, son, but I cannot allow you and Penny to
continue to destroy yourselves with my money. You
drink too much, you smoke too much, and you're
lazy. For that reason, I have decided to give the
majority of my money to the First Methodist Church
in Pittsville. I will leave you enough money so that
you can go to a top-rated college and get a good
education in hopes that you'll get a good job and
provide for your family.*

*Please, son, think about these words and make a
future for yourself and your family. You won't
regret it.*

Love, Dad.

Adam folded the letter and placed it back in the
envelope along with the will. *No point in reading the will,*
Adam thought. *I know I'm not mentioned in it since
Grandpa died two years before I was born.* Adam felt he
had a kindred spirit in his deceased grandfather. He never
knew anything about the man who died before he was
born—except for the negative verbal bashings he'd heard
from his parents—but he now knew that his grandfather

hated his parents' bad habits as much as Adam did. Knowing he could identify with another human being in this world made him feel like a part of a family for the first time. But knowing the only human being he ever identified with was dead made him feel more alone than ever.

Brainstorming

The day before Adam's parents returned from Tennessee, Clark went over to Adam's house to hang out for the afternoon. He told Adam, "Bobby's leave date was changed again, and he'll be home for the fourth. Helen's gettin' kind of anxious about Bobby comin' back. She says Kaladi still drives by the house every so often … acting like some weirdo. She told me he plays 'Help Me Make it Through the Night' real loud when he drives by so she'll hear it. I think she's afraid he's going to tell Bobby about the baby."

"If he does," Adam said, "you just have to tell Bobby that Kaladi's a liar."

Clark and Adam drove around town brainstorming ways that Kaladi might be persuaded to keep his mouth shut regarding Helen's pregnancy. Between Clark's weed and Black Sabbath, nothing really productive came of it. In fact, it turned out to be a wasted two hours that ended on a paranoid note when Clark pulled into the Pitt driveway and ran over Gop's sleeping head. Clark was so stoned that he didn't see the dog until it was too late, and Adam was rewinding his tape and didn't see the dog lying there. After backing up the car, they both got out and saw that the dog had been killed instantly.

Clark stayed to help bury Gop behind the garage before Adam's parents knew anything about it. "I really feel bad about this, man," Clark said. "I mean ... he's part of your family."

Adam cringed at the thought of his family. He told his friend, "Hey ... don't worry about it. The dog was old. My parents were talkin' about puttin' him to sleep. They'll just think he went away to die somewhere."

"So you're not going to tell your parents I ran over him?"

"They don't need to know. They'll probably be glad he's gone. It'll save 'em a vet bill."

It was the casual way Adam dismissed Gop's death that made Clark's mind believe, *If I'd run over Kaladi the same way I ran over Gop, I'd prob'ly feel no diff'rent than I do now.*

After returning the shovel to the nail on the wall in the garage, Adam said to Clark, "Too bad it wasn't Kaladi instead of Gop, huh?"

With Adam justifying Clark's thoughts on the matter, he began anew his brainstorming right there in the garage. He told Adam, "We should waste that idiot."

They went up to Adam's room and listened to more music while dreaming up ways to ensure that Kaladi didn't tell Bobby about the lost baby. Each idea they came up with was impossible to pull off without breaking the law, so they scrapped each one. They finally decided to just tell worried Helen that if Kaladi said anything to Bobby, they'd all deny everything and tell Bobby that Kaladi was just jealous because Helen dumped him for Bobby. "After all," Clark told Adam, "Kaladi can't prove anything."

"Yeah ... our word against his," Adam agreed.

Later that afternoon when Adam and Clark were in Clark's garage rotating his tires, Helen excitedly came into the garage from the house to tell them about the letter she had just received from Bobby. "Bobby said he's going to pay for my flight to San Diego, and that we can spend his leave together near the beach. He doesn't want to come back home for his leave and have all that fanfare about going overseas," Helen explained to her brother and Adam as they worked on Clark's tires. Helen was beside herself with this news because she felt like they'd either elope or at least get engaged during their time together in San Diego. If Bobby came home to Pittsville on his leave, Helen was well aware that his parents were likely to talk their son out of doing anything impulsive. She believed that's why Bobby wanted to spend his time alone with her in California. But Helen was not revealing any of these details to anyone—not even her brother, who now seemed relieved to stop thinking about how to get Kaladi to keep his big mouth shut.

Now Adam was unsure whether he'd even see Helen again once she left for California. He wanted to tell her and Clark about his plan to take the train north into Canada after the Fourth of July when their fireworks season was over. Only his parents and Grover knew about his plan, and Adam decided they were the only people who would know. Everyone else would have a difficult time finding out he was in Canada. His parents told him they would not tell a soul out of fear of being convicted by the Selective Service for harboring a fugitive or withholding information regarding their draft-dodging son.

Clark had been pumping gas for Jimmy Taggit over the summer as a way to earn some money to help his parents cover next year's college tuition. The day after Helen got Bobby's letter, Jimmy Taggit told Clark, "I got a letter from Bobby yesterday. Said he's stayin' in California for his leave. I bet that news'll break your sister's heart."

It was apparent to Clark that his boss was obviously unaware that Helen was flying out to be with Bobby. She had asked Clark not to tell Bobby's father that she was going to California to be with Bobby on his last leave before being shipped off to Nam. "Bobby doesn't want his parents to know I'm with him," she told her brother that morning when he went to work at the gas station.

Independence Day

Again, Adam worked the graveyard shift from midnight to eight in the morning starting June 25th selling fireworks from their trailer parked near the front of the Pitt driveway. The City of Pittsville had notified the Pitts that this was the last season they could sell fireworks from their property. The town council unanimously approved a new town ordinance that allowed fireworks to be sold only in a commercially zoned permanent structure that was at least five hundred yards from any residential area. Bill and Penny Pitt planned to appeal what they adamantly described as "the end of our livelihood" until they found out it would cost over five hundred bucks to file an appeal. At the beginning of every day shift, Adam had to listen to his parents griping and complaining about the new ordinance, and every customer heard about how those crooks at city hall had ruined their business and were forcing them out of their house.

But Adam knew that his dad would never sell the house that Grandpa Pitt gave him. They couldn't live cheaper anywhere else than the $1200.00 a year in property taxes plus utilities they paid for the Pitt House. Adam had even told his parents that they'd figure out something better to do—if they really needed to.

Every shift Adam would play his music from his cassette player, often without interacting or conversing at all with most of the endless stream of customers that stopped by the Pitt House to get their annual supply of fireworks.

Clark stopped by when Adam was working to tell him, "Helen called home a couple days ago. She said she's going off with Bobby ... that Bobby's going AWOL."

Adam was stunned and somewhat pleased with this news. "Are they going to Canada?" he asked Clark.

"She wouldn't say where she is or where she's goin' with Bobby. All she told my mom is that she loves Bobby and wants to be with him."

"Did Bobby tell his parents?" Adam asked.

"Not yet. He doesn't want his dad to talk him out of it. This'll kill Mr. T. for sure. I don't know how I can keep workin' there ... knowing this about Bobby and keeping it from my boss."

At first the news about Bobby made Adam want to tell Clark about his plan to go to Canada after the fourth, but he didn't. Instead, Adam listened to his friend go on at length about the war and how it was ruining lives and tearing apart families.

On the night of the fourth—the busiest time for the Pitts— Kaladi showed up drunk with Aaron Schick, a nervous tag-along inch-brow who thought Kaladi was cool. Aaron was known by his classmates as Dipshit. They wanted some firecrackers to toss out of Kaladi's truck while driving around town. Kaladi tried to act sober when he asked Adam, "So ... have you seen Helen around?"

The aproned firecracker vendor shook his head no. As Kaladi turned away from the stand, he lit a cigarette and acted like he was going to light the entire package of Black Cats he'd just bought. Adam turned off his music and called out, "Hey, Kaladi! No smokin' here!"

Kaladi and Dipshit ignored Adam. They were laughing while preparing to light the strand of firecrackers dangerously close to the trailer. Adam jumped down from the trailer and pushed both of them down to the concrete driveway, stepping on the lit cigarette that had fallen out of Kaladi's hand.

"Get your dumb ass outta here!" Adam warned Kaladi. The two drunks staggered to their feet, wanting no part in tangling with an angry Ape. "Back off, Ape!" Kaladi pointed his finger at Adam and stumbled toward his truck with Dipshit following.

Adam's heart calmed when Kaladi drove away, but soon the entire package of Black Cats was popping after Dipshit lit it and tossed it out from the moving truck on Pitt Street. *At least Bobby and Helen won't be bothered by that idiot,* Adam reasoned as he tried to calm himself after the incident.

Perhaps more than anyone else, Adam was aware that Bobby and Helen had the best reason to celebrate this day as a real Independence Day—both for themselves and their future together. Adam truly admired Bobby's courage to do what he had to do in order to live his life without the fear of being killed or injured in a senseless war. Now, Bobby and Helen would have to give up Pittsville and the people in their lives who would not forgive what they'd done.

They're better off staying away from here, Adam told himself several times during the remaining time of his last shift selling fireworks. Tomorrow he would help with the inventory and close up the trailer for the last time. Then he would count the money he'd made for his trip north and wait for the next Wednesday to arrive—Adam Pitt's Independence Day.

Wednesdays

The first Wednesday after the fourth, Adam just wasn't able to make his move as planned. All five days leading up to Wednesday, he'd talked to his parents about needing one of them to drive him to Union Station; however, when Wednesday morning came, he paced and circled the kitchen table. His words to them were anything but positive and confident. "I was awake all night ... couldn't sleep at all. Now I'm exhausted. I can't leave when I'm this tired."

"You can sleep on the train," his dad suggested dryly from behind his newspaper, obviously anxious to have one less mouth to feed since they'd seen the last of their fireworks income.

It was Adam's mother who showed some rare maternal support for her son's vacillation. "Yeah, you shouldn't travel when you're tired. Go next Wednesday," she smiled above her raised coffee cup before taking a sip.

"Yeah ... next Wednesday," Adam agreed and headed back upstairs to his room to get some sleep.

"He's too hard on himself," Penny told Bill after their son left the kitchen. "You know, once he's gone, we might never see Adam again. I mean, once he crosses the border, he might not ever be able to come back."

Bill Pitt put down his paper and lit a cigarette, exhaling his words with his smoke. "I'll betcha there's a thousand deserters doin' time in Leavenworth. I'd rather see Adam in Canada than prison. That federal penitentiary shit stays with ya a long time 'cause only the shit jobs will hire ya when ya do get out."

"Yeah," Penny sighed in agreement, then lit her cigarette with her lighter.

Adam awoke in the late afternoon, and the whole day he felt guilty and ashamed for not acting on his plan.

By the time the next Wednesday rolled around, Adam had convinced himself that there was no hurry to go north. *Unless the draft board orders me into the army*, Adam reasoned, *I may as well stay put and savor what remaining days I have in the United States.*

Adam started looking around town for part-time work. He wanted a job that he could leave in a hurry if he had to. He thought it was to his advantage to add as much as he could to his fireworks money before leaving, telling himself, *The more I save...the easier it will be.*

Early on the first Saturday morning in August, Clark knocked on the side door of the Pitt House. He made his way up to Adam's bedroom door after Penny let him in.

"WATCH YOUR STEP!" Bill called out in jest from behind his newspaper, referring to his sister's fall.

Bill Pitt's cynical comment made Clark think of his sister all the way to Adam's attic door. The KU sophomore-to-be was stoned on what he told Adam was the best weed he'd had in his life. Before knocking on Adam's door, Clark looked back down the dark stairway where Helen had fallen and lost her baby. Above his head he could see that there was still no light bulb in the overhead light fixture that hung from the ceiling. He knocked on the latched door that could only be opened from inside the attic.

Fast-approaching footsteps made Clark call out, "Open up, Ape! I got some news you won't believe!"

Adam was half-asleep and heading back to sit on his bed after unlatching the door to let Clark in.

"Helen just called from Vancouver, Washington. Bobby got caught by the feds when he tried to cross the border."

"Really? Oh, man ... that's not good," Adam groaned while seated on his bed, scratching his head and yawning toward the floor fan blowing on him below the front window.

"Bobby walked up to the border crossing station by himself while Helen stayed on the U.S. side. He didn't want her involved in case something went wrong. She watched the feds arrest Bobby. She called us this morning and said she wasn't coming home until she knew what was going to happen to him."

"Was she freaked out?"

"About as freaked as you were when I killed your dog."

"Really?"

"Yeah ... She told my mom that it's all for the best and that at least Bobby won't have to go to war or to Canada. She said he'll do some time and then they'll let him out. At least that's how Helen sees it."

"Now Mr. T.'s going to find out and, man ... Bobby'll never come back to this town. God, his dad's a big military guy ... an ex-Marine, for God's sake."

"Yeah, but at least Bobby'll be alive," Clark said to Adam's agreeing nod.

❖ ❖ ❖

It wasn't until the last Wednesday in August that Adam went to Union Station—just for a visit. He didn't go there to see Grover, since he'd be on his daily Wichita Express run. Adam had left the house early that morning, driving his parents' car. He wanted to see the 10:27 to Winnipeg up close. Sort of a trial run. In fact, he arrived at the station's platform at nine o'clock and boarded the northbound train just to get a feel for what it was like to sit in a coach car. To see the dining car and a restroom. And he wanted to see what the passengers looked like who would ride north with him someday. The night before, he had stayed up late poring over his books stacked at the end of his bed. He studied the weather tables and extreme cold weather he'd have to endure in Winnipeg. For an hour Adam stood on the platform so he could watch the 10:27 passengers arriving. They were mostly businessmen dressed in colorful polyester suits and sports jackets; they looked like they were headed for business dealings to the north. These were the people he would ride with if he ever heard from the draft board. Last week his father had read out loud to him from the paper that "one-point-four million young men have been drafted to serve in Vietnam so far, and twenty-five percent of the U.S. troops in Vietnam have been drafted ... compared to sixty-six percent in World War Two."

"And I'm not gonna be one of those twenty-five percent," Adam asserted to his parents at the breakfast table.

"And Bobby Taggit won't either," Bill Pitt smiled. He smiled because he knew Jimmy Taggit, Bobby's dad, very well. They had gone to school together. Everyone in school called him "Jimmy T."

"Wasn't Bobby sent to jail on a base in California?" Penny asked her son.

"Helen came home yesterday, and she said they put Bobby in a holding area on a base in Vallejo after Bobby told them he didn't want to be a Marine anymore."

"Yeah, they frown on that sort of thing," Bill chuckled, still smirking at the ironic thought that ex-tough-guy-Marine Jimmy T.'s boy was a deserter.

Right on schedule, Adam watched the 10:27's silver-steel cars move away from the station on its way to Canada. From the platform it looked so easy to just roll away and be on his way to a safe haven. Yet Helen had told Clark when she got home that Bobby didn't know that Canada was not a safe haven for deserters, since Canada also had strict laws against desertion. It was the draft-dodgers who were welcomed by the Canadians—the men who were not in the military yet. And for some creepy reason,

Adam was glad to hear that Helen and Bobby had not eloped like her parents feared they would.

On his drive back home from the station, Adam was curious about what Helen had told Bobby's parents. Clark told Adam that Helen had the task of breaking the news to the Taggits that Bobby had deserted and was now in the brig.

Not far from the Pitt House, Adam saw Helen walking on the sidewalk with a palpable sense of regret about her. She waved at him as he pulled into the driveway. She had just left the Taggit house after telling Bobby's parents everything he wanted them to know.

She stopped at the end of the Pitt driveway as Adam was getting out of the car and asked him to walk with her. He told her he'd be right back after he put the keys in the house. By the time he'd hurried back outside, he didn't see her. He walked around to the front of the house and found her sitting on the front steps with her face in her hands. He walked over and sat beside her without making a sound, waiting for her to say something.

Finally she said through her tears, "I feel like I just told Bobby's parents that he died. It was awful. They kept asking me to give them a phone number or an address where they could contact Bobby. I told them Bobby doesn't want to talk to anybody about this. He just wants to serve his time until they let him out. That's when Mr. T. said, 'Serve his time? He's better off dead. Deserters are worse than the enemy.' Then I told them that Bobby told me he realized that he couldn't kill anybody and that he'd be putting other Marines in jeopardy by going into a combat situation."

"You told Mr. T. that?"

"I told him and Mrs. T. It was awful, Adam," her head shook back and forth while she covered her face from view. "It was the way they looked when they heard about their son's inability to kill someone … like that was something too terrible to fathom. They hated the whole situation and hated Bobby for humiliating them. Bobby would tell me how his mother was more into the military and patriotism than his dad was, because her father retired from the Marine Corps. He always talked about how she validated and supported any U.S. military interventions or escalations in Vietnam. Even more than Mr. T."

"How long will they keep him locked up?"

"As long as they want. That's what Bobby told me just before we got to the border. He told me that if he was caught they'd put him in the brig for a few months and dishonorably discharge him. He also said that the ones who get the most support from home get out the fastest."

Adam nodded that he understood, adding, "It's still better than goin' to Nam." Adam's words were a reminder that at least Bobby would be coming home to her alive or in one piece. Then after a long pause, Adam decided to finally confess, "I'm goin' to Canada if they draft me."

She nodded positively, knowing Adam would be welcome in Canada and safe from the war. She told Adam, "Bobby talked about you a lot when we were in California. He could never understood why you wouldn't go to college on a track scholarship that would keep you out of the draft for at least four years."

Those words that Bobby had said to Helen about him were words Adam needed to hear. He had been rethinking his plan and seeing things in a different light. Adam was terrified of going to Canada alone and not knowing a single person when he got there—not to mention living the rest of his life as a draft-dodger. Ever since the Fourth of July, when he finally forced himself to make a decision about his future, his teenage angst and fear of starting over as a freshman had vanished. He could see himself walking on a college campus now and accepting the spotlight for his track achievements.

Helen had helped him see that he wasn't running away from the war, he was running away from Pittsville and all the real and imagined judgments and labels about his family—especially his grandfather who had employed then laid off half the town. But Adam knew the real story behind the mystery that had kept the town talking for more than twenty years.

Earlier that day when he was standing on the platform watching the 10:27 depart, the motion of the departing train made him whimsical and reflective. He tried to imagine his grandfather and even his father standing where he was and watching the trains leave for unknown places they'd only dreamed of. That's when Adam realized he wanted to be a part of a respected family like Helen's. And he could never have that if he left America. Ever. As Adam walked Helen home he told her, "I think I'm going to try to get into KU this fall ... if they'll still give me a scholarship." Helen was elated that Adam had changed his mind about college. She told him, "I'm going to write to Bobby and let him know that 'Ape's going to Lawrence!'"

Scratched

After dropping off Clark at his dorm in Lawrence, Adam drove over to the University of Kansas Armory, the massive indoor sports training complex where basketball practice and indoor track training was held. The athletic weight room was located in the Armory along with the coaching staff offices.

Coach Tubbs, the KU head track coach, had come to Pittsville to recruit Adam the summer before his senior year. Outside the Pitt House, the coach had told Adam that he could live off campus in a studio apartment paid for by the university, and that the school would help Adam find a part-time job off campus so he had a little spending money. Adam was resolute about living alone off campus, and he had to have a part-time job since his parents couldn't give him a dime.

Adam was impressed with the immense training facility—along with the big, fast, powerful varsity players scrimmaging. They were posting up aggressively in their half-court game, positioning themselves with a violent assertiveness he hadn't seen in high school.

At the long jump runway, Adam observed a tall, lean young man in sweat pants and a KU t-shirt with an expensive pair of royal-blue-with-white-trim track shoes draped over his shoulder. They were the most incredible shoes Adam had ever seen. He watched him walk-off his take-off point on the long jump runway and mark it before sitting down to put on his incredible shoes that Adam knew he had to have. The young man scratched, his toes over the foul line by at least an inch. Adam estimated his jump around twenty-five feet, though; and right away Adam knew that he was surrounded by a higher level of talent. He felt strangely comfortable and at home being in a place with hundreds of talented athletes who were all hungry for something that could help them reach their potential. About himself Adam thought, *With good coaching ... who knows?*

By the time Adam found Coach Tubbs's office, he was confident he could handle being a freshman all over again. He had to wait outside the coach's office for twenty minutes before he could talk to him. With each passing minute, Adam's self-confidence and anticipation of college life grew.

When Adam finally met with the coach, he was stunned by his sincerely compassionate rejection. "I'm sorry, Adam. I have all the jumpers I need. Every scholarship is taken. I didn't hear from you, son, after I talked with you last summer. I figured you scratched us off your list. I'm sorry, Adam."

Adam's mind was a blur with the stack of business cards and letters from other coaches at other colleges he'd tossed into the garbage can with Gop's dumpings. Back then he had thoroughly enjoyed rejecting their offers. But now he was wracking his brain trying to remember the names of coaches who had wanted him or the schools they'd represented. He was doing his best to grab anything out of his brain that could give him hope against the draft notice that could arrive any day.

It was nearly a mile's drive to Clark's dorm across the huge campus that Adam believed was bigger than all of Pittsville. As Adam got closer to Clark's dorm, his mind's fear grew—as if he'd been drafted already. *Maybe Clark can help me,* he kept trying to

211

calm his busy mind that was incessantly being chased by the government's crazy war. *It's a sacrifice I'm not goin' to make ... to be reduced to a number and then be dropped into another world where it's kill or be killed. No way. Not me. Not me.*

Clark was glad to see his friend from home, but soon Clark was disappointed to hear that he'd been scratched by the KU track coach. "God, Ape ... you have to go to some other schools that wanted you. One of 'em's sure to give ya a full ride."

"Yeah," Adam mumbled as they walked out of the dorm toward the cafeteria to have lunch before heading back to Pittsville.

"Helen's waiting for a call from Bobby today," Clark said, hoping the change of subject would help to momentarily assuage his friend's fears.

"Really?"

"Yeah, it'll be the first time they're letting him call anybody. And they only give him fifteen minutes. He's written her a few letters, but I guess they won't send 'em. And they won't let him have his letters from Helen, either."

"At least he's out of the war," Adam had to say, referring also to his own situation and still reeling from the sharp sting of rejection.

"Ape ... you really want to know what I would do if I was you?"

Adam nodded imploringly to his friend.

"If I was you and could jump like you ... with two national track records...I would go around to all the small colleges around here and let each track coach know about your records. One of 'em's bound to give you a full ride." After thoroughly chewing a bite of his sandwich he exclaimed, "Hey, I know! After we eat, we can go to the library here and get the mailing addresses of every college in Missouri, Kansas, Iowa, Nebraska ..."

"That has a track team," Adam injected.

"Right. I can type up a letter of introduction right there in the library for you to mail to the athletic directors of each school."

"Sounds good," Adam grinned, buoyed by Clark's take-charge attitude.

212

After lunch as they were walking to the campus library, the song "Ohio" was playing loud and clear on a student's tape player. To Adam this was a warning that the Selective Service was getting closer to sending him that dreaded draft notice that had the power to send him home in a coffin or body bag. Images of Reggie's coffin and funeral flooded his mind until the music was too faint to hear.

Clark went right to work in the library and found a reference book that listed every college with a track team. They used a copy machine to copy some twenty-six pages containing dozens of prospects that Adam could mail his query letter to. Then Clark composed and typed a letter of introduction that Adam could mass mail to each school's athletic department. In less than two hours, Clark had done more for Adam than anyone else in Pittsville had ever done. He had given his talented friend hope—and possibly even saved his life.

After making several dozen copies of his letter of introduction, the two young men walked to a nearby post office where Adam bought thirty-seven pre-stamped, business-sized envelopes. They stood in the post office lobby at a counter signing, addressing, sealing and mailing all thirty-seven letters to college athletic directors throughout the Midwest.

On his drive back to Pittsville, Adam couldn't stop thinking about how the once-eager University of Kansas track coach scratched him from his scouting list of high school prospects and made zero effort to find a way to give him a scholarship. But then Clark's positive action of getting out that letter of introduction out into "the track and field universe" and speculating that Adam would have his pick of schools, once again gave Adam hope and confidence in his future. *I hope he's right,* Adam said to himself as he drove his parents' car out of Kansas and crossed the Missouri state line.

The Waiting

The first days after mailing his letters of introduction dragged by for Adam like the humid, pollen-rich month of August always had. Each interminable day brought nothing for him in the mail; however, Helen had heard from Bobby that he hoped to be discharged from the service by Christmas.

Helen walked over to the Pitt House to share the good news with Adam. Both had been suffering through a long spell of waiting for news and getting nothing. "He wants me to just bring my clothes and be there wherever he's discharged. He said he doesn't ever want to come back here," Helen confided in her friend.

After sitting on the front porch steps in silence for a few moments, finally Adam asked her, "Where do you guys think you'll go?"

Helen shrugged her shoulders, unsure about their future.

Wanting to help her stay positive he said, "I think you're both lucky to be waiting for your new start together this way … instead of waiting for him to come home safe from a war."

"Yeah," she agreed, "but it still makes me sad that Bobby would never want to return home and that we'd hardly ever see our families ... or Pittsville."

Still trying to keep her positive he responded, "I'd be glad if I never had to come back to this place. Your families can visit you ... and you know they would. Mine? Yuck!" he demonstrated with a twisted mouth of disgust.

Helen laughed and then complained: "I just hate all this waiting! Waiting for Bobby to come home ... waiting for him to get out of the service ... waiting to get a good job. It just gets old ... all this waiting."

"Yeah. Seems I've been waiting my whole life. Since waiting is the biggest part of our lives now, why don't we teach ourselves to enjoy the waiting ... somehow?"

Helen perked up right away, saying, "You're right, Adam. We should teach ourselves to enjoy the waiting. It's like Bobby said, 'We have to make the best of it.' Like right now ... why don't we walk to the library and research some places we'd like to live?"

They walked the five short blocks to the one-room library and pored over travel reference books with colorful pages of cities and points of interest for tourists. Leaving the library, they talked about their favorite places with an infectious enthusiasm. Laughingly, they both agreed that was a much better way to live.

As they got to Helen's house she told Adam, "You know, I think I want to walk around town a little more ... instead of just sitting around the house waiting."

"I know exactly how you feel. I'll be happy to walk with you," Adam suggested.

"That would be positive for both of us," she agreed.

They walked until they reached the old Pitt Gravel Yard, still and quiet but in its day bustling with dust clouds of activity this time of year. Neither of them had been born yet when Grandpa Pitt closed down the town's largest employer in 1950. As they stood there looking at the abandoned business, there were still no trees or grass growing on the ground that remained an industrial wasteland and eyesore for the town—a constant, negative reminder to those who had had to go without income for many months, or the many who lost their homes and had to move in with relatives, or the scores who just moved away altogether.

"I wish my dad hadn't stayed here when Grandpa Pitt closed this place down."

"Why did he close it down?" Helen was curious

"He wanted to retire in California. He gave my dad the house and took off for the Golden State."

"Why didn't your dad run the business?"

"He partied too much. He was no business manager and too lazy to work. He has just lived off the inheritance and the fireworks stand. And now that the town has said my dad can't have his fireworks stand, he told me last month I've got to move out or pay him rent. This damn draft has me stuck! If I don't get a track scholarship, I'll have to go to Canada or be drafted. It all just sucks."

"Yeah," Helen understood as she scanned the old gravel pit that covered hundreds of acres. Then she said, "Bobby says we can't live near his parents. I think we'll probably end up living in Oregon."

Adam wasn't surprised to hear Oregon was a possibility. He'd surmised that when they were in the library and she had enthusiastically shown Adam pictures of towns and cities in Oregon that were particularly appealing to her. "Why Oregon?" he asked her.

"Bobby heard that the people there are more liberal-minded toward young men who leave the service early."

"That would be good for both of you," Adam nodded.

"Clark said you mailed out a bunch of letters to schools," Helen said, changing the subject. "Did you get any responses?"

"Not yet. It's too early. Maybe I will soon … I hope."

"Yeah, I do hope you hear good news soon. Clark thinks you'll get several offers."

"It might be too late, though. Whatever."

"C'mon … let's keep walking."

Three miles later they stopped at the Dairy Freeze, and Helen bought them each a slushie—a "guaranteed brain freeze," Adam called it. They sat on the top of a Dairy Freeze picnic table slurping their cold drinks with their backs to the parking lot and facing the undeveloped lot that was mostly weeds and prairie grass stretching all the way to the railroad tracks. Seeing the tracks remind Adam of his father's accusation that morning that he had chickened out of going to Canada, and then his ultimatum that he pay rent or pack up.

"Since the town shut down our fireworks business, my dad has let me know in no uncertain terms that he wants me out of the house ASAP."

"That must be hard to be around," Helen said with a genuine empathy he'd only heard from his mother a few times in his life, but not at all since he had decided not to go up north. Helen changed the subject by asking him, "So where do think you'd like to live?"

"Anyplace but Nam or Pittsville," he answered seriously.

Just then behind them they heard a familiar sound that made both of them instantly apprehensive. They turned back to the Dairy Freeze lot and saw Kaladi parking his new truck. He was alone and dressed in black Bermuda shorts, a white tank top and sandals, his muscular body tan from the summer. Kaladi stared at them from his open door as if he hated them, then he slammed the door shut hard after getting out and heading for the Dairy Freeze.

"What a jerk!" Helen quipped to Adam when they turned back toward the empty lot.

"Last time I saw Kaladi was when I pushed him and Dipshit away for smokin' at the fireworks stand. They were both drunk."

"At least he won't bother us like we were afraid he would last spring."

"Yeah, that's true."

Soon they heard the scraping sandals of Kaladi's arrogant walk as he made his way back to his truck, but this time they didn't turn to look at him. Kaladi again slammed his truck door, and they could feel his angry glare boring into their backs. Helen and Adam looked at each other and started giggling, which Kaladi must have heard; and when the spoiled rich kid started his engine, he began revving it as if angry. Kaladi burned rubber all the way out of the driveway, childishly expressing his anger at being laughed at and ignored by his ex-girlfriend and "that Ape." When they finally looked at Kaladi's moving truck, they saw Kaladi flipping the bird at them as he fishtailed away down Main Street. They laughed until they both got a brain freeze from absently sipping too much of their slushies, which made them laugh even more.

A bit later when Adam and Helen walked past the Taggit gas station, they waved at Clark who was checking the oil for a customer parked at the island. Evelyn Taggit spotted Helen and came out of the station calling her name. Adam walked over to Clark so Mrs. T. could speak privately to her son's girlfriend.

"Tell Bobby that we love him and to be patient with us. Do you know when he's getting discharged?" Evelyn asked with genuine concern in her voice.

Even though Helen was under strict orders from Bobby not to say anything to his parents, she couldn't keep quiet when she saw Evelyn Taggit's sad and searching eyes. She told Evelyn, "Bobby is hoping to get out of the brig by Christmas. I know after that he wants to travel for a while."

A grateful mother squeezed Helen's hands while thanking her profusely, almost to the point of embarrassment, before she walked back into the station.

When Adam saw that Helen was alone again, he walked over to her and asked, "Everything okay?"

"Yeah," Helen answered softly. "She's just worried about her son."

"Well, I guess I understand that," Adam replied. Then he changed the subject and said, "Clark told me to ask you if you want to go with us to the drive-in movie tonight."

"Yeah, I'll go," she was happy to get away from the waiting and the concerned eyes of her parents.

It was another no-mail day for Adam at the Pitt House. After a dull supper with his parents, Adam was soaking in the bathtub before getting ready for the movie. He was relaxed and thinking about the waiting that Bobby must be enduring until he would be free to be with Helen. *At least he has someone to wait for,* Adam thought, trying not to be jealous.

The Sting

The Pittsville Drive-In on the north edge of town had one screen. It cost three bucks per person to get in, or twelve bucks per carload of four or more people. Adam sat in the middle of the back seat so he could see the screen between Clark and Helen.

It was Clark who first noticed Kaladi had parked his truck at a speaker directly behind his car. "Guess who's here," he groaned cynically.

"Who?" Helen asked.

"Your ex-boyfriend."

When Helen started to turn her head, Clark hissed at her, "Don't look at him!"

From the front passenger side-view mirror, she could see Kaladi's ominous black truck. "Who's with him?" she asked her brother.

"Dipshit," Clark answered.

Clark felt uneasy about Kaladi watching them from behind. He had heard about both the incident at the fireworks stand when Adam had an altercation with Kaladi and Dipshit, and also about the incident at the Dairy Freeze. The sound of beer cans popping open behind them made the trio feel even more uneasy. Clark was no fighter and wanted no part in any violence. Just before the feature movie was about to start, Clark wanted to go to the concession stand with his passengers but didn't feel he could leave the car unattended with Kaladi behind them.

"Lock your doors," Adam suggested.

"No, that idiot might smash my windows or flatten a tire."

"You guys go. I'll wait here. Bring me back a small Coke and small popcorn," Adam handed Clark his money.

Clark looked at Helen and she said, "Okay, let's go."

Adam watched Helen and Clark walk to the concession stand. Because the volume was turned up on the speaker hanging from Clark's driver's window, Adam didn't hear Kaladi's truck doors opening or closing behind him. Each pair of black pointed-toe cowboy boots took a straight path to each side of Clark's two-door Nova—Kaladi on the left and Dipshit on the right. Kaladi put his beer can on the roof of the Nova before reaching into the front window to turn down the speaker. Kaladi's face appeared to Adam to fill Clark's window as he lit a cigarette and blew his smoke into the interior of Clark's car. "Hi, Ape!" Kaladi grinned at the confined backseat passenger.

Standing close to the rolled-down passenger-side window was Dipshit. Dipshit was chain-smoking a cigarette with his right hand, and his left hand was behind his back. They reminded Adam of the myriad times throughout his childhood when his father would be drunk and teasing him.

"Go away, Kaladi!"

Quickly Dipshit and Kaladi each used their lit cigarettes to light a strand of Black Cats, and they tossed the sizzling strings of firecrackers onto the backseat on either side of Adam.

Trapped in the back of Clark's coupe, Adam had no way out of the car. He was forced to cover his face and take dozens of stinging explosions, mostly to his legs and arms. Then came a high-pitched siren blaring between his ears—his brain's warning that it had been assaulted.

Nearby vehicles had seen the fireworks display in the backseat of Clark Bach's smoking Nova. Kaladi and Dipshit retreated to

Kaladi's truck and were laughing and driving away spitting gravel. Adam was curled up in agony on the backseat.

In the hospital's emergency waiting room Helen said to Clark, "Luckily Adam's face wasn't burned." It was the very same place where the Bachs and the Pitts had waited anxiously for news about Helen when she had fallen and lost her baby.

"Yeah ... at least he has that much going for him," Clark answered, exhausted from helping his friend out of his car and into the emergency room.

The burns on Adam's body weren't serious enough to leave permanent scarring; however, the stinging was the most intense pain poor Adam had ever experienced. Aching from firecracker burns in two dozen bandaged places, he was released from the hospital after three hours. Helen and Clark helped him into the front seat of Clark's Nova that was still littered with shreds of Black Cats.

"You gotta press charges, Adam," Clark said.

"You should," Helen agreed. "They can't get away with this," she added with nearly palpable enmity.

"Yeah, Ape ... you can sue both their asses. Well, Dipshit doesn't have any money ... but it's a cinch Kaladi does. A good lawyer could get you enough money to pay for a year or two of college ... so you wouldn't have to depend on a track scholarship."

Helen scared Adam when she added, "That's right, Adam. Your hospital bills are going to be big. Hundreds of dollars."

"Maybe more," Clark inserted. "Tomorrow morning I'll take you over to the police station to press charges and then to my parents' attorney in Kansas City. You have good witnesses. Jerry Bales and his girlfriend saw Kaladi do it. Hey, Ape! Just think ... Kaladi might've saved your life!" Clark laughed, referring to the lawsuit settlement Adam would surely be awarded for his injuries—money that would keep him in school and out of Nam.

He declined Clark and Helen's offer to help him up to his room and made the painful trek by himself. He didn't want his parents to know anything about the incident. He believed they would do everything possible to capitalize on his misfortune, circling over him like greasy vultures to try to get his money. They would charge him room and board and swoop down on him to pick apart at his money until it was all gone. He'd be stuck in the prison of the Pitt House until the government dragged his sorry bones off to a war that had already ruined all his hopes and dreams of living a productive, independent life after graduating high school.

The next morning when Adam tried to get out of bed, the pain he endured with every movement was the most physical pain he'd ever felt. Despite the pain, he knew he had to think clearly and figure out his every move. *I can't wear dress clothes to see the attorney because those vultures downstairs will be suspicious. Besides, I should wear shorts and a t-shirt to show the police and the attorney my injuries.*

Adam came downstairs dressed in gray sweat pants and a long-sleeved Kansas City Chiefs sweatshirt over his boxers and t-shirt. Bill and Penny figured he was training for track since he was still hoping for a response to the letters he'd sent. His parents didn't see his painful descent from the top of the attic steps to the last step at the bottom of the staircase. The burns around his knees were so painful that he had to wipe the tears from his eyes before entering the kitchen. That's when he had to do some acting, especially when he sat down to eat his breakfast. Luckily his father was buried in his paper and his mother's back was to him at the stove.

Clark and Helen picked up Adam and drove him to the dinky Pittsville police station. The Bachs wanted to support their friend and make sure Kaladi got what he deserved. The town cop interviewed Adam, Clark and Helen, and took pictures of Adam's legs and arms. He then inspected the interior of Clark's littered backseat. "That's everything I need to file charges and arrest Steven Kaladi and Aaron Schick for assault. I'll make the arrest before noon, but I want you to know that both men will likely be released on bail before the end of the day. I'll also interview the two witnesses this afternoon and get their statements entered into the official file on this matter."

Leaving town to go to the Bach family lawyer in downtown Kansas City, the trio felt good knowing that Adam's medical records from his injuries would be secured, and both credible witnesses at the scene of the crime would be contacted right away.

Union Station was only a few blocks from the attorney's office. *Maybe I can stop and see Grover,* Adam hoped as he gingerly extracted himself from Clark's car.

The meeting with the attorney went well for Adam. They all noticed how the lawyer seemed to get more interested in Adam's case when Helen revealed that Kaladi's father owned a new car dealership.

"Cross when you can!" Adam voiced during his hobbled jay-walking across the busy streets of the city on their short walk to Union Station. Adam decided not to say anything to Grover about what happened at the drive-in since he didn't want to alarm his friend.

Clark and Helen were more excited after the meeting with their attorney than Adam was, mostly because it was always hard for Adam to get excited about anything. But as they closed in on the station, Adam was excited for his friends to meet Grover in his office on the train.

When they got to Grover office, he wasn't there. Adam offered to buy his friends lunch at Rudy's, since Grover might be there.

Clark was really impressed with the train station, "Man, I haven't been here since I was a little kid. This place is really remarkable. I didn't remember how massive and visually appealing this place is!" Seeing all the uniformed servicemen made Helen sad about Bobby's situation while Clark kept admiring the architecture of the historical landmark.

Walking into Rudy's, Adam was disappointed that Grover wasn't to be found there either. He wished he'd asked somebody on the Wichita Express where Grover was, instead of assuming he was having lunch. They sat at the counter with Helen between the two boys. It wasn't long after they ordered that Helen suddenly burst into tears from lack of sleep and worry over Bobby.

After lunch, Adam's arms and legs were burning and itching so badly under his bandages that Clark had to walk back alone and get his car so that he could pick them up at the front entrance to Union Station.

Two letters from colleges rejecting Adam's scholarship request had arrived in the mail.

"They're not interested," Adam groaned at his parents' gaping faces as the trio were seated at the kitchen table.

As Adam gingerly got up and walked away in the same sweats and sweatshirt he had worn that morning, his father asked, "What happened to your legs?"

"Pulled two hamstrings," he groaned while ambling for the dreaded staircase. With each painful step up to his room, he reminded himself that the new school year enrollment deadline was less than three weeks away.

Three more rejection letters arrived Monday and one on Tuesday. With no positive response to his letters, Adam decided to take matters into his own hands and go right to the source of his problem: Kaladi.

One Shot or Die

It took Adam a few more days to muster the courage to walk into Kaladi's car dealership and make Joseph Kaladi, Steven's father, a settlement offer. In exchange, Adam would drop all charges against his Steven and withdraw the lawsuit.

After four more rejection letters that week, Adam got a copy of his high school transcripts. He called the University of Kansas finance office and found out he'd need four grand to cover a year's tuition, including room and board, books and fees. Five thousand dollars, plus whatever repairs were needed for Clark's damaged backseat, was the figure Adam wanted from Joe Kaladi to drop his lawsuit. The extra grand was for the hospital bill and living expenses until he could get a steady job. Adam called this bold move "One Shot or Die"—a last-ditch effort to save himself from a war he wanted no part of.

Night after night before deciding to make his offer to Joe Kaladi, Adam had terrifying dreams of dying in Vietnam like Reggie. Right after one such nightmare—upon awaking on sweat-drenched sheets and unable to move a muscle because of his injuries—Adam resolved to approach Joe Kaladi first thing in the morning with his offer. Bill Pitt had always referred to Joe as a worthless crook. But Adam was aware that his dad went to school with Joe and that his dad was jealous of the fact that Joe became a successful, well-respected businessman.

Adam knew that if he lost his resolve and failed to secure his settlement, he deserved to be dragged off to war. Or to live life piled on the same heap of ciphers like his father—losers who gave up on living well.

Step by step, Joseph Kaladi's image behind his glass cubicle was becoming larger and more imposing. Joe looked rich. Adam could see the flashy diamond rings he wore on both of his manicured, well-tanned hands that held some important piece of paper in front of his eyes.

The Italian-American car dealer looked up from his papers and saw the Pitt kid approaching his office door. He set down his papers and motioned for Adam to enter his office.

Adam opened the office door and entered the room that reeked of British Sterling Cologne, the same fragrance Steven would repulsively splash on after gym class or after basketball games in the crowded locker room. He had three seconds to think about his rehearsed pitch to the senior Kaladi, but the exact order of words escaped him as he stood before the imposing man his father hated just as much as Adam hated his son.

"Mr. Pitt! Please have a seat. What can I do to ya?" the sharp salesman laughed, exposing his bleached-white, capped teeth.

"You do know about the charges I filed against Steven and the pending lawsuit?" Adam asked while gingerly sitting down, his wounded skin tearing some and burning around his knees.

"Yes, I'm aware of the lawsuit," the man stiffened with a grim mouth that now hid his teeth.

"I'm willing to drop all charges against Steven and the lawsuit in exchange for a five-thousand-dollar payoff settlement, plus repairs to Clark's car. That's just enough money to enroll me in college," Adam explained without blinking or averting his eyes from the experienced salesman.

Joe Kaladi sat back in his high-back swivel chair, puffed out his flabby cheeks, and exhaled words that surprised Adam. "And that includes all medical expenses for your injuries?"

227

Clark's warning about a big hospital bill sprang to his memory, but he didn't want to blow this deal. "Yes, I'll cover my medical expenses ... if I get a check for five grand today."

The dark-haired senior Kaladi shifted in his chair and said nothing. Then he picked up his phone and called his secretary. "Joan, please come to my office."

Before lunchtime, Adam was driving away from the bank after cashing his check for five thousand. On the dash was a copy of the letter Adam and Joseph Kaladi had both signed and had notarized agreeing to the terms of the settlement. Steven Kaladi was off the hook and Adam could go to school.

At the police station Adam dropped the charges against Kaladi and Dipshit. Upon returning home and hiding his envelope of money under his mattress, he walked over to the Bach house and asked Clark, "Can you call that attorney and let him know I dropped all the charges and I want to drop the lawsuit?"

"Really?" Clark was surprised.

"I settled with Kaladi's dad for five grand."

"Plus hospital bills?"

"No, I'll pay that over time. I needed the money right away so I could enroll at KU Want to go with me tomorrow when I register?"

Clark was happy about his friend going to Lawrence— especially since Steven Kaladi was paying for it. He just hoped the hospital bill wouldn't be too high.

Crap Happens

The next day Clark rode along with Adam to register for classes in Lawrence. Adam wasn't waiting for any more letters. He had made up his mind to go to the University of Kansas where at least he knew Clark and could count on his friend to give him rides home to Pittsville. Clark tried to get Adam in the same dormitory he was moving into, but they were full. Adam got a room in another all-male dorm that was located within a block of Clark's dorm. Adam was very satisfied with his room and the building.

After lunch at a campus cafe, Adam and Clark walked around the sprawling campus so the new freshman knew how to find his classes.

Later, they ended up at a friend's house off campus to watch the Olympics which were underway in Munich, Germany. Adam was interested in his field events, since he believed his national records were close to being good enough to qualify for the Olympic team. Randy Williams of USA won the gold medal in the men's long-jump with a leap of 8.24 meters, just a notch over twenty-seven feet. *And who knows how far I can jump with the professional training and coaching that's available here*, Adam mused.

Even though his injuries were, for the most part, now healed burn scars and would be hidden by hair growth in time, he wasn't as paranoid about being around a crowd of gawkers like he used to be. And yet from time to time a nagging doubt swept over him knowing he could no longer use Helen as his motivation to jump.

A week later while watching the Olympics with Clark in his dorm, gut-wrenching news interrupted the games about "The Munich Massacre." Innocent athletes had been killed by terrorists. This brutality of the attack reminded Adam that the world was violent enough without Nam.

On their walk to Adam's dorm, Clark couldn't stop talking about the tragedy in Munich. "This kind of crap happens because the world is so violent."

"I don't see how anything good can come from this violence in Munich. Just more guns and more fear," Adam said.

"It's the kind of crap that keeps all of us stuck in a world that gives attention to violence and war," Clark said.

After consistent time spent in the Armory watching experienced triple jumpers going through everything from warm-ups to their final landings in the sand pit, Adam knew he was not physically built to compete in the triple jump on a world-class stage The event was much better suited for the tall, giraffe-legged athletes who dominated it.

Meanwhile, Penny Pitt kept forwarding to Adam his rejection letters from schools, along with his $1,200.00 hospital bill. He had to get a job to pay the bill. But as the weeks passed and Adam grew more and more comfortable with college life, he knew he wanted to try out for the track team in the spring when walk-ons were given a chance to earn a spot on the team.

It always seemed very strange to Adam that his parents weren't at all curious how their son managed to go to college; however, he was certain they were relieved that there was one less mouth to feed. He hoped they were relieved also that he had been spared from being drafted for a year, but neither of them had ever expressed that sentiment. Now that Adam was exposed to other young men and how they were connected to their families, he realized he deserved more than what he called the "normal insanity" at home. His country was also his home; but he didn't like the war, the discrimination, and the growing attitude of "me, me, me and screw everybody else."

By late October Adam was really into the college scene. His roommates were serious students who didn't bother him. He got a part-time job at a large full-service gas station where Clark also was working. Clark worked ten hours a week on weekdays while Adam worked twenty hours a week and only on weekends. Adam had no desire to ride home with Clark every few weeks. Adam had a big bill to pay and didn't miss his family like his friend did. Peace-loving Clark was becoming a left-wing liberal complainer, griping about every single thing that was wrong with the government and that "conservatives are supporting the war and ruining any hope for young people like Bobby and Helen to live without guilt or fear of punishment for wanting to live a peaceful life."

Adam continued to find small blocks of time to observe older athletes working out in the Armory. With every visit he'd pick up some new stretch or technique used by the experienced long jumpers on scholarships and use it himself. He would see them lifting weights to increase leg strength, along with running forty-yard wind sprints. Since the Armory was open until ten o'clock every night of the week, the kid from Pittsville would take what he observed and diligently lift or stretch and sprint as if he were on scholarship and preparing for the upcoming spring track season. At the end of every self-imposed workout in the Armory, he would eventually find by trial and error his starting spot on the long jump runway and locate his perfect take-off point on the board without fouling. He never jumped for that first month of using the expansive sports training facility, but he was confident his scarred but healed injuries did not appear to have diminished his speed or his anticipated jumping ability.

One Thursday evening as Adam was in the weight room lifting weights, it occurred to him he hadn't thought of himself as "the

Freak from Pittsville" since he started college. His self-confidence was growing, and he no longer needed an external stimulus—like Helen Bach—to help him achieve his goals. While he still adored Helen and cherished her as one of his best friends, he knew he had within himself the ability to earn a place on the KU track roster. He smiled to himself as he realized, *It was inside of me all the time. I just needed a positive, creative, encouraging environment to really grow.*

Out of his $110.00 weekly paychecks, Adam was sending fifty dollars to the hospital. He also put away ten bucks a week for the new clothes he planned to buy when he had fifty bucks saved. His face was nearly clear of pimples because he was eating good food and drinking better water that came out of the taps of Lawrence, Kansas.

Helen was the one to notice and remark how good Adam looked since he started at KU. She went to Lawrence every other Saturday to visit her brother and to swim in the Olympic-size indoor pool on campus. Helen would hang out with Clark at his friend's house off campus where she would play pool and listen to good music—all things that helped to take her mind off of Bobby and whether they'd ever have a life together.

Todd Lynch from Wichita was Clark's friend and one of four roommates in the house where Clark and Helen would spend their Saturdays while Adam was working. Todd was handsome and had a great personality. He'd play pool with Helen and really listen to her situation with Bobby. Todd was involved in the campus anti-war movement and had helped other young men like himself who came close to enlisting in the service to avoid being drafted. He told Helen, "They have to let Bobby out. But they'll take their sweet time unless a politician or some retired veteran calls the base commander where he's being held and appeals for some kind of hardship release on Bobby's behalf."

"Like what kind of hardship?" Helen was more than curious.

"Say, for instance, if he's needed at home to work in the family business, or if there's some medical situation at home and he's needed to help support the family."

"His father was a Marine. So could he call the base commander and help get Bobby released or discharged?"

"Yeah. All it really takes is for someone to express an interest in Bobby ... someone they respect and who makes a good impression."

At last Helen had some real hope and could try to help Bobby get out of the brig. She was certain now that they weren't delivering her letters to Bobby. That was her main motivation to do something, the fact that she wasn't getting any communication to or from Bobby.

Turkey Day

Thanksgiving morning was the first time Adam had been back to Pittsville since he started school in Lawrence. He rode back with Clark, and both of them were anxious about Helen's meeting with Bobby's parents that morning. She planned on appealing to them both, asking them to write a letter or call the base commander to tell him Bobby was needed back home to help run the family business.

Clark stopped in front of the Pitt House to let Adam out with his black gym bag that held enough clothes to last him till Sunday. Clark invited Adam over to his house for Thanksgiving dinner and Adam accepted, since he never saw a turkey dinner at home— except for the year his mother won a twenty-two-pound turkey in a raffle at the Pittsville Sunshine Grocery when he was in grade school. The only reason Adam came home at all was to borrow his parents' car Saturday to go see Grover at Union Station.

Bill and Penny were having coffee after breakfast when Adam came into the kitchen from the side door. They weren't expecting him and didn't seem the least bit happy or excited to see him entering the kitchen.

After the very awkward, stony-silent reunion, Penny asked, "So how's college?"

"It's okay," Adam shrugged. Again it bothered the Jayhawk freshman that neither of his parents had ever asked him how he managed to enroll. "I'm training for the long jump," he added.

"That's good," his mother said.

His father nodded after finally putting down his newspaper.

"You have some mail," Penny said as she got up from the table. She handed him his last bunch of letters from schools he'd queried for a scholarship.

Adam decided to open them later in his room when he hung up the clothes he had folded in his gym bag. Adam felt compelled to start establishing some kind of a positive relationship with his parents. He wanted to talk to them about something—anything—so he sat down at the table and said, "I'm really doing much better in Lawrence than I was here in Pittsville. College life has been really good for me. It's forced me to be more proactive about living and more interactive with the people around me since I didn't have the security of my bedroom to hide in."

Bill and Penny nodded in silence, not offering any kind of a response or indicating that conversation was of interest to them at all.

Not surprised by his parents' passive response Adam added, "I'd like to borrow the car Saturday morning … if you're not going anywhere."

His parents took a quick look at each other and agreed that they weren't going to need the car Saturday and that it was okay for him to take it. Adam nodded and said he'd put some gas in it.

"Make sure you *leave* some in it," his dad smiled cynically, which made his mother chuckle while lighting her cigarette.

Alone in his room standing in the middle of the narrow, sloped-ceiling attic, he stared down at his twin bed with its box springs and mattress that had no frame or headboard. His eyes went to his set of encyclopedias standing in a row against the foot of his bed and held in place by the plastic bookends he'd bought for a dollar at Ben Franklin. He thought about how most of the information stored in his brain came from those books. And even his fame as a jumper that he'd resisted for so long was because of those thick, brown books his mother had bought him after he flunked the fourth grade. For the first time in his life, Adam could see that being held back a year was a good thing. It delayed his graduation and gave him a whole year to improve his jumping ability as the opposition to the war increased, putting more leverage on Nixon to get out of Nam.

He went for a long walk around town on that colder-than-usual Thanksgiving Day, noticing every so often how much smaller Pittsville seemed after having been in Lawrence for the past few months. The houses seemed even shabbier now that the January-like wind had blown all the green from the town's yards and trees. And the people living in those shabby little houses all knew his grandfather nearly turned Pittsville into a ghost town, like one of those Midwest towns far from any highways or railroads that could never grow. This town would never let him forget his family's bitter legacy. It was in the eyes and on the faces of the town's elders, business owners, and teachers; and it had been passed on to his generation of faces. Adam's peers had been raised on the negative talk of Bill's peers who resented the Pitt family for crippling the economic future of Pittsville. Countless times in his life, Adam could read the spiteful, unforgiving looks of repulsive disgust that revealed unspoken thoughts of the townsfolk about his family's standing within the community. Yes, he could read them. *That's a Pitt. His parents are drunks living off that greedy old Pitt who took all the rock out of the ground and left the town unemployed.*

But then Adam's track records made them all shut up about his family's dark past and brought a renewed respect to the Pitt family name. "That Pitt kid long jumped over twenty-five feet yesterday. Man, that's a state record!" "How far'd he jump yesterday?" I heard it was twenty-six feet. Man, he's gotta national record now!"

Now for the first time in his life, Adam could finally see that he forced them all to accept the Pitt name as a name to be respected again. And he did it all by himself. There were no teammates or even any coaches who helped him break those records. Only Helen had helped him, and she wasn't even aware of it.

Helen! At that very moment Adam knew Helen was at the Taggit house pleading with Bobby's parents to take action that would help get Bobby out of a military jail that she knew had to be killing his spirit. That was one of the things Helen had told Adam late one Saturday night earlier in November. He had stopped by Clark's dorm when he got off work at the gas station and Helen was there visiting her brother. She told Adam she had called the base commander's secretary, a friendly woman who advised Helen to have Bobby's father write a letter to her boss requesting the release of his son because he was needed home to help work the family business. The secretary went on to give Helen an exciting tip: "If your boyfriend's father personally comes to the base to talk with the commander, there's a better chance he'd be released sooner."

Around three in the afternoon, Adam walked over to the Bach house for dinner hoping to hear good news about Helen's talk with Bobby's parents. But the news wasn't good.

"Mr. T. was inflexible and wants nothing to do with getting Bobby out of the brig. The whole scene was awful," she told Adam when she finally came out of her room for dinner after a two-hour crying session.

Table talk during Thanksgiving dinner was subdued, to say the least.

Later that evening while Clark and Adam were in the Bach garage cleaning the interior of Clark's Nova, Clark admitted, "God, it was like somebody just died. I don't ever remember such a pathetically depressing Turkey Day."

"They gotta let Bobby out sooner or later. So why make it harder by thinkin' Mr. T.'ll ever do anything to get Bobby out? He's an ex-Marine and he always will be. He's got his beliefs to protect."

"You mean *ego*," Clark corrected Adam, knowing his ex-boss would never forgive his son for deserting the Corps, especially when his country was at war.

"I don't think there were near the protestors when Mr. T. was in the service," Adam said.

237

"I'm not so sure about that," Clark had his own theory after a year in college. "Back in Mr. T.'s day fewer people went to college, and the news didn't show protestors and carnage after battles. Now we see every night thousands of college men and women against the war, making it cool to be against it. If more mothers, wives, and girlfriends refused to support their men going to war … wars in other countries would be very difficult to get started. I think that's what happened to Bobby."

"What do you mean?"

"Well, Helen tells Bobby about everything she thinks and feels about everything. I know she used to always put down Mr. T. the way he treated Bobby like he was his drill sergeant. You know how even in a football scrimmage Mr. T. would get all over Bobby if he missed a tackle or made any kind of mistake?"

"Yeah, I've seen him get all crazy at games."

"Bobby liked the way Helen stood up for him when his dad busted his chops. She made Bobby see a better side of himself … like when he'd read the books she liked to read just to understand her better. And Bobby would talk to Helen about how strict his dad was at home and how his mother would always take his dad's side whenever Mr. T. was tough on Bobby. So Helen ends up being Bobby's champion, and Helen's opinions now carry more weight with Bobby than his parents'. Helen is opposed to the war and doesn't want Bobby going off and getting killed—or worse—so now Bobby's a deserter. And I know Helen feels bad about the whole scene because she can't do anything about it."

"I think it's like Todd said; they gotta let him out."

"Yeah," Clark agreed.

Wichita Express

A massive ice storm hit the area Sunday. Adam was stuck in Pittsville; the University of Kansas had canceled classes for the week because of road conditions and power outages. Tuesday morning Adam was shocked out of his early morning stupor by the ringing of the kitchen wall phone as soon as he finished his first cup of his mother's very strong percolated Folgers. The Pitt phone never rang. Nobody ever called them, and they never called anybody. Not even each other. Adam answered the third ring. It was Bobby Taggit and he sounded scared and desperate. "Hey, man, I'm glad I caught ya at home," he said talking fast. "I used my last dime in this pay phone and I only have three minutes. I really need your help, man."

The sound of Bobby's urgent words scared Adam because he'd never heard tough Bobby T. sound like this before.

"Listen, buddy, I got nobody else I can call who would do me a big-time favor. I can't call my folks, and I don't want to get Helen's parents involved."

Bobby had escaped by walking off of the base while on clean-up duty, but he didn't tell Adam that. He had taken two city buses for twenty-five long miles to a truck stop where a sympathetic young truck driver gave Bobby a pair of sweat pants and a red Georgia Bulldogs sweatshirt. He then had given Bobby a ride all the way to Denver, and another trucker had taken him all the way to Wichita. In Wichita Bobby spent all his money on a train ticket to Kansas City. Bobby couldn't tell Adam any of this; he had to lie.

"Ape, they let me out a couple days ago. I'm takin' a train to Union Station, and I'll be arriving there at four-thirty this afternoon. I really need your help, Ape."

By the time Bobby's fast phone call was over, Adam's head once again heard the same wailing siren as when he was assaulted by those Black Cats at the drive-in. Because Adam's parents were in the kitchen the entire time Adam was on the phone with Bobby, he had to be discreet and could only listen and say "uh-huh" to his fast-talking friend.

By the time he was off the phone, Adam's head was swimming with the myriad details Bobby had given him frenetically. He told his parents Clark needed his help with his car right away, and he left the house with only a strong cup of coffee in his belly. He was most anxious to deliver Bobby's message to Helen, which was sure to change her life forever since Bobby was apparently free now. And yet he didn't sound free at all. He sounded desperate, like he was in trouble.

Bobby's instructions were clear. Adam was not—under any circumstances—to let anyone but Helen know he called. A few fast strides after turning onto Helen's block and he saw his track shoes overhead. He walked even faster knowing he had broken his vow to himself to never jump again, yet energized because he knew he had made the right choice. Since starting school in Lawrence and getting his job at the service station, combined with the higher level of training he was observing at the Armory, he knew what it took to prove himself to the world. And he didn't feel ugly now.

Adam knew all the Bachs would be home. He knew where Helen's bedroom window was; but in order to get to it, he had to pass by the front of the house and another side of the house unseen by anyone, including Helen. If Henry or Carol Bach saw him, it would be the end of Bobby's plan that he trusted Adam to carry out for him. *Besides that, they'd think I'm weird,* Adam muttered to himself as he successfully slipped past all of the Bach windows unnoticed. He tapped lightly on Helen's bedroom window but got no response. He tapped again, and finally Helen parted open her curtains and was surprised to see him. Adam quickly put his index finger to his lips to indicate that she shouldn't say anything to alert the rest of the family that he was there. She opened both glass windows and whispered, "Adam, what are you doing?"

Adam talked in a rushed whisper with his face close to her window screen, wanting to get out everything fast that Bobby told him to say. "Bobby just called me. He wants you to meet him at four-thirty today at Union Station on the platform when his train arrives. He said to pack light, and I'm s'posed to drive you in his Mustang to Union Station. He said you have the keys to his car. And he said don't tell anybody or let anybody see ya leave town."

"Where was he?" Helen asked.

"He wouldn't say."

Helen stopped breathing. Her brain was trying to assimilate the unbelievable words Adam was saying. Finally she whispered back, "They let him out?"

"Yeah, but he doesn't want anybody to know. *Not anybody.* He said to get the car from his house at noon when his mom takes Mr. T. his lunch at the station."

Helen's mind was racing with packing and getting out of the house without being seen and not saying a word to her family. "I'll be at your house a little before noon," she whispered to Adam.

Adam nodded and headed back to his house feeling like he had forgotten to tell Helen something Bobby wanted her to do. Oh, how he envied Bobby right now—running away with Helen after telling the military he won't fight in a war he doesn't believe in. Then he remembered that he had forgotten to tell Helen that Bobby wanted her to bring as much money as she could. He stopped on the sidewalk and debated whether or not to go back and tell her. *No, we've got till four-thirty. We can stop at the bank. No big deal,* Adam reasoned and continued on home.

241

From eleven o'clock on, Adam stood behind his front bedroom window watching for Helen walking down the sidewalk. Again, he was thinking how lucky Helen and Bobby were to have each other and to be on their way to having a life together. On top of that, he was a part of it all. Of all the people in this world Bobby could have called, he called Adam to deliver his girl safely to him. And Helen's terrible fall was partly because of his dark attic steps, which resulted in her losing her baby. That was another reason he was glad to have a part in bringing them together and giving them what might possibly be their last chance to live lives free from war and away from the cynical faces of Pittsville. Adam knew firsthand the small-minded gossipers would never stop making their snarling negative comments, never once giving Bobby and Helen—or their children—a day free from their petty, hypocritical judgments and labels.

Adam remembered there was one more thing Bobby said to do in his rushed phone call before his payphone time ran out. "You have to call one of my parents. Not Helen. You, Ape. You have to tell one of them I gave you permission to use my car until you can afford to buy one yourself. That way they won't call the cops and tell 'em my car was stolen. Helen knows the phone number." Adam was really dreading that call to Mr. or Mrs. T. He was also starting to get confused about how he would get back home, but he quickly dismissed his concerns and told himself he'd get back somehow or maybe Bobby would drop him off close to town.

Until he could see Helen walking down the sidewalk toward his house, Adam calmed his nerves by doing his mail-order calf exercises on four stacked encyclopedias near his front window, balancing himself by touching the wall. For about twenty minutes he did the simple exercises he had been doing daily for over ten years—exercises that had made him a celebrity in Pittsville. When he saw Helen stop on the sidewalk in front of his house, he called down to her that he'd be right down.

Helen stood on the sidewalk with her biggest purse slung over her shoulder bulging with items and her packed medium-sized olive-green suitcase in her hands. She had managed to exit her house unnoticed since Clark was in the garage and her parents had left to visit some friends.

When Adam reached her, he told her about Bobby wanting her to bring as much money as she could. "I already got all the money I have," she said.

❖ ❖ ❖

Bobby looked and smelled like he hadn't slept or showered in three days. His black beard stubble covered his neck and face. He hoped he could shave and at least clean up in some head on the train before he met Helen in Kansas City. He was seated on a long bench in the Wichita train station. His eyes were closed but he was resisting sleep since he couldn't board his train for at least another thirty minutes. He was too tired to feel anything; he only knew that he was never going back to the brig. For nearly four months he had been working in the mess kitchen scrubbing pots and pans by hand for twelve hours a day, then he spent the other twelve hours locked in a solitary cell with only a bed and a toilet.

Bobby Taggit did what he had to do. The week before he escaped from the base, he heard a rumor from other inmates that the military had stopped dishonorably discharging deserters and now planned to keep them confined without pay until U.S. forces were all out of Nam. With no end to the war in sight, he bolted with his plan to drive Helen in his Mustang to northern Maine to an obscure border crossing that would allow them safe passage into Canada undetected by either side. He felt good about his plan.

Sitting in the Wichita station, Bobby's head-nodding bits of respite were interrupted by harsh-sounding boarding announcements and glimpses of servicemen in spotless uniforms coming and going all around him, each one a possible threat to his freedom. Freedom was a precious thing Bobby had truly learned to cherish in the military jail.

He wanted to board the train early, but that would only draw more attention to his slovenly appearance. When he finally heard that he could board his train to Kansas City, he moved his tired body outside to the platform boarding area, up the iron steps into a

243

passenger car, and sat down exhausted in a window seat. Heavy boarding started soon with passengers getting their seats all around him. He tried to keep his eyes closed, but fear of getting caught kept him fluttering them open to see if military or government men were on the platform looking for him. Just as he was about to doze off, he spotted a pair of cheese-nosed, inch-browed men in dark suits that he was certain were government men hunting for deserters. He watched the men enter the car ahead of his with other boarding passengers, which caused Bobby to get up and walk quickly to the next car and then through the dining car. As he quickly walked through the empty dining car, he checked every door he passed for a possible hiding place.

Just as the Wichita Express started to move, Bobby found an unlocked door and entered it fast, certain he was unseen. He was in a dark, small office, and he locked the door behind him. Then he opened another door in the office looking for a place to hide, and he found a private little bathroom that had a toilet, a shower stall and a small sink with a shaving kit on a table beside it. He locked the bathroom door. Although exhausted, he shaved and showered faster than he ever had in boot camp, Pendleton, or the brig.

As soon as Bobby finished putting on his dirty clothes, he saw the red initials G.C. on the exterior of the black leather shaving kit. By now Bobby was more awake and more paranoid about being caught as the train picked up speed leaving Wichita. In the brig he had heard about bounty hunters who would bring back deserters in handcuffs. He heard they traveled in pairs and split expenses— along with the considerable bounty they were paid for every deserter they handed over to any military base in the country. The "killer instinct" Bobby had developed on the football field and in boot camp took over. He had to assume that those inch-brows on the platform were on the train and looking for him now.

The deserter from Pittsville tried to clean up the bathroom like a Marine, leaving it spotless—the same way he had found it— except for the damp towel he left hanging on a hook beside the shower door. His skin felt invigorated after his quick, hot, soapy shower and freezing cold rinse. *That sure woke my tired ass up,* he thought to himself.

He exited the narrow door of the bathroom and was back in Grover's dark, dinky office. He moved his tired body over to the cramped space between Grover's chair and desk. Then Bobby heard a man's voice outside the door of the moving cubicle office that felt as confining as his windowless cell in the brig. Quickly Bobby turned on the desk lamp looking for a weapon. He saw the letter opener near the base of the lamp and reached for it.

❖ ❖ ❖

Adam and Helen watched from behind a row of bushes as Evelyn Taggit left the house to take lunch to her husband at the service station. As soon as her car disappeared around the corner, Helen led the way to Bobby's car that was parked on the side of the Taggit garage.

Adam started Bobby's Mustang and remembered something else Bobby told him on the phone. "Helen, one other thing Bobby said was to bring him some clothes."

Helen got out of the Mustang and used the key Bobby had given her the last time she saw him to get into the Taggit house. She slipped down to Bobby's room in the basement, which was still military clean like he had always kept it. She pulled down a small suitcase from the closet shelf and quickly filled it with clothes until she found a cigar box inside one of the suitcase compartments. She opened the box and saw a bunch of military service ribbons and medals, including a wrapped Purple Heart Mr. T. had received after being wounded in combat. She closed the box and put it on the closet shelf. She was reminded how hard this would be on both Bobby and his father, a wounded and decorated veteran.

Jeans, shirts, underwear, socks, and two pairs of shoes—one of them his favorite white Converse—all managed to fit inside his small suitcase. Since Evelyn would be at the service station all afternoon working on the books and there was plenty of time until Bobby's train arrived, she looked around his room to see if there was anything else he would want her to bring. She walked over to a framed black-and-white photo on his nightstand, a picture taken when Bobby was seven. He and his dad were fishing on a dock, and Jimmy's tattooed, muscular arm was affectionately draped around his son's shoulders. She put the photo inside Bobby's packed suitcase and closed it, then left the house and relocked the door with her key.

Meanwhile, Adam was worried that one of the neighbors would see Bobby's idling car and call Mr. T. at the station.

Leaving Pittsville in Bobby's black Mustang was dangerous because everybody in town knew that car. Adam stopped at the same Sinclair truck stop where Bobby had punched Kaladi. Helen waited in the car while Adam called Taggit's gas station.

"Mr. Taggit ... this is Adam Pitt. Bobby wanted me to call you and tell you he's letting me borrow his car to get back to college. Clark won't be going back to Lawrence until the weekend, but I have to get back earlier to study. Please don't report his car stolen."

Adam paused for Mr. T.'s response, but there was only the sound of the mechanic's nasal breathing close to the receiver.

"He said to tell you he loves both of you ... and everything will work out fine."

Again, Adam got no response and hung up the phone.

Behind the wheel again, Adam left Pittsville in Bobby's Mustang. Both he and Helen were unsure whether or not the cops were now looking for them on their drive to Union Station.

What Happened

The next March at the University of Kansas Armory, Adam was stepping off his take-off point on the long jump runway. This was his walk-on tryout for KU's track season that was starting in two weeks. The kid from Pittsville, along with two other walk-on long jumpers, was trying to make the track team. In all, thirty-six athletes—all of them KU students at every grade level—were trying to run faster and jump or throw farther than the talented athletes already getting full scholarships from the Big 8 track program that was known for its long-distance runners.

Adam coincidentally wore number 14 pinned to the front and back of his blue track jersey—the same number he had drawn in the Draft Lottery and an ominous reminder that he was jumping for his very life. Every track and field coach from colleges and universities throughout the Midwest was there to spot talent.

One of the scholarship long jumpers was jumping close to twenty-five feet his junior year at KU. The other long jumper on scholarship was a freshman from Wichita who jumped twenty-four feet, nine inches to set a Kansas high school record. Adam was well aware that since he was from out of state, he'd have to out-jump both scholarship athletes in order to have a good shot at making the track team and getting a scholarship for his sophomore year. The worst part of the tryout, though, was that the rules stated each athlete got only one attempt to prove themselves.

It was time for Adam to use his new motivation, his reason to jump. And it was no longer Helen Bach. Rather, it was what happened the day he drove Helen to Union Station in Bobby's Mustang. The images of that cold November day were as clear to him now as they were when he brought Bobby's girl to him. As he had a thousand times before, Adam went over in his mind again exactly what happened that day at Union Station.

Bobby was holed up in Grover's tiny office on the Wichita Express, desperate and ready to defend himself against anyone who tried to take him back to the brig. Bobby was standing in front of Grover's chair when he heard Grover's booming voice outside his office door. Grover tried to open his office door, but the door was locked. Grover never locked his door unless he was going home for the night. Bobby turned on Grover's desk lamp to find a weapon; and just as he reached for the letter opener sitting at the base of the lamp, he saw the very same newspaper clipping that every person around Pittsville had saved as a collector's item when Adam Pitt jumped into the record books and broke the national high school long jump record. That same clipping was now illuminated by the lamp on the desk on the Wichita Express. Then the small office door opened and Bobby saw a towering Negro man in a chef's white linen uniform and chef's hat enter in. To Bobby's surprise, though, Grover quickly entered his office and shut the door again, as if he didn't want anyone to see the frightened young man standing behind his desk pointing a letter opener at him.

"Sir, I bought a ticket," Bobby said, "and I didn't steal anything. I showered and shaved, that's all."

It must have scared Bobby when Grover closed his office door behind him, showing no fear in those big brown bulging eyes of his. He asked Bobby in his calm and powerful voice, "Son, what are you running from?"

248

Bobby put the letter opener back on Grover's desk next to Adam's newspaper clipping and answered, "I'm a military deserter. I escaped from the brig."

"Army?"

"Marine Corps."

Adam was certain Grover had to have been thinking about Reggie as he stepped over to one of his two folding chairs in front of his desk and sat down. He invited Bobby to take a seat in his chair behind the desk, which Bobby did.

"You were in Nam?" Grover asked.

"I was headed there. I knew I couldn't make a kill. I froze in training. Couldn't do it," Bobby confessed to this stranger who had Ape's clipping on his desk.

Grover reached over to his office door and locked it. He told Bobby, "Two government men are on the train looking for you. They showed me your picture."

About that time Adam had parked Bobby's Mustang near Union Station. Helen and Adam were unsure whether or not they should bring their bags into the station or leave them in the car. Helen said, "Maybe we'd better take them in … just in case Bobby plans to get on another train. Better safe than sorry."

Helen was walking so fast in the station that Adam had to remind her there was still a lot of time before Bobby's train arrived. Adam wanted to buy her a late lunch at Rudy's. He knew it was perhaps the last time they would ever spend together.

They sat in a booth and talked during and after their meal for two solid hours. They talked about their lives in Pittsville. Bobby and Clark were in many of the humorous memories they shared. Then the conversation turned serious.

"Helen, I want to apologize for not havin' a light bulb in the attic stairway. Maybe you wouldn't have fallen and lost …"

She cut into his words and said, "Shh. You know, it haunted me for a long time that I never wanted to know the gender of my baby. I guess that was my own guilt and shame over what I had done. It wasn't your fault, Adam, and I never did blame you. I knew it was dark when I reached your room."

"It was an 'unconscious accident.' That's what Clark called it."

"I know. He told me that the first time we talked about it after I lost the baby."

"It bothered me when you dated Kaladi so soon after you and Bobby broke up. He's always been a jerk to me."

"That's the same thing Clark says about him," Helen said, and they laughed together. Then Helen surprised Adam when she told him, "The whole time Steven and I dated, he never said a bad word about you or Bobby ... not even after Bobby punched him. Joe Kaladi wanted Steven to sue Bobby for his medical bills, but Steven wouldn't let him do it."

There were two walk-ons ahead of Adam. He continued to focus his thoughts on the remarkable events of that day—a discipline Adam trained himself to do to replace Helen as his motivation to jump into the University of Kansas track team's scholarship roster his sophomore year.

Adam and Helen were standing on the platform after finding out that the only train arriving at 4:30 was Grover's Wichita Express.

Bobby had pointed to Adam's newspaper clipping under the glass on Grover's desk and asked Grover if he knew Adam Pitt. They were both amazed that they each knew Adam.

Grover asked Bobby, "So what's your plan, Adam's friend?"

Bobby answered, "My girl is bringing my car to Union Station. We'll head north, and I'll drop off Adam near Pittsville. Then we'll ..."

"Wait a minute," Grover held up his giant paw to stop Bobby. "You tellin' me Adam is gonna be waitin' for ya at the station?"

"Yeah, he drove my girlfriend there."

Grover listened patiently to Bobby's plan—how he was going to drive Helen to northern Maine in his car, then they'd walk across the border into Canada at a safe place he'd heard about from a reliable source while in the brig.

Grover got up to get Bobby a Coke. They traded chairs in the cramped office, and Grover sat quietly in his chair thinking about the situation while Bobby literally gulped down the Coke. Grover handed him another one from his little fridge.

After several minutes of pondering the situation, Grover took over and changed Bobby's risky plan after telling the deserter the government agents would grab him as soon as he off-boarded at Union Station. And if he did manage to get himself and his girl out of Union Station, the authorities were certain to have every highway patrol car in the country aware of his car and plates. Grover then added, "I'm very concerned that Adam's involved in this. Aiding and harboring a deserter is a big deal to Hoover and his G-men, Bobby. You got the FBI on your behind … so you best have another look at your plan."

What Adam found out later was that Grover gave Bobby the same plan he'd been saving for Adam in case he needed it. Losing Reggie was the reason Grover off-boarded his train at the Union Station platform at 4:30 wearing his old Red Cap uniform with the navy-blue suit and shiny black dress shoes he'd worn when he was a Pullman porter and baggage handler for many years at Union Station. Grover had grabbed a luggage dolly parked on the platform and went looking for the pretty redhead her boyfriend had described to him.

There was only one long jumper ahead of Adam as the rest of the events that day at Union Station unfolded in his relaxed mind.

Adam had gone to Union Station to see Grover shortly after the first of the year. It was during lunch at Rudy's that Grover recounted the details of how he had helped Bobby and Helen.

"I could see the woman with red hair standing next to you with her bags. I knew you didn't recognize me in my Red Cap uniform because you was anxious and busy watching for Bobby to off-board the train. I loaded her bags onto my cart, and then you recognized my voice when I told her that Bobby was waiting for her on another train and to follow me. I was hoping you would just keep quiet and do what I told you to do when I told you discreetly that you was to drive Bobby's Mustang to the K.C. airport parking lot, leave the keys in the car, and wipe down all the door handles, steering wheel … the whole interior with the rag I handed you. Boy, was I glad when you took that rag and turned around and left without saying a word!"

"Yeah," Adam interjected, "I didn't even ask you how I was going to get home from the airport; I just did what you told me to do. I could see you were protecting me from something."

"I always felt bad about that part of the plan," Grover said. "I couldn't ever work out how you was going to get home after you left the airport. I just said a prayer for you, and I knew the Almighty would work that part out for me."

Grover went on to tell Adam that he had taken Helen and their bags to a lone sleeping car on the idle and empty 10:27 to Winnipeg that would leave the station the next morning. Helen helped the old porter load their bags onto the coach car and then into the locked private drawing room that had a queen-size bed and a full bathroom compartment. Bobby opened the door wearing a kitchen crew uniform. Grover had told him to put on the uniform and the puffy white cook's hat before they left Grover's office so that he would not be suspicious-looking. Grover left the embracing couple in their private room and locked the door after telling the grateful couple that he was going home to his wife.

About the time Grover reached home, Adam was walking away from Bobby's parked Mustang in the airport parking lot after wiping it down thoroughly as Grover had instructed. It was at least a twenty-mile walk to Pittsville, and it was getting colder by the minute. There was nobody he could call. Because of his role in aiding and abetting a military deserter, it was too dangerous for him to call anyone to give him a ride home. He had figured Grover was doing everything possible to protect him from being charged.

After about three feet-freezing miles into his walk on the shoulder of Highway 2, a familiar truck passed him and stopped abruptly some fifty yards ahead of him to give him a ride. Of all the people who could have possibly stopped, it was Steven Kaladi! Adam was wary of approaching the black truck that sat idling on the shoulder.

It was announced that Number 14 was on deck to jump after the walk-on before him, Number 13, had fouled by stepping over the line. Adam tried to stretch a bit and looked around the Armory as if trying to spot someone. Adam was confident he had his mark. He had to have a clean jump so that it could be measured and recorded by the track coach and his assistant. According to the rules, fouls were not measured and no second chances would be given. As a student helper raked the sand in the landing pit after the last walk-on fouled, Number 14 took his time removing the worn gray sweatpants he'd worn at every track meet since high school. He saw what he was looking for—Clark and Coach Tubbs engaged in dialog.

Adam was completely oblivious to the fact that every coach and athlete in the Armory—whether playing basketball, lifting weights, or warming up and stretching before their event—had all stopped what they were doing to watch the Kid from Pittsville who held both long jump and triple jump national high school records.

Following the plan Clark had worked out with Adam over the past two weeks, Adam was to "take his sweet time" removing his sweat pants and stretching his legs as if his life depended on it. Everyone present in the Armory that day thought they were about to witness history, so they waited and watched Adam's every little move. He was up next, and he had the unmitigated gall to place his cassette player beside the runway close to his mark and crank up the volume. The whole Armory could hear Crosby Stills Nash & Young singing "Woodstock" as Number 14 approached his mark on the runway.

But the only thing Adam could see was the passenger window of Steven Kaladi's truck on that dark, cold and empty highway. Adam had spent the last few freezing miles thinking about the stories he'd heard on campus in Lawrence and at work at the gas station about how students were getting their draft notices soon after turning nineteen and had to go through big hassles to prove they had a college deferment and that their grades were up to the minimum standards. He'd even seen actual orders for students to report for induction and a physical exam in thirty days. Failure to report to the Induction Center in downtown Kansas City was mandatory jail time. Adam would be twenty in two days. Because he had flunked the fourth grade and was a year behind his peers, he feared it wouldn't be long before he received a similar letter with his name on it.

"What are you doin' out here, Ape?" Kaladi yelled at Adam.

Adam wasn't sure what to do; he was shivering cold and miles from home. It had gotten dark early and fast after he'd left Bobby's Mustang at the airport with the key in the ignition. But he was so cold and still so far from Pittsville that he was glad to see Kaladi's face lit by his truck's fancy interior lights.

"Get in!" Kaladi waved him inside the warm vehicle that smelled new, except for the pungent smell of English Leather. That smell made Adam think of Helen and the gift she had given him right when she broke up with Kaladi. Adam felt dumb all over again.

"So what in the heck are ya doin' out here in the middle of nowhere walking in this freezing cold?" Kaladi asked Adam.

Adam could tell Kaladi had been drinking so he quickly tried to think up something simple and believable. "Car broke down and I didn't have any money for a tow or even a long-distance phone call home. You know how it is with us starving college students."

"Well, that won't ever happen to me," Kaladi snorted. "I enlisted in the army, so I'll be skipping college."

"Really? I'm shocked to hear that, man. With your family's money, you could go to any college in the country. Why would you enlist in the army?"

"'Cause I hate school," Kaladi grinned. Then right out of left field he added, "I'm sorry 'bout the Black Cats, Ape. That was a shitty thing to do, and I always wanted to tell you that. I was upset about Helen choosing Bobby over me, and when I thought she was pregnant and it was mine ... well, I guess I just kinda lost it for a while."

As they crunched along the snow-caked road in silence for several miles, Adam finally asked, "Steve, I always wanted to know if you saw me put that box of Hershey chocolate bars in that mailbox."

Even Adam had to admit it was funny when Kaladi humbly nodded yes. "I saw you put something in there, but I couldn't tell what it was till I opened the mailbox and looked."

They both laughed over the incident that happened fourteen years earlier. Adam extended his right hand and they shook hands over another incident in their past lives that had kept them from being friends. When they got to Pittsville, Steven stopped at the grocery store and bought two dozen Hershey candy bars and gave them to Adam. They both laughed again.

Adam was relieved to see Clark walking with Coach Tubbs over to the assistant coach near the pit who was watching for fouls and measuring and recording each walk-on's jump. Adam breathed a little easier and relaxed his mind. He turned off his music box right when "Woodstock" ended. Adam started to head over to his mark on the runway, but Coach Tubbs waved at him to hold his mark.

Coach Tubbs leaned down to speak to the assistant coach, "There's a bit of a rule change here, uh ... has any walk-on fouled out?"

"Just one," the younger assistant answered his boss while pointing at his clipboard, "Number thirteen."

"Thirteen ... it figures," the coach chuckled. "Where is thirteen?" the coach called into the growing crowd of spectators for the recently ousted walk-on.

Clark gave a discreet thumbs-up symbol to Adam. Clark's plan had been to convince Coach Tubbs to take away the one-jump rule for long jump walk-ons. "It's the one thing that can blow your chance," Clark had told Adam two weeks ago. Then of his own volition, Clark had called every track coach he and Adam had sent letters to last summer. He convinced each coach to call Coach Tubbs and let him know they were interested in Adam Pitt's distance at the upcoming try-outs. Coach Tubbs's office had been flooded with calls. Because of Clark's argument to the proud head coach that his reputation among his intercollegiate colleagues could be at stake, Coach Tubbs barked to his assistants and the two remaining jumpers, "Number thirteen and fourteen, you need to get a clean jump! If you foul … you jump until we get a clean jump!"

Adam was relieved knowing he didn't have the pressure of fouling. He sat down and wrapped his cassette player in his jacket before lying back, stretching out his bowed legs, and looking up to the Armory ceiling that had to be as high as the Grand Hall in Union Station. He closed his eyes knowing it would be his time to jump when Clark tapped one of his new red track shoes he had broken in over the winter while training for this chance to stay at home in his country.

Adam's mind went back to the day after Helen and Bobby went north. It was Adam's twentieth birthday. Government agents went to the Taggit house in Pittsville asking Bobby's parents if they knew where Bobby went. They said they had found his Mustang in the Kansas City airport's long-term parking lot, and it had been wiped clean of any fingerprints.

Jimmy Taggit had covered for Adam and lied to the G-men who were looking for his son and anyone who would have helped him. "Haven't seen him and don't care to," the ex-Marine said coldly with his wife sitting beside him on their sofa.

The feds handed Jimmy the key to his son's Mustang and told him it was still parked in the same spot at the airport.

Evelyn Taggit drove her husband to the airport to get Bobby's Mustang. She waited near the pay booth at the only exit from the parking lot. Jimmy saw the parking stub Adam left on the dashboard. When he started his son's car, the song "For What It's Worth" on Bobby's Buffalo Springfield tape started to play. Instead of turning it off, Jimmy listened knowing it was Bobby's music. The hardened, decorated ex-Marine realized Adam was sending an important message to the father of a deserter.

Adam closed his eyes, hearing Number 13 sprinting past him down the runway. Soon he heard the assistant coach call out, "Foul!"

In his mind, Adam was able to see Grover secretly watching the honor guard respectfully unloading Reggie's coffin from the train onto an obscure platform in the yard that was hidden from public view. He could see clearly Grover's sad, brown eyes flooded with liquid memories that ran down his cheeks as the six-man honor guard carried Reggie's coffin into a government truck. Adam could still hear the words Grover had said to him in Rudy's at a private booth in early January.

"Standing there watching his coffin carried into that old truck, I could feel Reggie's presence like I always could. And then it left me when they drove away. I was standing there alone in that empty yard ... and I felt just as empty. I don't remember walking back to the Grand Hall. I just walked 'round aimlessly; I was numb from seeing that boy coming home like that. Then I heard that one song you said you liked that time it played in Rudy's, but I couldn't remember the name of it. So I walked over to this long-haired young man who was playing that song on a little music box ... not a radio but a tape player that was standing on the bench next to him. I sat down right next to him on the bench and just listened to that song. While I sat there and the song played I asked him what the name of that song was, and he said 'Woodstock.' *Yeah, that's it,* I told myself. After the song played I asked him what the song's message was. He turned off the little box, smiled and said, 'We've got to get back to the garden,' he used his fingers to express quotation marks around 'back to the garden.' I was confused and he said, 'Yeah, man, back to the times when we helped each other live off the land and really cared about each other.' I nodded that I understood and he rewound the song and played it again and again and again."

Then Grover told him what happened that Wednesday when he showed up early for work wearing his usual crew chief's uniform. He escorted Helen and Bobby and their bags to a coach car that was located down a few cars from that private drawing room on the 10:27 to Winnipeg. Grover told Adam that Bobby was wearing the same kitchen crew uniform he had worn the day before when he off-boarded the Wichita Express for the idle sleeping car on the 10:27. Grover said that after they got Helen situated with their bags in her coach seat, he handed Helen the ticket he'd bought for her Tuesday night before going home. Grover said he had called his dispatcher and told him he wanted to train a new crew member

257

Wednesday on the 10:27 and requested a three-day transfer to work the three-day-run roundtrip.

Number 13 went sprinting down the runway on his third attempt. "Foul!" the assistant coach barked louder. The beautiful way Grover had described the scene made Adam smile—then at Rudy's and now in the Armory. "Helen was seated at a linen-covered table in the rolling dining car when she saw Bobby in his kitchen crew uniform bringing her a cup of coffee and serving her on a silver tray. I was standing back, watching them smile at each other so lovingly. I felt good when I saw that, and I knew I did the right thing."

Adam had leaned forward at that booth in Rudy's and told Grover, "And you helped Bobby right away ... even before he asked you about my clipping on your desk."

Grover handed Adam the last letter he'd received from Reggie. It arrived the day after his funeral. It was the same letter he kept under the glass top covering his desk right next to Adam's clipping.

While still on his back Adam bent his legs, a cue to Clark that he was ready to jump. Number 13 got a thumbs-up signal from Clark near the sand pit, and Clark started walking toward the spot where Adam was resting. As Number 13 sprinted down the runway for the fourth time, he made a clean jump. "Sixteen feet, one inch!" the assistant called out after measuring the jumper whom Clark had paid twenty bucks to foul until Adam was ready to jump.

All Adam had to do was lie on his back with his eyes closed and recite Reggie's last letter to Grover. Adam had memorized every word and had been using it as his new motivation to jump ever since Grover told him at Rudy's that he wanted to give him Reggie's letter to remind him how important *real freedom* is:

Dear Grover,

I've only been over here a little more than a week and I have this strange desire to write more on the subject of going to school to get my education. I see now that I should've tried harder to stay in

258

school like you always wanted me to do. Even though I've only been here such a short time, I already look forward to the day I can fly home and start my life over. Tell Adam if he can fly out of Nam by jumping, do it, man! Please tell him that for me, Grover. I see so many guys here like me that don't really want to be here. Man, I wake up scared every day because everyone else does. I can feel it. Gots to go now. Love to you and Mrs. C.

Adam felt Clark's gentle tap on the side of his track shoe. It was time to jump. Adam opened his relaxed eyes and saw his friend's smiling face looking down at him.

"Ape … it's time to fly outta Nam."

Fistful of Sage

In early June Adam rode home with Clark for summer break. Adam was given a full scholarship for his sophomore year to long jump for the University of Kansas after jumping an incredible twenty-seven feet, one inch—an inch further than Randy Williams had recently jumped in Munich to win the gold medal. That walk-on jump was two feet farther than anyone had ever jumped in KU's history. So remarkable was Adam's first and only clean jump that the Kid from Pittsville was once again a celebrity—only this time on a much bigger stage at a major university with serious talk all over campus about bringing home Olympic gold from Montreal in '76.

Clark was now Ape's self-appointed manager for the part he had played in helping Adam reach his goal to be on full scholarship. Clark couldn't stop thinking or talking about that moment in the Armory when time stood still for every person who witnessed that incredible leap by Adam Pitt. As they drove home in Clark's Nova, Clark recalled, "I still hear the silence when you were sprinting down the runway. Man, that was just plain and simple beauty. It was beautiful! And when you were in the air for so long and stretched out like you did … The best part was during the cheering by the crowd, I saw the looks on the faces of the other two long jumpers on scholarship. They weren't happy for you, I could see that. And that was big-time envy-ugly. So I knew you did something that scared them. And Coach Tubbs … when they measured how far you jumped, I saw right away that he knew he better sign you now or he'd be the one everyone was talking about if you went to another school."

"That's for sure," Adam replied.

Well, one thing's for sure … you definitely jumped outta Nam! You know what I find really amazing, though? All those girls on campus who are openly flirting with you. I've never seen anything like that before … especially with you!" Clark smirked. "But the best part is that you just seem different ever since that jump. Like, you're not that introverted hick from Pittsville anymore. Why is that, Ape?"

Adam answered matter-of-factly: "I'm not stuck in my past like I used to be. It's like everything that used to bother me was erased."

"That's amazing!" Clark laughed.

"I'm free to live my life now," Adam smiled with a clear complexion for the first time since childhood. "I'm even breathing better. It started when I realized that most of the people I know and meet are stuck just like I was my whole life in Pittsville. Now I see so clearly that I've been given this gift to jump, but I've been hiding from using it and enjoying what I can do with it. The other day I was in the cafeteria, and these two big football stars came over to my table and asked me for my autograph. I was surprised and thrilled … and even humbled. Before when kids in Pittsville would want my autograph, I'd get all embarrassed … like I was ashamed and afraid of the attention I was getting."

"I get that," Clark replied. Then changing the subject he said, "Why do you think Mr. T. wants to see us?"

"I don't know. It's prob'ly about Bobby. Prob'ly wants to know if we've heard anything."

"Like what? I mean … aren't there some things we shouldn't tell him?"

"Like what?"

"Like that Helen called and said they're doing well in Winnipeg? Or that Bobby and Helen got married two weeks ago? If Bobby didn't tell his parents that stuff, then Bobby doesn't want them to know … right?"

Adam agreed and yet felt weird about not telling Bobby's dad what he knew about his son. Especially since Mr. T. was so cool about not telling the feds that Adam was involved when he knew Adam was the one who drove the Mustang to the airport and left it there as a diversion.

When they arrived in town, Clark and Adam stopped first at Taggit's Gas Station to get their dreaded meeting with Jimmy Taggit over with. Their apprehensions vanished when Jimmy offered Clark and Adam each thirty-six hours a week over the summer to work the gas station so that he could focus on mechanic work during his busiest season. They were both flabbergasted to get such an offer for summer work, considering they were coconspirators in Bobby's exodus to Canada. Since they both needed to live at home over the summer, they gladly accepted the work Mr. T. offered them. Clark was more than happy to get the work because he wanted to help his parents by paying for some of his junior year at KU.

When Clark and Adam left the gas station, it was Adam who went back inside to tell his new boss, "Bobby's happy in Canada. They got married two weeks ago. Helen called home to tell 'em. Just didn't feel right not tellin' ya."

Mr. T.'s nod was positive, and the veteran mechanic looked grateful for the information about his son.

Both Adam and Clark were looking forward to working at the station over the summer and right away figured out together how much money they'd make before going back to school in the fall.

"I decided I'm going to give my parents half of what I make at T.'s," Clark announced during their short drive over to Adam's house.

Both of them knew that half their wages would be about sixty bucks a week. They were both looking forward to the next school year because Adam had been told by Coach Tubbs that he'd make sure Adam could room with his buddy/manager Clark in Clark's dorm on campus. Besides that, before they left Lawrence they had been guaranteed their part-time hours for the upcoming school year at the Sinclair station not far from the school.

Clark parked on the street in front of the Pitt House. The car was gone and it seemed strange to Adam that the fireworks trailer was gone, leaving visible the only clean patch of cement where it always had been parked off-season until the town revoked their permit.

Clark pointed at a patch of wild sage growing alongside the empty Pitt driveway in the overgrown lawn and said, "That's wild sage. My mom keeps it in the kitchen to purify the air. Mind if I get some?"

"Take it all," Adam shrugged.

After Clark drove off with a fistful of sage, Adam put his suitcase down and pulled out a fistful of sage. He carried it to the back of the garage after dropping his bag by the side door and planted the gray-green sage over Gop's grave. He made up his mind right then and there that he would give his parents sixty bucks a week for room and board over the summer. He knew they would appreciate that, since he was certain the town would never approve his father's planned appeal to get their permit renewed.

Upon unlocking the side door and entering the kitchen, he set down his suitcase and looked around his childhood home with his new attitude and his new way of looking at life. He saw things that had been there before he left for school but had never really noticed. Like how the same clipping of his record jump in high school that Grover had in his office was magnetized to the refrigerator door. And the letter from the City denying them a permit for their fireworks business was right beside his clipping. He hoped they would be happy that he got a scholarship and didn't have to flee the country. He thought perhaps he'd borrow the car in the morning and drive to Union Station to tell Grover that he got the scholarship Reggie wanted him to get. He could also let Grover know that Helen and Bobby were married and doing well up north—thanks to him.

Adam walked through the quiet old house. His legs felt powerful under him as he scanned the furnishings and household items that told him he was home. Nothing was different, except he was seeing these things differently. Now he could see the Pitt House for what it really was—the simple home his parents made for him, the only home they were capable of giving him because of who they are. Gone were those old feelings of disgust and shame he'd always felt inside those four walls.

"I'm home," he said out loud as he hurried through the house. He carried his bag upstairs to his room to unpack, anxious to see his room for the first time through the eyes of his new attitude. At the bottom of the attic steps he turned the light switch. Amazingly, the light came on and the attic steps were lit for Adam. Maybe he wasn't the only one changing.

Adam opened the door to his bedroom and set down his bag. He walked between the sloped ceilings to look out his front window. There was the tall grass of the front yard in need of mowing with fallen twigs and pieces of blown paper littered about the yard in several places. He smiled at the familiarity of the scene and thought he'd pick up the yard and mow it before his parents returned home from happy hour. He looked down at the trash can standing near the window. His track ribbons were still there where he'd thrown them the summer before when he was fearfully planning his escape to Canada. In the ether of new life he realized something that never really had sunk into his brain before. He had made the right choice—even if it was for the wrong reason—by not competing in sports his senior year. Because he had flunked a grade, he realized it wouldn't have been fair for him to compete in track or basketball his senior year. By not competing his senior year, he could always say that his records were made when he was high school age and not when he should have rightly been starting his freshman year of college. He stood there looking out the window, laughing at all the silly reasons he hid behind for not competing his senior year.

Adam turned around to see his twin bed and his encyclopedias standing at the foot of his bed, not far from the sloped ceiling where he must have done a million Atlas repetitions to improve his jumping ability. Now he was genuinely grateful for these books that literally had given him an abundant life by sparing him from a war that terrified him. He wondered how much farther he could jump now that he'd be using all the equipment in that modern training facility in the Armory.

He dusted off his set of books and realized how grateful he was also that his parents had bought him these books. They, too, played a part in saving his life without even knowing it.

Adam went down to the garage and put some gas in the lawn mower. He saw his dad's twelve-foot aluminum extension ladder, and he carried it over to Sycamore and set it up under his dangling track shoes. He carefully removed his faded red, soggy, weathered, record-breaking shoes from the power line. He valued them now as if he'd found a lost treasure—a part of his past that could be worth something someday.

Back at the Pitt House, Adam retrieved Grandpa Pitt's wooden box from the shelf in the garage. He put his weather-beaten shoes inside the box and returned it to the shelf. For an instant he recalled that moment when he knew he'd nailed his long jump attempt in the Armory. His first thoughts were of Grandpa Pitt and the legacy he had left to his grandson. He recalled that as a young boy his goal was to make a name for himself that would diminish the negative talk about his family, and he had done that. But now Adam was starting to see that he had a responsibility to leave a legacy for future generations of the Pitt family. The family line would not end with Adam Pitt, and Adam was determined to once again make the name of Pitt a name that was respected and appreciated within the community.

As Adam pushed the lawnmower onto the front yard, he spotted a shabbily dressed salesman walking down the opposite side of Pitt Street carrying an oversized brown sales case. He reminded Adam of the salesman who had changed his life so many years ago. *I wonder if he has any idea that his sale literally saved my life. I wonder how many other lives he has touched without even realizing it. But maybe that's how it works. Going through life, doing good, helping others ... making a difference. In this case, the difference between life and death ... merely existing or thriving in life.*

Adam pulled the cord on the mower, eager to do something good for his parents.

The End

"Writing a novel is like leaving a safe and worn path in order to take a route nobody has ever taken. It's dangerous and risky, and all for the hope of finding you, my reader."